The Fathers' Club

The Last Housewife
The Family Stalker
Death by Station Wagon
Sign Off

JON KATZ

The Fathers' Club

A Suburban Detective Mystery

DOUBLEDAY
New York
London
Toronto
Sydney
Auckland

PUBLISHED BY DOUBLEDAY
a division of Bantam Doubleday Dell Publishing Group, Inc.
1540 Broadway, New York, New York 10036

DOUBLEDAY and the portrayal of an anchor with a dolphin are
trademarks of Doubleday, a division of Bantam Doubleday Dell
Publishing Group, Inc.

Library of Congress Cataloging-in-Publication Data

Katz, Jon.
The fathers' club: a suburban detective mystery/Jon Katz.—
1st ed.
  p. cm.
1. Deleeuw, Kit (Fictitious character)—Fiction.   2. Private
investigators—New Jersey—Fiction.   3. Suburban life—New Jersey—
Fiction.   4. New Jersey—Fiction.   I. Title.
PS3561.A7558F35   1996
813'.54—dc20   95-43549
CIP

ISBN 0-385-47921-2

Printed in the United States of America
June 1996
First Edition

10   9   8   7   6   5   4   3   2   1

To Bob Mellman and Susan Buckley, and Ben and Will

The Fathers' Club

One

OVERNIGHT, the maintenance staff at the mall had Halloweened us.

I'd noticed the transformation immediately, passing through on the way upstairs to my second-floor office. The Food Court fountains, normally bathed in cheesy Esther Williams-ish aqua lights, had turned dramatically orange. The Muzak, usually a syrupy wash of Henry Mancini or string-heavy versions of old Motown hits, had been replaced by a soundtrack of shrieks and moans. Every doorway had been draped in orange and black bunting, every store window stuffed with plastic vampires and leering jack-o'-lanterns.

Halloween is what gets the fraying fifties-era American Way Mall through those bleak weeks between back-to-school promotions and the Christmas marathon. The mannequin family in Cicchelli's Furniture Store window, usually the most clean-cut and Rockwellian of families, had been joined by a frayed polyester bat hanging over the plaid sofa and a new pet—a stuffed black cat with mean yellow eyes that narrowed menacingly precisely every thirty seconds.

Murray Grobstein, sneaker entrepreneur, applies the same special acumen to this holiday that he so successfully applies to footwear the rest of the year. He devotes an entire corner of Shoe World to costumes, notably the *craze du jour*. I don't know where he gets his intelligence, but it is impeccable. Murray knew all about Ninja Turtles even before the mall's toy store. And he'd picked out this year's hot costume months ago, when the windows were still full of Easter bunnies. "Power Rangers," he'd whispered to me, after peering around to be sure no competitors were within earshot. "It's all Power Rangers this year." Sure enough, right after Labor Day stacks of polyester Mighty Morphin Power Rangers costumes appeared—then swiftly disappeared. He was almost sold out.

And it wasn't even October yet.

Another week and the first luminous plastic tombstones and ecologically sound nonaerosol "spider webs" would sprout on the front lawns and shrubbery of nearby Rochambeau.

Halloween really is scary in the New Jersey town where I live: all those forty-year-old attorneys and securities analysts parading around in their Frankenstein costumes, the small masked and caped children who tag along with them almost an appendage to the great fun the grownups are having. Every time the doorbell rings, you are expected not only to exclaim over how scary Suzie looks or how sweet a bunny rabbit Johnny is: you have to praise their larger, middle-aged companions as well.

At first I had thought the parents were coming along for safety, to make sure nobody bothered their kids or slipped tainted Snickers into the goody bags. But they could have accomplished all that without costumes. Like sports, trick-or-treating has become another former province of childhood that's been annexed by child-obsessed parents.

Halloween was undoubtedly on the mind of the woman sitting across from my old scarred desk that fall morning. She had two young children to outfit, pumpkins to carve, supplies to acquire.

"How much candy do you buy?" she asked, glancing at the picture of my wife and kids on the window ledge behind me.

"At least three times more than I should," I replied. "Then I shovel handfuls out to the latecomers."

She laughed. "I tell my kids to go late—a bit before nine. That's just before people start turning their porch lights off, and they're candy-dumping. They don't want to keep the stuff around the house or *their* kids will wind up eating it."

Sound strategy, I agreed. "But do you secretly throw away half of the candy your kids bring home?"

"Of course, right away. Before they count it and know what's there to the very last Gummi Bear. I grab the stuff that's hardest on the teeth—licorice and caramels and Raisinets—and chuck it right out."

We both chuckled a bit and traded costume anecdotes.

I wondered how many of the American Way's patrons knew or cared that a private detective's offices were right over their heads. While teenagers wolfed tacos and frazzled mothers shouted pointless warnings to their children to sit still, stop slugging Martha or quit whining, Deleeuw Investigations was going full tilt just a stairway away. It was an odd location, but I wouldn't have traded it for Rockefeller Center.

It was rare for me to joke around with someone whose business I didn't even know yet. Clients could present me with trouble of many varieties, and it was rarely funny. But Linda Lewis seemed more comfortable than most.

"What are your kids dressing up as?" she asked.

"My son Ben is thirteen and way too cool to dress up," I reported, "but not above going door to door with a large plastic shopping bag." I had to be careful not to sound testy about Ben; we'd been sparring lately. Transient adolescent surliness, I hoped. Emily, my daughter, three years younger, was still debating what her costume should be. Last year—in a major test of parental inventiveness—she'd gone as a VCR. She'd even had a slot cut into her cardboard costume, through which you could actually insert a videocassette.

Lewis laughed. Her five-year-old, she told me, had spurned any costume involving a skirt last year, but this year demanded three-inch heels in order to trick-or-treat as Barbie. Her mother was offering a compromise: turquoise eye shadow in exchange for a flat pair of Mary Janes.

Lewis turned out to be unusual in other ways, as well.

Most of the divorced women who hire me to track down their deadbeat husbands and get them to pay what they're supposed to pay are either desperate or furious, sometimes both. Some would be delighted if I beat the hell—along with the support check—out of their exes. Though once they see me, they drop any such notions. "Jeez," groused one, "you look like my kid's history teacher, for Chrissake! You sure you're Kit Deleeuw, the private eye? The Suburban Detective?" I am sure; I've been an investigator for five years now. And for the record, I've been shot once, slugged now and then. I've solved a couple of high-profile cases—I've even made enough money to paint my house. Next year, maybe, the garage.

In the course of all this I've heard plenty of sob stories about what rats ex-husbands can be. But Linda Lewis seemed profoundly embarrassed, uncertain that she should even have come. She kept telling me what a nice guy her ex was. In fact, she insisted, only some dire problem could have caused him to have missed three months of child support and his last two weekly visits with the kids.

"You don't know Dale," she said firmly. "He's a wonderful father. Something must be very, very wrong." Right, I thought—like the high cost of black leather sofas for Tiffany from the office steno pool to perch on when she comes over to try his fabulous new Cabernet. My cynical reaction dismayed me: was I finally becoming successful enough to turn into one of those hard-bitten, wisecracking private eyes?

I admit it, I'm prone to anger and self-righteousness when the question of men and child support comes up. But in my book there aren't any good excuses for letting your kids go hungry.

Frankly, my experience with my fellow males has been predominantly guarded, unpleasant or unfortunate. The male friends of my youth communicated with basketballs, water guns, fists or spitballs . . . when they communicated at all. Then came the Army, where I learned my investigating skills—no need to elaborate there. Working on Wall Street for a decade did nothing to improve my notions of other members of my gender, especially those who ran American business by bullying, firing, attacking and taking over one another. Wall Street execs are the last legal big-game hunters, stone killers with elephant guns. I lost any friends I'd made at my firm when an insider-trading scandal blew it apart in the late eighties. I wouldn't cooperate with the U.S. Attorney's office, so I was run out of Wall Street for life, even though I'd done nothing wrong. Because I wasn't indicted, my former associates all avoid me. And because of the scandal and my odd new career, middle-class Rochambeau professionals give me a wide berth, too.

So my two closest male friends are an eighty-one-year-old Quaker gardener and an elegant Cuban immigrant of indeterminate age—a famed criminal lawyer in his own country, the manager of a burger franchise in ours. I love them both, and enjoy every moment I spend with them, but neither exactly qualifies as a contemporary soulmate. And you don't meet a lot of empathetic, sensitive men in my trade.

With my wife Jane Leon working day and night toward her psychology degree at NYU, I feel flashes of loneliness at times, especially when both kids are out of the house. I wouldn't mind a close male friend or two, somebody to have lunch with once in a while or check in with on the phone, but I don't have much expectation of finding any. And keeping close tabs on a moody thirteen-year-old boy and a vibrant ten-year-old girl doesn't leave many spare hours for friend-shopping.

I suppose working as a private detective only heightens my knee-jerk reactions to and suspicions of my own gender. Much of my early work consisted of locating unfaithful, irresponsible, abusive or negligent husbands and fathers. I was all too often enraged at the suffering of the ex-spouses and children of men who seemed to have no trouble paying for expensive meals in New York with their new girlfriends. I admit to profound satisfaction in tracking these men down and intimidating them into coughing up at least some of what they owed their kids. Where were all these new males I kept reading about? I saw a few here and there, but nothing to match all the hype.

This is, I know, neither a fair nor typical portrait of most men who, like me, are just trying to do well by the people in their lives, to help keep home and hearth together and somehow squirrel a few bucks away for the kids' college. Their lives are no picnic either, especially these days, when costs continually soar and job security plummets.

Still, in her assessment of her ex, I sized up Linda Lewis as somewhere between excessively forgiving and completely naive. Some women are simply suckers for abusive men. But Lewis didn't sound so gullible.

"Dale is a good man," she said again. "If he's not paying child support, and hasn't called the children in two weeks, then he's in trouble. I'm really worried about him, Mr. Deleeuw. I want you to find him, talk to him, make sure he's okay."

"And do you want me to encourage him to write a check?" I asked, deliberately giving her a sharply skeptical look. I had already been down this unhappy road a few times in my short life as a private investigator. I liked her, but even if I hadn't, I wanted her to understand what she was getting into. Hiring a private investiga-

tor isn't like having a buddy call your husband and plead with him to do right by the kids. It's a serious step. Finding out what's going on in somebody's life just isn't a discreet matter. We make waves, talk to employers and neighbors, rattle and embarrass people and sometimes frighten them. That's what makes guys pay up.

Lewis's reply was level but quite decisive. "I'm not a bubblehead, Mr. Deleeuw. Or a victim. If Dale was screwing my kids financially, I would be plenty angry about it. But this isn't like that. Our marriage didn't work. Dale just couldn't handle a relationship. He has a lot of serious emotional problems that aren't his fault, and it made things rough. He gave up on us; I think the whole thing was just too painful for him. But Dale is on the high end of the evolutionary scale for men, believe me. He's even joined a men's group. A dads' group. They call it the Fathers' Club. He takes his parental responsibilities *very* seriously."

Okay, definitely not naive. It's easy to underestimate or misjudge women these days, especially in a suburb like Rochambeau. You meet somebody you think, from her schlumpy sweatpants at the supermarket, is a housewife—and she turns out to be a world-renowned geneticist. You meet somebody in a business suit you assume has just made partner, but she's actually a cell-phone-equipped SuperMom who logs three hundred miles a week ferrying kids to practices and play dates. The point is, no stereotypes or generalizations apply anymore.

Linda Lewis was an artist, she had told me. Early thirties, wiry in her worn jeans and work boots, close-cropped brown hair and dark eyes with just the start of laugh lines at the corners. Appealing and, it seemed, perceptive and tough. But that didn't make her right about her ex-husband. I wondered what would make a guy leave a woman like this. So I asked.

"What sort of emotional problem does Dale have, Ms. Lewis, if you don't mind my asking?"

"Mr. Deleeuw, I don't want to put my whole life on the table. Dale was often depressed, especially as his business began to fall apart. He wouldn't get the sort of help I thought he needed, and I couldn't live with somebody who suffered so much and wouldn't do something about it. We would never have split up if he'd been seeing a therapist, I'm convinced of it, and I'd take him back tomorrow if he would. But so far . . ." She sighed, shrugged. She didn't seem to have a lot of expectations in that direction.

I phoned out to Evelyn de la Cretaz, the retired librarian-turned-secretary and assistant sleuth who, well, who really runs Deleeuw Investigations. I asked her to send in our new—our only—associate.

What we needed now was Willie, the fearsome Deadbeat Dad Tracker. He bounded in a few seconds later, notebook in one hand, Snapple bottle in the other, his long blond hair flopping down over his forehead. Though Willie had run the computer operations of a massive credit-reporting agency in the Jersey exurbs six months ago, he looks like a teenager. From his appearance, he could have been a varsity lacrosse captain, a roadie or a roller-blade champion. This of course makes him deadly on undercover work. The fact that he's a hunk doesn't hurt his face-to-face information-gathering opportunities, either.

But he often doesn't need face-to-face questioning to learn what he wants to know. Willie believes every American leaves a computer trail as distinct as a moose walking through mud, and he knows how to follow it. Anybody, anywhere, who used a credit card, made a purchase of more than a hundred dollars, applied for a mortgage or a lease—Willie would know about it in minutes. Back when I was slipping him envelopes of twenties, I never knew how he found stuff out for me and now that he worked for me I sure didn't want to know. But Willie's hacking had located many a corporate thief, phony nanny (checking out child-care people was the fastest-growing part of my business) or insurance hustler.

I introduced him to Linda Lewis, which for most people would be a cue for a firm handshake, but Willie just smiled and gave a little wave, then draped himself over the remaining chair in my tiny office, his endless legs sticking out halfway across the room.

Lewis smiled back at him. Everybody likes Willie.

"What do you think could have happened to your husband?" I asked her. "What sort of terrible thing?"

"I don't know. He's had a lot of money troubles. His business—he was trying to start a development firm that would specialize in low-income housing—fell apart. He and his partner declared bankruptcy. It was pretty ugly, but Dale wouldn't say much about it. I know he hasn't shown up at the Fathers' Club for a couple of weeks, even though he was fanatic about staying with it. And he hasn't called to explain why he hasn't sent any checks, or even to ask about the kids, which he usually does almost daily. I teach painting at the Rochambeau Adult School and exhibit in a gallery in the city; he's well aware that I don't produce any real income.

"Besides, Dale also knows that I would understand if things were rough temporarily, that we'd work something out. We always did, at least until . . . I don't know. I'd try to get my son into day care—he's two—and I'd look for work that paid something, until Dale could make the support payments again. I've taken a part-time job already, just to keep our apartment. I'm typing computer programs two mornings a week. Not what I went to Parsons for, exactly, but I'm not afraid of working. And I have some watercolors on exhibit at the Rochambeau Art Museum; that might lead to something . . ."

She stopped then, as if she recognized that she was giving herself a pep talk as much as answering my question. She seemed to square her thin shoulders. "I'm sure I sound like a lame-brain to you. The truth is, I have no idea what's happened, but I do know Dale. We were married for seven years and living together for several before that. He's sometimes overly ambitious, and overreaches. But he wouldn't just bail out like this. Do I want him to pay? Sure. But I also want to know if he's okay, because only something very wrong would cause him to act like this. He loves Liz and Noah too much for this."

This was a rare and surprising attitude for an ex whose two children were stuffed into a tiny walk-up in nearby Clifton, who was working two jobs to keep a roof over their heads, and whose husband had skipped the last three months' support checks without explanation.

"Well, I understand your feelings about him, Ms. Lewis, but I have to be candid with you, too," I said gently. "You're taking a very generous view. I should warn you that what I usually find—"

"I know what you usually find," she interrupted. "I've read enough about deserting fathers. But Dale isn't like that. He was a wonderful father and a good husband. He would never just refuse to return my calls like this. I've been by his apartment. There doesn't seem to be anybody there. Nobody answers. Something's wrong. I can feel it, you know, the way you can when you know somebody so well?"

Evelyn edged in with a tray carrying three cups of takeout coffee and some doughnuts, undoubtedly from my friend Luis Hebron's Lightning Burger ("Food in a Flash") downstairs. She must have liked Linda Lewis, because the formidable Evelyn wouldn't fetch coffee for just anybody. It wasn't in her job description.

"What can you tell me about this men's group?" I asked, moving on. "Do they beat drums in the woods?"

"Dale hated when other men made cracks like that," Lewis said crisply. "Every men's group doesn't beat drums, you know. They really help each other. Don't you think that's possible?"

I felt boorish. "I'm sorry," I told her. "It's all that Robert Bly gobbledygook. He gave men's groups a bad name. I apologize for being insensitive. I guess I'm just trying to prepare you for finding out that Dale may not be such a saint after all. I hope I'm wrong, but I do worry that you're not going to like what Willie and I find."

She seemed to accept my apology and my cautions. We talked about my usual fee—now up to a $2,000 retainer plus $175 an hour for corporate clients. Linda Lewis was proud; she wouldn't accept charity but didn't have a spare two grand. "I will pay you at your usual rate," she said firmly. "It might take me a while, but I will."

I wanted to help her, and had little doubt that Dale Lewis wasn't as nice as she thought he was, so I took a check for $150 and told her I would make some preliminary inquiries, then decide if there was any point in pursuing the case further.

I was pretty sure Willie would find that this guy had lit out for Hoboken or SoHo. And if he had money and was spending it, it wouldn't be easy breaking the news to Linda. But she had to hear it and I might be able to squeeze some money out of him.

She gave me the names of his Fathers' Club friends, one of whom turned out to be his business partner as well, the address of his apartment and office. I asked for a photograph of him, which she pulled out of her wallet. It clearly reflected better times. They must have been a neat couple: attractive, laughing faces, small kid bouncing on his shoulder, another in her arms, dog looking mournfully into the camera. Whatever Dale's emotional problems, the picture showed an easy smile, a lean, runner's frame. He looked like a nice guy. I sighed my families-are-fragile sigh. Two nice people who cared for each other and for their children—why weren't they together?

"You said his office was closed, but do you happen to have a key?" I asked, just in case I wanted to "browse" through his files. She did have one; she didn't ask me why I wanted it.

Willie tossed her a few questions—what kind of car did he drive, what kind of music did he like, did he go to malls much. She tried to answer, having little idea, I think, that within an hour Willie would know how many and which CDs Dale Lewis had purchased with his MasterCard.

"Look, Mr. Deleeuw, I'm a grown-up," she said, standing up to go, shouldering a leather backpack. "I can deal with whatever you find—another woman, the posh apartment you seem to think he's spending his money on. I just need to know two things. Is he okay? And can I count on him for some child support? If not, then I'm not looking to punish or sue him, but I have to get on with my life. And if he is having trouble, I want to help him. It's corny maybe, but I think marriage vows transcend even the marriage sometimes, don't you think?" I nodded. Yes, I did, very much so. "So my interests are clear and so are your responsibilities. Do we understand each other?"

"Perfectly," I said. Then we all—even Willie—shook hands and she left. She was pretty impressive. I hoped we could do right by her.

"Dale Lewis. Fetch 'im," I said to Willie when she'd gone, pointing to the adjoining office I had rented for him a few months ago.

"Right, Chief," he said, ambling back to his darkened cave. After the first few visits, I preferred not to go inside, and Evelyn absolutely refused. Willie's office bore an unsettling resemblance to Ben's room, overflowing with piles of CDs and tapes, 'zines, posters of deranged metal bands, and enough computer equipment to eavesdrop on the National Security Agency. But Willie seemed to love his new job and his research was impeccable. We made a great team.

The schedule Evelyn kept for me looked pretty clear for the afternoon, until Emily's piano lesson at 4 P.M., followed by dinner preparations. Jane wouldn't get home until nearly midnight. Before her graduate studies entered their final phase, this would have been dinner-and-a-movie night. Now, I often hit the Route 20 Gargantua-plex by myself. Em might go with me to kids' movies and comedies, if she wasn't with her friends, but Ben adamantly refused to be seen in the same theater. Since I loved movies dearly, that usually meant going alone. Life would be like this for us for at least another year, maybe two. I'd come to understand how those

1950s housewives felt, listening for the door to slam when Harry came home.

Like a housewife forty years ago, there was a lot weighing on me—my work, shopping, chauffeuring, dog-walking, a raft of household chores. For a while I'd reveled in domesticity, but lately I'd found myself fantasizing a bit about getting on that train and heading for Wall Street to make our fortune.

But there was at least as much pressure on Jane. She's a mother; she sees desperately needy clients at a clinic in an impoverished neighborhood of Paterson; she carries a brutal load of study, research and commuting. Jane's job as a psychiatric social worker had made it possible for me to rebound from my shattered Wall Street career and now it was my turn. I thought it churlish to complain and, some weeks, I even managed not to.

I had an instinct about where to go first this afternoon, especially after I dialed Dale Lewis's apartment and heard only unanswered rings. I thought about the serious emotional problems Linda had vaguely described, and how they might have been exacerbated by his disintegrating business. Those were dangerous circumstances for men conditioned to equate providing with success. Which was a lot of men. So much is being asked of men these days—that they work harder for less security and manage, along the way, to reshape themselves into sensitive, nurturing creatures. Yet nobody tells them how. They never seem to find personal relationships fulfilling enough to compensate for trouble at work. If Dale wasn't entertaining a honey, he might be off brooding somewhere—missing his kids, mourning his career, feeling a failure.

I drove to the address Linda had given me, on the southern edge of Rochambeau's downtown. Here there were pre-World War II brick office buildings and converted warehouses where small design firms and architects found ample space and a cheaper rent than on the main drag. Kimball Associates, Suite 301, was still on the small directory posted next to the front door.

While Willie was back in our mall office searching for electronic traces of Dale Lewis, I was looking for the physical, the man himself. When there was no response to the bell, I climbed three flights of stairs. A computer-typed announcement taped to the door of 301 tersely informed me, "Kimball Associates closed," with a number to call for further information. The realtor trying to rent the space had posted an "Office for Lease" sign next to it.

To my surprise I didn't need the key; the door pushed open easily. I saw no sign of an alarm system, but I could probably talk my way out of trouble even if there was one, assuming Police Chief Frank Leeming's eager young recruits didn't show up and gun me down before I could open my mouth. Leeming might be momentarily saddened by my loss but would quickly recover.

Kimball's outer office still contained furniture, but there were marks on the receptionist's desk where I presumed a computer had once stood. I saw no paper, mail or other signs of recent activity, but the office wasn't musty either. I guessed it had been rather recently cleaned out; in another week it might be empty.

I flicked the light switch on and walked through the outer office, with photographs and sketches of presumably low-income apartment complexes on the walls, to the door with Dale Lewis's name still mounted on it. It opened. It shouldn't have. The chill that shot up my spine made me shiver.

In record time, I had found Dale Lewis. He was slumped in his desk chair, his complexion the color of computer paper. I shook off my shock and stepped inside. There were no visible injuries, no signs of any struggle, nothing askew, broken or out of place. He was just sitting back motionless in his chair, his arms hanging down beside him, his eyes and mouth gaping. I held the back of my hand to his nose and mouth and felt nothing. His skin was cold. He had no pulse. He was dead, probably had been for hours.

I shouldn't have, of course, but I patted down his pants pockets, felt some cash in his right one and a wallet in the left. Then I pulled my new cellular phone out of my jacket pocket and dialed 911.

Linda Lewis was right: there had been a terrible problem.

Two

I WAS SUPPOSED to meet Linda Lewis at nine-thirty, but I got to Rochambeau Municipal Park half an hour early. I wanted—needed, maybe—a little time to walk and clear my head. I'm not the sort of private detective who's gotten used to encountering dead bodies or who recovers quickly from the sight. I knew I wouldn't be sleeping well for weeks.

It took the detectives half an hour to totally convince themselves that *I* hadn't killed Dale Lewis, as opposed to being merely the unlucky fellow who'd found him dead. It wasn't lost on them that I had no business being at Kimball Associates, and my declining to explain why I was didn't improve their opinion of me. It was only when Chief Leeming showed up, groaned at the sight of me, shook his head in disgust and proclaimed me too dumb to figure out how to kill a tadpole that the detectives reluctantly dropped the idea.

"Sweet Mother of Jesus, Deleeuw, I'll never understand how an amateur like you can get himself in the middle of every goddamn mess that happens in this town. And this was supposed to be my quiet reward after all those years in Brooklyn. Lord," Leeming muttered. "I get heartburn every time I see your damn face."

While he groused, the crime scene unit quietly and efficiently took pictures, foraged through drawers and behind cabinets, dusted for prints, picked up threads and fibers. "Deleeuw," the beefy chief growled, "you'll have to tell us who hired you. You understand that, right? Otherwise, I will not only lock you up again, but this time I *will* go to the state licensing board."

The first, I knew, was no idle threat. Leeming had once locked me in a cell for five hours when he discovered I'd withheld crucial evidence in the case of a murdered husband and an accused, grieving wife. Would he actually go to the licensing board? I wasn't sure.

We had become reluctant comrades, each developing a grudging respect and affection for the other. But we were just too different to get very close. Leeming would never think much of my investigative skills, and he would never quite get the suburbs. A former precinct commander in Red Hook, the chief had seen more than I ever had or ever wanted to—too much more. I think a part of you has to go permanently numb to survive what he'd seen.

He'd expected a cushy stretch in an affluent New Jersey suburb as his reward after all those years knee-deep in serious crime, but he didn't get it. Rochambeau had recently endured a series of sensational murder cases, and Leeming had discovered the hard way that suburbanites have a peculiar notion about criminal justice: their version of the American Dream doesn't include any crime. Nor does it include high enough property taxes to pay cops well. Next to school superintendents, who never seemed able to educate any town's kids well enough to suit their parents—the taxpayers— police chiefs had the highest turnover. Leeming was actually into his seventh year as ours, a testament to his savvy and professionalism.

A stickler for the rules, Leeming would have little choice but to come after me if I didn't cooperate. Withholding relevant—in this case vital—information in a murder investigation is perhaps the fastest way to lose your investigator's license in New Jersey or any other state. I had already seen one career collapse; I couldn't afford to lose my second. I just wanted to let Linda know first. Client courtesy. So I couldn't answer the chief's increasingly hostile questions.

My buddy Detective Danielle Peterson was on the scene right after the chief. The first African-American female to make detective in the Rochambeau PD, Peterson was, not surprisingly, tough and direct and possessed of a strong sense of irony. We had become good friends on my last case, one that had made friendship a welcome commodity.

I doubted the chief knew the full extent of our communication. We traded information all the time, no questions asked on either side. She cut through bullshit like a bullet through butter. If she had an investigative weakness, it was her inability to comprehend the upper-middle-class suburban lifestyle. "I'm sorry, Deleeuw," she'd confessed at lunch one day, "I know how a drug dealer's mind works, but I can't understand people who spend as much on their dogs each week as I do on groceries." Actually, that was where I came in. I *did* understand those people; they were my friends, neighbors and clients. In many ways, they were me.

"No visible cause of death," Peterson had murmured to me after the body was gone and Leeming was elsewhere, brandishing his radio. "Could be suicide, I suppose, except there was no note or anything. Could be a coronary or a stroke, I suppose. Could be poison." We agreed to stay in touch. Unlike Peterson and Leeming, Willie didn't need a warrant to go clacking around people's lives and spending habits.

It was no simple transition to put a meat loaf in the oven and oversee the kids' homework after watching a corpse get zipped into a bag and carted off. Later that night, I'd called Danielle at home.

"Okay," she said without preamble when she picked up the phone. "What *were* you doing there? I presume the wife hired you? What for?"

"Deadbeat Dad stuff," I said. "He missed some payments. She was worried about him."

"Worried about him? Why not be furious with him? As in wanting to strangle him," Peterson mused with characteristic subtlety.

"Forget it, Danielle. Absolutely not the type. For one thing, she wasn't mad at him; she was concerned. Besides, why kill him? He's got no money, and if he's dead he's never going to be able to provide child support. For another thing, I'm sure you'll find she was home with her two kids—"

"We already have found that, Kit, or she'd be sitting at the station now answering a lot of pointed questions. Believe it or not, us civil servants aren't as dumb as we look on TV. The sitter and neighbors and her adult school students can account for her all day today." Peterson sounded disappointed. "I just wanted to get your reaction. You know these kinds of cases: you don't often go wrong if you suspect the spouse. You got anything else we should know?"

"No, I just got the case and went straight to the body. Couldn't it be natural causes?" I wanted it to be.

Peterson sounded skeptical. "Young, fit guy. If it isn't a heart attack, which will be easy enough to tell, then it's probably murder or suicide. I heard one of the lab guys say he had some threads in his nose and mouth. You know, fibers inhaled when he reflexively gagged for air, maybe panicked."

"As in . . . ?"

"Smothered, dummy. Shit, the chief is right about you. I keep forgetting that your investigative experience was on Wall Street. *Suffocated*. And did you smell the liquor on his breath?"

"Uh, no . . ." I said, a bit embarrassed. Danielle was half kidding, but she was entitled to be arrogant about her skills. She saw lots of things other people didn't see. Or smell. I hadn't even thought to sniff Dale Lewis's open mouth; merely touching his cold skin made me feel creepy and nauseated. As I often told my kids, I am a *thinking* detective. Like Hercule Poirot. Only he loathed children and was undoubtedly too fastidious to have even stepped into the smelly, cranky old Volvo station wagon I pilot around town.

"Kit, if he was drunk—or drugged—it wouldn't be all that hard to smother him. 'Cause how could he have killed himself sitting in that chair? I see somebody—male or female—coming up behind him. He's probably asleep or at least drowsy. Perp clubs him on the head, maybe; I thought I felt a lump. Pulls something over his neck to hold him back, presses something else to his face with the other hand. Takes two, three minutes if the victim is impaired. There were no signs of a struggle, nothing under his nails, no obvious bruises, nothing knocked to the floor or broken. Suggests to us that he never resisted; maybe he was in no condition to. But that's very unofficial, okay? The medical examiner will know more soon.

"One strange thing," she added after a pause, as if she was debating whether to tell me or not. "The FBI showed up not long after you left. All ticked off that the body was already gone. Asked about two hundred and fifty questions. Wouldn't answer any of ours, of course."

"The FBI? What the hell brought feds into a local murder?"

"Hey, I'm the last to know that," Danielle said glumly. She'd obviously been pondering the same question. Did all cops hate the feds? Probably. "Maybe this too will be revealed to us. Stay tuned." She hung up.

The morning paper carried a brief story about the death, inside on page 13, but the police had said nothing to the press about the possibility of foul play. And no autopsy findings had been released. I bet Leeming had delicately hinted Lewis's death was a suicide, which always caused the local daily to be relatively low-key. Nobody dwelled much on suicide here. Give up on the American Dream? So, blessedly, Jane and I didn't need to talk to the kids about one more death, at least not yet. My last case had attracted sensational publicity—the usual vicious-murder-comes-to-placid-suburbia stuff—and had struck too close to home in many ways: Ben's middle school principal had been the murder victim, and a parent had been accused of the killing. We did *lots* of talking with the kids about that one, and for months afterward. Rochambeau's many family therapists were probably still doing a brisk business.

I called Linda Lewis that morning, as soon as the school buses had come, to see how she was and to ask if she wanted to talk. "I'm glad you called," she said simply. Her voice sounded husky with tears. "I was hoping you would. It's funny, but there aren't a lot of people I want to talk with at the moment." It was her suggestion that we meet. Why, I wondered, would I be the one she did want to see? She must have other confidants. Her mother, for one, had rushed in from Connecticut to help with the children, she said. Maybe Linda thought that somehow, I could explain her husband's death to her. The thought made my heart sink.

"Mr. Deleeuw, it's hard enough that he's gone. But they obviously think he's been murdered. Could that really be possible? Dale never had an enemy that I knew of . . . at least not in that way. He had a gift for enraging business partners, I guess, but enough to kill him? God, I've got to understand this. I'll never have any peace if I don't. I've got to be able to tell Liz and Noah." She sounded numb, in shock, and I felt a surge of protectiveness for her. It surprised me. I often felt sympathy for my clients, but this was something different.

I decided I should wait until we were face-to-face to tell her that Chief Leeming was asking questions. And that Danielle Peterson had called me, first thing this morning, with fresh and ominous, though not totally unexpected, information. Dale Lewis had, in fact, suffered a blow to the head; his blood alcohol content was three times the legal driving limit, and there were barely visible but unmistakable contusions to the neck. "Doesn't make it a hundred percent. There are other scenarios you could construct. But it sure looks like somebody brought him or followed him to his office, then killed him," Peterson reported. "That would make it somebody he knew well enough to let in.

"And," she added bluntly, "somebody who was either really pissed or obsessively thorough. Probably knew he was tanked or helped him get into that state. Because, otherwise, you have to be real strong, confident and experienced, to do something like that. If you mess up, he can come back at you. It isn't as quick or sure as a bullet to the head.

"Question is," she went on, "did someone go drinking with him? Was he sitting in his office drinking? But then, we didn't find a bottle or even a paper cup. Or did he get drunk somewhere else and just go there because it was nearby? We're canvassing the bars, but he could have had a few drinks anywhere. Who knows what he'd been up to? He was out of work, hadn't picked up his business mail in days. His answering machine had messages from his ex and his creditors going back a week."

Leeming would never have given me so many details about a crime, but Peterson knew I wouldn't tell him—or anyone—that we'd talked. There was a lot to think about. We agreed to stay in touch if answers to these or any of a hundred other questions materialized.

The Rochambeau park always seemed to embody the promise, bustling family energy, even the occasional beauty of suburbia. I'd suggested to Linda Lewis that we meet there. The enormous old oaks were beginning to turn yellow, but the grass remained a lush green, and bikers, strollers and canine play groups seemed to be taking advantage of every corner of the place. Only the soccer field, where overinvolved parents turned their kids' recreation into referendums on their own parental achievements, was empty.

I loved to walk Percentage, my black Lab, here. This was the place to study the distinctly different stages of suburban life: the newly arrived young couple waiting to have children; the Manhattan émigrés pushing toddlers in strollers or yakking with friends around the sandbox. Your mid- to late-thirties couples tended to sit on the benches to watch their kids climbing on the jungle gym. (Frisbee-catching canines invariably appeared at this stage of life.)

By their forties (Jane and I would fit here), adults cheered kids on from the edge of the soccer field or softball diamond. I often saw older adults walking by themselves, sometimes with pedometers on their ankles.

More and more, there were new kinds of families: African-American and interracial ones, gay and lesbian ones, Iranian and Ghanaian ones. This bastion of white foursomes had quietly but noticeably given way to a true melting pot.

And of course, at every step along the way, there were the casualties: divorced dads with armloads of sports equipment, soaking up every minute with their kids to make it count, their anxious faces reflecting how short their time was with some of the people they loved most. And divorced moms looking sometimes wistful, sometimes lonely, always harried.

Lots of happy people, too; I shouldn't forget that.

Every stage rushed by so quickly. I couldn't fathom that it wasn't just yesterday I was pushing Emily on those swings, pretending to ignore her fake shrieks of alarm, or puffing down the path alongside Ben's first bike. He had slammed into just about every tree. One edge of the park, where a pack of goodhearted Labs and retrievers romped, was where I'd first met Shelly Bloomfield, the Last Housewife. Shelly had left Rochambeau, but I still saw her dog Austin from time to time, entrusted to the loving care of one of Shelly's dog-crazed neighbors.

Here you were reminded that all the dumb clichés of life were true: you blink and your kids are grown up and gone. You take your family for granted and suddenly it's shattered, ripped apart by divorce or illness—or death in a swivel chair.

I saw Linda Lewis step out of a small blue Toyota dwarfed by two giant four-wheel-drive, cellular-equipped suburban combat vehicles fully stocked with roof racks, child seats and dog cages. In my office yesterday, I hadn't quite focused on how attractive she was. I don't leer at women much; aside from the fact that they don't like it, I feel cheap doing it. But watching Lewis, in her jeans and a tweedy jacket, hoist her leather pack gracefully over one shoulder and stride down the hill toward me, I wondered again what sort of emotional problems would have caused Dale to let a woman like this go. Those warm eyes, the gamine hair—she was attractive, substantive, and suddenly profoundly in need. It was a compelling combination.

Everybody feels crushes from time to time, I cautioned myself. It isn't wrong to feel it, just to act on it.

This had happened before, once or twice, so it didn't really bother me. Women often told me I had a giant MARRIED sign stamped on my forehead. And it was true, I couldn't talk to most people for three minutes without bragging about my wife or relating some cute story about my two kids—at least, until the older one had turned moody and uncommunicative, a poor source of winning anecdotes. There was little danger of my screwing up all that for a fling; I had mopped up professionally after too many foolish men who had.

Linda was red-eyed but in control. She shook hands and nodded when I said hello. We walked over to a wooden bench near one of the park's three ponds.

"I haven't told the kids yet," she said after a brief silence, staring at the ducks paddling about. "I'm going to this afternoon. I called a therapist and she suggested ways to handle it. She said to be straightforward and direct, to tell them Daddy wasn't coming back, but that he loved them very much and we would all find ways to remember him and keep him in our lives. She said not to lie or sugarcoat something it isn't possible to sweeten. Then to really work hard at reassuring them that I was okay and would be taking care of them. Sounded a bit blunt, but it makes sense." She sighed softly. "You always want to protect your children from reality. Noah's so little—how can he possibly understand? I guess I've protected them from Dale's troubles, but there's no way I can protect them from this. I just feel we both failed them in the most basic way at the very age they most desperately need a real home with a mom and dad in it."

I agreed with her therapist. "I have learned the hard way never to lie to kids. Whether it's surgery or the death of a grandparent, you tell them the truth. They always figure it out anyway. They may have to deal with tough stuff, but at least they don't have to hate you for lying to them."

She smiled crookedly, then turned to look at me. "I'm sorry you had to find . . . him. That must have been dreadful. Are you okay?"

I nodded, pulling my jacket collar up against the breeze that had begun sweeping across the park. It was a startling question; I couldn't actually recall a client asking me that before. People in trouble expect the people they hire for help to be strong, not vulnerable. Nobody thinks private investigators have trouble with anything.

"Thanks for asking. I didn't sleep much last night. But I'm the detective here, remember? I'm supposed to be worrying about *you*. I know how much feeling you still had for him."

She leaned back on the bench, her brown tendrils ruffling in the wind. "I have sort of come to terms with the death of our marriage. I think I understand that Dale just couldn't pull himself together enough to have a real partnership. But it's very hard to think of him gone. And it's just beyond comprehension to think he could have been murdered. You didn't know him, but when we got married, he was so enthusiastic, so up, so . . . full of energy and promise. I just don't understand how he could have fallen so hard."

There was nothing I could say to that. A sob racked her and she crumpled and buried her head on my shoulder. Two women pushing strollers turned to look, but nobody else seemed to notice. The wind was getting brisker now, and as I sat there, letting her cry, I saw mothers with small kids bundling them up and heading for their minivans and station wagons.

She snapped her head back up, struggling for control although the pain in her face was evident. "Sorry," she said. "You're a detective, not a pillow. And I barely know you. You must think I'm a total ditz."

I mumbled something banal about her having every right to be upset.

"Kids without a father, ever. Jeez," she said flatly. "This wasn't supposed to be the way the family album was going to look. Do you think it actually was murder?"

I nodded, not wanting to give away anything Peterson had told me. "I think that's what the police will find. But we should wait and be sure."

"Will you stay on the case?"

"To do what, exactly, Linda?"

"To find out what happened. Somehow, I'll get a better job, I'll find a way to pay you. I just can't leave it like this. I need to know." The resolve in her voice was replacing the tears; she dried her eyes and studied my face, waiting for my answer.

I crossed my arms and pulled my blazer closer. The sun seemed to have lost its warmth; I was shivering.

"Well, the police will probably find the murderer. At least you ought to give them a chance. Save yourself some money."

"But that's only a part of it," Linda continued. "I want to know who killed Dale. But I also need to know what happened to him, to his life. I don't want to cast suspicion on anybody, Mr. Deleeuw, but there's something I want you to know and I'm not sure I want to tell the police. Because it involves good friends of Dale's, and I don't want a shadow to fall on them . . ."

"Let's try first names, shall we? Linda, can I ask you an honest question?"

She looked wary but nodded.

"Are you sure you want me to go on with this? Are you really prepared for what I might find? I mean, I didn't know your husband, and you are admirably loyal to him. Maybe he *was* just too emotionally ill to make it in the world. But maybe there was something else. Anything from drugs to women. Maybe he wasn't so upright. Maybe he was spending his money on something other than his children. It hardly matters now, and you have the option of not having to know. That's not so terrible a choice, really, for you or your kids. Because once I take the case I'm going to find out. And I owe it to you to tell you what I find, I won't patronize you. You can head all that off right now, just by shaking my hand and going home and letting the police do their job and find out who killed him and why."

While she was considering that, I took a breath and plunged on with the rest of the speech. "Another thing, Linda. I can't swear that what you tell me won't make its way to the police. If I think it's relevant to solving a homicide, I'm legally bound to do that and ethically bound as well. So please think very carefully before you tell me to go ahead."

She gave it a minute or two, eyes on the mallards in the pond. I think she'd never really bought the idea that I might find something that wasn't praiseworthy, that might force her to reevaluate her notions of her former husband, that might eventually prove difficult for her children to handle.

"I want to know the truth," she said finally, looking me square in the eye. If she had any doubts at all, they didn't show.

I sighed. "Okay," I told her. "We'll mail you a contract to sign and return. Pay me what you can when you can." Evelyn would squawk. Her favorite aphorism was, "Kit, we're not the United Way."

Linda nodded and cleared her throat. I suggested we walk. We got up and headed toward the jungle gym. Linda and Dale had probably brought their kids here too.

"Dale has always been subject to manic depression, lots of ups and downs, grandiose plans one morning, so depressed he can't get out of bed the next," she began. She had slipped unconsciously into the present tense. "During these periods, he drinks too much. This Fathers' Club has been a big support for him. A friend of his who lives out there invited him to join. Sometimes they go out to dinner, sometimes they go fishing, most weeks I think they just talk. He's very faithful about going, even though Springdale's pretty far away."

I had driven through Springdale before; it wasn't far from the Pennsylvania border, closer to Philadelphia than New York. Maybe driving three quarters of an hour from Rochambeau let him be more open with those guys.

"I don't know the details, but Dale came home one day and told me that David Battelle, one of the men in the group, had offered him a business deal, a land-development partnership . . ."

"Is that the business that went bankrupt? Kimball Associates? The one that involved low-income housing?"

"Yes. Dale set up an office here in town. He kept insisting that Kimball Associates was going to be huge, that it would make a lot of money. But then something went wrong. It was a terrible blow to him, coming right after we had decided to get divorced. The final paperwork isn't even through yet, you know. Dale told me there was some bad blood between him and David. They were fighting about something. That surprised me, because David seems so controlled, so smooth, at least to me. But Dale said he could be pretty hot-tempered. And I know a lot of people don't like him. Dale said things between him and David had gotten pretty intense."

I interrupted. "That was the word he used, 'intense'?"

She nodded. "And it gets even more complicated, Mr. Deleeuw. Yes, okay, *Kit*. Because Dale also borrowed a lot of money—I don't know how much, but a substantial amount—from Jim Rheems, a stockbroker who's also a member of the Fathers' Club. Jim actually even took a second mortgage on his house to help them out."

We turned in the general direction of Linda's Toyota and strolled on. "So there were tensions in the group," she said. "All Dale would tell me was that it was 'personal,' but I could see that he was upset about it. He felt that even his men's group wasn't a refuge anymore. But by that point he really wasn't confiding in me all that much."

She sighed again. "One other thing. David Battelle is divorced. He asked me out a couple of times. And I went. I actually grew somewhat fond of him. David's smart, interesting and affectionate, once you get past the cynicism. But I didn't know if I could really be involved with anyone just yet. I just wanted you to know about it."

"Linda, did you mention the Fathers' Club to the police?"

"No. I didn't. I wanted to think it over first. I didn't like the idea of the police crashing in on the group. They did so much for him; they've all been so supportive. Two or three of them have already called, offering to baby-sit or bring dinner. I don't know . . . Should I have told the police all this?"

"Eventually we have to," I said. "But let's hold off a bit."

"Why?"

"Because I'm about to join the Fathers' Club," I said. "And I hope you're right about their not beating drums."

Three

IT WASN'T HARD to locate Charlie Montgomery. His law office was listed in the phone book, a few towns over, in Livingston. When I told his secretary I was calling in reference to Dale Lewis, Montgomery, the man Linda said was the club's liaison to the outer world, came right on the line.

"Mr. Deleeuw. Gemma tells me you're calling about Dale?" Montgomery sounded open, friendly, but pretty down; there was a grim tone in his greeting.

"Yes. I know he was a friend of yours. I'm sorry about his death; that had to be rough news." Silence. Montgomery was, after all, a lawyer; he wasn't going to say anything until he heard more. "I didn't know Dale well," I continued, "I'm closer to his wife—his ex-wife. The reason I'm calling, other than to express my sympathy, is that I'm interested in the Fathers' Club. I have two kids; my daughter is ten, my son's thirteen." So far, no actual falsehoods.

"What do you do, Mr. Deleeuw?" Montgomery wanted to know who and what he was dealing with.

"I work in corporate security, mostly. A consultant, sometimes an investigator." Telling at least part of the truth meant that, if Mongomery or anyone else in the group had ever heard my name or read about me, I wouldn't seem a complete liar. But I'd only gotten publicity on a couple of cases, and I'd avoided giving interviews. And the other fathers lived pretty far away . . .

"Dale's wife Linda has mentioned the club to me several times, and I've actually been meaning to call. I'm sorry to say it took hearing about Dale to do it. I hope this isn't too awkward a time to add a new member."

"Maybe not. Dale would surely have wanted the club to continue. Why are you interested in joining us?"

I paused on that one. "I'd like to be better at it . . . being a father, I mean. With two kids heading toward adolescence . . ."

"Yes, we all need help then. My oldest crossed that threshold a couple of years ago. It was a tricky time."

I plunged on. "I'm also having a bit of trouble with my son. It's almost impossible to talk to him these days. He seems sullen and angry a lot of the time. I don't know, I feel as if we're almost never communicating well." The odd thing was that this wasn't a ruse; it was true. Everything I said to Ben seemed to grate on him or sound like a lecture. Everything he did seemed to me to border on the impulsive or the irresponsible. Beyond that, I was starting to worry about him. I'd seen some Cs, even one D, on school papers he'd left lying around. And he didn't always tell me where he was going when he left the house, although he was supposed to leave a note or call in.

I knew from my own work that those could all be symptoms of serious trouble—drugs, depression—but they could also be a rough patch some kids just went through. Mostly, I thought I ought to give my son a wide berth for a while. Since I seemed to infuriate him so, why not make myself scarce so he wouldn't have as much to get angry about? I didn't expect that the Fathers' Club was going to help me decide whether that was a wise response or not, but my concern was real enough.

Montgomery chuckled understandingly. "Say no more; I've been there." He cleared his throat, was quiet for a moment. "Well, Mr. Deleeuw . . . I don't know what to say. We're all pretty shaken up by Dale's death. I haven't really absorbed it yet. We've been through some pretty intense stuff with him, and we all believed we had helped him. Now . . ."

I said I was aware that this probably wasn't the best time to approach the group. "But Dale's death made me feel some sense of urgency, you know? Made me stop wanting to put it off. I could get hit by a car tomorrow. Or . . . something else."

Montgomery was mulling it. I wondered if he thought Lewis was a suicide. "Can you come by my office this afternoon? Perhaps about three? That will give me a chance to call a couple of the others, see how they feel about it."

I thanked him and said I'd be by. So far, I hadn't really lied—except about the most important thing, why I wanted to join. It wasn't simple to figure out the ethics. In an investigative sense, gaining access to the group clearly seemed the appropriate thing to do. My client's ex-husband was dead, almost surely murdered, and his closest connections were with this group of men. He was quarreling with one member, Linda thought, and might have had problems with others. Kimball Associates was partly funded by a club member. In any case, they all would know more about his life than anybody else would. On the other hand, these were men opening up to other men in good faith, and I would be participating under distinctly false pretenses.

But murder took precedence over social niceties. And if they were like most men I knew, they didn't get all that personal anyway.

I tried to call Jane at her clinic, got the all-purpose "She's in conference" response, which probably meant, "She's trying to prevent some desperate addict from prostituting her thirteen-year-old." Maybe I'd have better luck calling at lunchtime.

Meanwhile, I leashed the enthusiastically wriggling Percentage and headed out for a short walk. There were lots of commands he missed, but the implications of clipping a leash onto his collar generally seemed to get through.

Afterward, I'd call the office, see if Willie had turned up anything on Dale Lewis, check my mail, return my telephone calls. I was expecting to hear whether a ball-bearing firm, one shipping more ball bearings than it was getting paid for, wanted to contract for my services. I was less interested in industrial theft, though, now that I had another murder on my mind.

It was surprisingly easy, usually, to figure out who was stealing from a company. You just got a list of employees and looked for expensive new additions to their houses, flashy new cars, vacations in the Caribbean. These were all things Willie could sniff out in minutes. Then you followed your suspect for a week or two and inevitably wound up in the company parking lot around 2 A.M. while some underpaid, on-the-take security guard left a back entrance unlocked for a few minutes or temporarily clicked off the video surveillance camera.

These cases were lucrative but not very fulfilling. I hoped Willie could handle most of them, once he learned the ropes.

Though I never say this out loud, I secretly think of much of my own work as family-saving. Finding out if a kid is on drugs or under the influence of dangerous friends. Checking to see whether a nanny really left her previous job under pleasant circumstances or was fired for drinking herself into a stupor while the baby cried untended. Determining whether a father really can't meet child support or is faking it.

I'm no Mother Teresa of private investigators. I can hardly afford to be altruistic. Even with business picking up, it looks like Ben and Em will have to panhandle their way through the colleges of their choice. It's just that family work is so much more satisfying. Doctors specialize in family practice, why can't I?

Percentage hobbled alongside with surprising agility. I wondered if the dog had any idea that one of his legs wasn't working—or if he had any ideas at all. He'd been poisoned earlier in the year by somebody trying to warn me off a case. The creep had laced a chunk of meat with arsenic and thrown it into the house, correctly assessing that Percentage would gulp down a brick if it smelled like ground beef. Dr. Camerson, the town's beloved vet, had saved him, but Percentage had suffered some permanent nerve damage in his rear leg.

At first, watching him hobble around broke my heart. But then I realized his injury didn't bother him in the least. He retained all the same skills he'd always had: wagging, eating, sleeping, retrieving (on occasion) and eliminating. He had the same inexhaustible reservoir from which to mark every tree, bush and hydrant in his path. And, on the bright side, he was off the hook, hunting-wise. Now, he had a permanent excuse for missing the squirrel or crow or rabbit.

Some people think Percentage is stupid: I prefer to see him as deeply introspective.

Before she got quite so busy, Jane and I walked the dog together almost every day. Having the ear of an almost-psychologist is a great fringe benefit. Jane knows how to read kids' behavior, how to tell moodiness from serious depression, passing rebelliousness from a possible drug problem. She has a gift for putting inexplicable actions into a comprehensible context. But I couldn't recall the last time we'd strolled together.

Which wasn't to say I wasn't pleased to help Jane realize her ambitions. She'd done the same for me, putting in plenty of twelve-hour days at the clinic so we could pay the mortgage while I turned detective after my fall from grace on Wall Street. Even with her encouragement, paycheck and health plan, for the first few years it seemed inconceivable that we'd get through. We sold off the stocks and bonds I'd expected to pay tuitions with, eroded our savings, dipped deeply into home-equity money. I doubt we'll ever fully replenish our reserves. It still gets dicey some months. But here we are. I'm a private detective with a new associate, an expanded office, even a modest measure of local celebrity. And Jane is zeroing in on her lifelong dream of being a shrink.

But I miss my damn feminist wife. Jane and I have become partners in the most literal sense of the word, and it's tough working without your partner. Right now, I'd give a week's pay to get her advice on Dale Lewis's emotional symptoms. Jane would tell me all I needed to know about manic depression.

It wasn't only her professional advice that I missed, though. She just wasn't as available for dealing with the innumerable daily crises of family life. Should we talk to the teacher about Emily's social studies struggles? Limit Ben's MTV watching? Enforce the 11 P.M. weekend curfew he so bitterly resented? What should we tell Em when Monday's best friend wouldn't speak to her on Tuesday? Was $95 too much to spend for the latest solar-powered sneakers that would not only help Ben play defense but probably launch him into space? And should his sliding grades factor into the equation?

Most of these weren't UN Security Council-level problems, but they were very real and had to be resolved, and I had to deal with them on my own. So did millions of divorced or single parents, I knew, but I liked to have all the help I could get—especially now when my relationship with Ben seemed so precarious. Aware of near constant undercurrents of resentment and resistance, I was not at all sure of how I should respond.

Jane was torn, as were so many women we knew, struggling to balance work and family. "These are some of the most important years of my kids' lives, and I'm turning into an absentee parent," she said sadly and often, exaggerating considerably. But we both knew that she would shrivel without work.

Before the insider trading investigation that had demolished my firm, Jane had spent years at home with our kids. Some women just aren't domestically inclined. Jane found life on the home front repetitious, draining, diminishing. She didn't want to function as social adviser to her children, to build her afternoons around shopping excursions, or have extensive discussions with the piano teacher, let alone sit admiringly for thirty minutes while Emily stumbled through her fifth rendition of "Für Elise."

Even before we were broke, and in desperate need of the salary she could earn, Jane didn't care to set out pots of impatiens in the spring or chrysanthemums in October. To my knowledge, she has never purchased a poinsiettia at Christmas and would gag at the idea of corn husks on her front door at any season. As for cooking, she was delighted to phone the neighborhood pizzeria, slice a few carrot sticks to salve her conscience, then sit down with the kids to eat supper and watch "The Simpsons."

The truth was, Jane needed to work. Loving her children wasn't enough to keep her brain from going mushy. Work was part of her identity; she needed the stimulation and sense of value and independence it provided. And she wanted to do it the best she could, which mandated an advanced degree.

So, in a curious twist on suburban tradition, we'd become one of those families where Dad doesn't get home till late, gets briefly filled in on the family's doings, then trudges off to sleep. Only Dad is Mom. And Dad and Mom hardly got to make love anymore, snatching quickies at odd times during little windows in our busy schedules.

I'd have to wait till the weekend, maybe, to learn more about manic depression.

What else did I know about Dale Lewis? He was warm, a loving father. If he were a manic depressive, that would square with the possibly grandiose notion of building housing for poor people when he couldn't sustain his own career or his marriage, let alone keep a roof over his family's head. His emotional problems must have been severe for him to have left his kids, given how attached to them Linda insisted he was. He was obviously struggling with some issues in his life. Not many men joined Fathers' Clubs, though a whole lot probably could have benefited from one.

I watched Percentage investigate a crumpled candy wrapper and wondered which category of suburban man Dale Lewis belonged to. There were several.

You had your standard *House and Garden* men, of course, a popular and familiar subspecies, with the closest ties to suburbia's founders. They've worked like the devil to get hold of a slice of the dream, and damnit, that slice is going to look spiffy.

Few Saturday mornings go by without at least one visit to the hardware store or lumberyard. The lives of such men seem to revolve around eternal home-improvement projects. They never seem to find time to shop, help clean the house or meet the pediatrician, but they have immaculate cars and superbly equipped workbenches; they build great shelves.

I thought they were somewhat sad figures. However much Saturday afternoon digging, raking, mowing, sawing or assembling goes on, these men never quite join the flow of family life. Their wives do all the stuff that counts. It's as if the men are standing by a rushing stream and once in a while stick their toes in to feel the temperature.

I remember when life was like that for me, and to tell the truth, even now such a life did have some appeal. You got into bed and slid between clean sheets. You opened the drawer and found a laundered shirt. You flushed and the toilet worked. The plumber joked with your wife and maybe even knew your kids' names, but if you bumped into the guy at the barbershop, you'd never know that he'd been unclogging your drain the day before. Kids learned to play the sax, made friends, rode their bikes through the park—all out of your sight and grasp.

Despite sporting events and weekend trips to the video store, these dads never catch up. They are strangers in the houses they paid for and fuss over. All would have said they do everything for their families, yet their families get less of their attention than their gutters and shrubbery.

I was generalizing, of course. Life in suburbia is evolving too quickly for rigid categories. Still, there are types.

The Sports Men teach their children early on that males have major problems with competition, communication and problem solving. Sports Men scream at their kids' coaches, at parents from the opposing team, often at their own tense sons and daughters. They keep alive the inane homilies of the sports world—"Come

ON, Julian. Defense!"—while slamming their fists into their palms, rolling their eyes in exasperation, even getting into occasional shoving and belly-bumping with other berserk parents. The Coach's strategy is never sound enough and invariably fails to take into account the special needs and emotions of their children.

Remote Men tend to be law partners, bond traders, doctors, the hard-working, high-earning white collar professionals who leave early for work and come home late, and spend much of their weekends on the phone or in the office cleaning off their desks. They can never really let go of the heady business of running the planet and will no doubt spend their retirement years wondering why they aren't closer to their kids.

I think a lot of men compensate for this distance by overexerting their authority when they *are* home. By issuing dictums, giving lectures, making demands on their children, they try to demonstrate that, even if they aren't especially connected, they are forces to be reckoned with. They may never take a kid to a movie or learn to play a video game, but they always have plenty to say about study habits, morals, responsibilities and the insidiousness of television. Rules, rules, rules. Speeches, speeches, speeches.

Here and there you glimpse an actual Shithead, a man who screams at his wife and kids in public or gets off on smacking them around from time to time. A dwindling minority hereabouts, but they exist, I know that from my case list. And there are Divorced Dads, of course, alone in apartments during the week, struggling to make their weekends with their kids special.

As for the much-ballyhooed New, Sensitive Dad, he seems to live mostly in magazine pages. In Rochambeau, I can still count on one hand the fathers I know who have actually taken a paternity leave or a day off to stay home with a sick kid. Most men are doing better than their fathers did, but the reality hasn't caught up with the myth, at least not from my perch.

Transitional, Struggling-to-Find-Their-Way Dads are, on the other hand, a big group. For all the obsession with gender roles, most families in Rochambeau are still financially supported by men, most homes purchased with the long train rides and draining days of men's jobs. These guys love their kids and want to be part of their lives, but there is only so much energy to go around. I never feel more grateful about my own reinvented life than when I see these suburban warriors dragging their tired butts off the train at 8 P.M., ties loosened, jackets slung over their shoulders, Lands' End shoulder-bag straps wrinkling their shirts. By the time they eat dinner, their kids will be headed to bed. These men do the best they can, struggling to get home early for teacher conferences and school plays, showing up late at soccer games, occasionally going through elaborate scheduling contortions in order to drive on a class trip. They don't get a lot of points for any of it, either.

Which category did Dale Lewis belong to?

I walked home, hung up Percentage's leash and called Willie.

I don't really know what time Willie gets to the office each morning. He's usually there before I am—maybe he sleeps there?—but it doesn't really matter. Willie isn't the type who needs to be reminded of his responsibilities.

Besides, in our shop, schedules need to be flexible. With Jane so busy and two kids at home, my freedom to move around is somewhat limited. I don't mind being out one or two nights a week, but I want to be present for the kids, to make healthy low-fat dinners, to roust them from the TV, to go over homework, prod them to make tomorrow's paper-bag lunches, set more or less reasonable bedtimes. That's one of the reasons I hired Willie.

It had been a great move, even if he did go off surfing or dirt-biking on Friday afternoons. He had the world's best disposition and, when it came to getting information, he was a vacuum cleaner.

"Morning, Willie. How are you?"

"Great, Chief. You?"

"Good. I'm on my way in. I just wondered—do you have anything on Dale Lewis yet?"

I heard his computer beeping and clacking in the background. It was much the better for both of us if I didn't know what he was doing with it.

"Well, there's no unusual credit card activity," he reported. "In fact, his MasterCard was canceled a few weeks ago. So was his AmEx. He wasn't going to fancy restaurants or buying much with them anyway. Mostly necessities—food, clothing. Nothing to indicate a girlfriend or a fancy new apartment. He applied to Jersey Central for a business loan a few months ago, and he was asking for a lot of money for a guy whose credit cards are getting canceled: $200,000. But I don't know yet what he wanted it for or whether he got it. If he was spending money, he was using cash. I'll keep looking."

Deadbeat Dads busy setting up new social lives love to acquire furniture, to squire their new friends to elegant eateries. But Dale sounded genuinely broke. So what made him think he could get a $200,000 loan?

What sort of suburban male was this? From what Linda told me, he'd been an ambitious, promising young man. And he'd been on the sensitive end of the fatherhood scale when his depression and work troubles didn't weigh him down. But once they did, he'd been a Disappearing Dad. Then a dead one.

Four

WHEN I PULLED into the mall parking lot, work crews were installing spiffy new "American Way" signs, bright plastic trash receptacles and potted shrubs around the lot. New lighting, too, to reassure shoppers during the latest carjacking scare, though any carjacker with two brain cells would skip this lot and head for the Lexuses and BMWs and Rangers at the bigger, newer and more upscale malls down the road. Who would hijack an eight-year-old Chevy sedan? Or a beat-up Volvo with leaky oil seals?

The American Way was continuously, heroically, transforming itself, the little strip mall that could. Or at least wanted to. When I'd first moved in five years ago, the thirty-year-old mall was on the edge of extinction, which is why I could afford to rent space here. The Amway, as its tenants call it, was one of the first generation of malls, and probably belongs on the National Register of Historic Sites. I can actually picture it stuffed into one corner of the Smithsonian's Museum of American History.

Originally, I'm sure, it was all the rage. By the time I moved in, however, the floor tiles were curling up, a general air of dinge prevailed, and Murray Grobstein was almost single-handedly keeping it alive. Aside from his shop, yet to be expanded to its current high-profit dimensions, there had been a record store, a couple of sad five-and-dimes, a pet shop that was eventually raided by the local animal welfare society. Our Christmas Santa was an East

German immigrant who spoke no English at all, but answered all the kids' requests with an enthusiastic *"Ja! A gut* Christmas!" The mall remained fairly low-concept, lacking architect-designed atriums, fern-fringed restaurants or hip catalogue stores selling thousand-buck Stairmasters. It worked comfortably, if not prosperously.

The things people pouring into the megamalls to buy seem to grow ever weirder and pricier. Who needs cleated Goretex hiking boots to negotiate suburban culs-de-sac anyway? Maybe they just go nicely with those rugged $50,000 Land Cruisers people drive. The more built up the suburbs get, the more people who live here want to look and act like they raise livestock in Montana.

But evolve or die is the core ethic. The Amway was battling back, reinventing itself in endearing, gloriously tacky, sometimes even successful ways.

There was the new computer discount store and the brand-new International Food Court, complete with Pitaville, Yogurt World and Creative Potatoes.

Small carts had popped up in the mall's aisles and courtyards, selling inexpensive jewelry, sculpted candles and personalized knickknacks—way stations for immigrants, retirees, laid-off Madison Avenue account executives and entrepreneurial housewives in transition.

In transition, too, was Plain James, the slatternly transvestite who peddled R&B and soul music from his DDT Tapes and Records cart. Open cross-dressers being somewhat rare in our neck of the woods, the mall manager thought he was renting cart space to a "knockout dame," as he later recounted it. And certainly James *is* striking: six foot three, with platinum-blond hair and a penchant for short skirts and outrageous accessories that brings mall strollers to a dead stop when he reports for work. He'd just won a bitter battle with heroin and had impulsively decided to move away from dealers and users. In search of "someplace pure vanilla," he'd rented an apartment above a dentist's office in Clifton, where few questions had been asked, and gotten into retailing. It took Luis, who loved blues passionately, two milliseconds to spot the fact that James was a knockout but not a female.

None of us fellow tenants cared much. And even though passersby were occasionally startled, and teenage boys snickered, the mall's customers didn't seem to mind much either. Suburbs can be surprisingly tolerant places, as long as you're not messing with lawns, schools or property taxes. Still, it wasn't the East Village, and there was the inevitable bit of trouble.

"This ugly woman with a fat ass came walking by with her daughters yesterday," James reported indignantly one morning. "I had taken my wig off because it itched like hell and this awful little child shrieks, 'Look, Mommy, that woman is a MAN!' And the mother squeals, 'Oh, my God,' and grabs the beastly infant and runs—I mean RUNS—away. As if I could ever look as frightening as that woman in her running shoes and spandex pants!"

After a brief flurry of complaints, mall management briefly considered trying to run James out. But Luis and I warned quietly about the prospect of lawsuits and bad publicity and all sorts of trouble if anyone bothered Plain James, who kept his cart clean and attractive, was doing a pretty fair business, and was meticulous about paying his rent. So James was told to keep his wig on and his fashion critiques to himself and permitted to remain. He still greeted me with affectionate hoots, daring me to get an earring or "Do SOMETHING to spice yourself up, honey." I hoped he stayed forever.

And of course there was Murray Grobstein's ever expanding Shoe World, a sneaker emporium attracting teenage boys from all over the county.

Murray spent part of each weekend cruising Newark and Brooklyn. It was market research: whatever city kids were wearing, he ordered dozens of pairs immediately. He was now given to high-fiving and shouting "Yo!" and "Chill!" at friends and customers. Murray conceded that he didn't exactly understand why middle-class white suburban kids wanted so badly to emulate gangsta rappers, but he was grateful and quick to stock multicultural rages like the down-over-your-brow knit hats that had spread from the inner cities to the outer lawns. These met what Murray said were the three basic criteria for a successful cultural transplant: "Black kids wear it, it's expensive, and it looks silly." Murray just hoped this strange cultural phenomenon didn't evaporate before his youngest got through Yale.

Anyway, add in the numerous special events staged for recreational and shopping pleasure—elders' walking clubs, free blood-pressure readings, crafts fairs—and it looked as though the American Way was going to survive, if not precisely boom.

My pal Luis hadn't figured out how to integrate his Lightning Burger into the Food Court's international theme, but I pointed out that his Cuban ancestry probably covered that. If he felt sad about never practicing law again, Luis never showed it. But I suspected that helping me strategize, as he often did, felt like a return to his earlier, more aristocratic and pre-fast-food life. We were in fact planning to have lunch that day.

Evelyn was sipping herbal tea and fussing with her computer when I came in. I'd finally figured out—with Willie's help—that Evelyn, who was pushing seventy but unwilling to disclose just how hard, had joined a seniors' conference on one of the big computer bulletin boards. I had signed us up for the legal news and other help offered on a new international investigators' conference. Willie and I often e-mailed requests for information or background checks to participating members in other parts of the country and returned the favor when we could. But Evelyn was spending a lot of time on more personal message boards. We suspected an on-line boyfriend.

"Uh . . . good morning, Kit," she said, clearing her throat and flushing. "There are some messages, but nothing important. You know," she continued brightly, logging off, "there are a lot of library applications for this technology. I must speak with the library trustees." I nodded.

His name, Willie had whispered to me several weeks earlier, was Digital Thunder. "Came across some e-mail in our mailbox," Willie said. "I couldn't help noticing." Digital Thunder. Love springs eternal.

Evelyn had rescued me, sort of, from my chronic disorganization. When she'd joined me almost a year ago, she'd promptly stuffed mounds of paper into bags for sorting, tossed the three-foot-high pile of newspapers and magazines, immediately established a file system. She screened oddball calls, prepared a daily telephone call and return list, badgered me into buying a computer and fax, sent out bills. Only her forceful intervention had repaired the frayed relations with several insurance companies increasingly frustrated by my delinquent reports. Evelyn considered my reports in the same way she undoubtedly had viewed tardy book-returners: she wouldn't have it.

In a way, I'd rescued her too, I thought. She'd felt useless and lonely after her retirement from the library. My chronically chaotic office and methods were constant creative challenges to her. She'd taken to mothering Willie—who thought nothing of wearing the same sweatshirt for two weeks—with a vengeance. She had also begun to dabble in investigation, going out on carefully selected surveillance missions.

I had to admit Evelyn and Willie were lethal in the field. Nobody would ever peg either of them as a private investigator and almost everybody talked openly to them. Evelyn had once sat on a park bench for two hours with a tiny video camcorder pointing out of her purse while the plant manager of an electronics firm illegally sold stolen computer parts right in front of her. He almost fainted when she got up to testify at his trial. "Serves him right, too," she'd sniffed. "I hate a thief.

"And of course you remember," she now added firmly, "your appointment with Mr. DiNato of Wauheeken Industrial." And of course I hadn't. DiNato, an affable ex-state cop, was seeking help with a suspected industrial espionage problem. "He's in your office," Evelyn said menacingly, as if I'd bolt.

So he was, looking prosperous, straining his shiny gray suit, leafing through my four-month-old magazines. I liked Al. I'd met a lot of ex-cops like him. There was a certain wariness to them, but once they got to know you they were generally warm, generous and easygoing. I had run some background checks for his company, and I'd sniffed out the clerical worker who was carting office supplies out at night and selling them at a flea market in Queens.

Attractive as the money would have been, though, I turned down Al's case. The truth was, though I could hardly tell DiNato this, I wasn't really in the mood. Dale Lewis's pale, stiff face kept popping into my mind, as did Linda's warm, animated one. I had the sense my immediate future would be taken up with Dale and Linda Lewis and the members of the Fathers' Club. So my meeting with Al this morning was friendly but brief.

A few minutes before my scheduled lunch with Luis—I'd called to "reserve" our usual table overlooking the highway—Willie tapped on the door.

"Boss, I've got the names of all the Fathers' Club members. Typed them up for you." Casually, he tossed me a computer printout. Willie is always nonchalant about all the information he wangles. He flopped down on the beat-up sofa that Al had just vacated, watching my reaction as he gulped from the Snapple bottle that seemed permanently attached to one hand. He liked the more exotic flavors—mango, I think this one was.

"Good grief. How'd you get this?" I asked, shaking my head.

"Well, these guys meet in a Methodist Church library—one of their wives told me so when I called up and said I was embarrassed, but real interested in joining. The group had to sign an agreement with the church, so I called and chatted with the church secretary, said we were considering a mailing about men's role in fighting domestic abuse. She said I could stop by. I did, and she showed me the insurance and emergency forms everybody has to fill out when they use the facilities. Church secretaries are not into lying, Chief. Then I picked up the rest of the info through, um, computer sources."

I read aloud from the list. "David Battelle. Linda mentioned him. He was Dale's partner in this ill-fated low-income development partnership. Dated Linda a couple of times too, she says. He's forty, I see. Got a bunch of real estate properties and projects. Lives in Clayton. Divorced, no kids—that's weird. I thought this club was for dads. Frank Dougherty, forty-six, a schoolteacher, two teen-age girls. Jim Rheems. He's a stockbroker—Dale borrowed money from him. Charlie Montgomery. I spoke with him a little while ago—I'm going over to his office this afternoon. Hal Etheridge, forty-four—married to a biologist at Rutgers, two kids . . . Amazing amount of detail you've collected here, I've got to say. Impressive." Willie beamed. "And Ricky Melman, thirty-four, three children, social worker. Belongs to the same church as Montgomery. Dale would have made seven."

Willie swigged from his Snapple. "You want me to run down financial data on them all?"

"Yes, please. I'm especially interested in any connections they had with one another or with Dale. But we need to be super-discreet on this, Willie. Don't spook anyone. I'm planning to join the group."

"The Fathers' Club?" Willie looked mildly repulsed. It clearly wasn't on his list of top ten things to do in your spare time.

"Well, I think it's my best shot at figuring out what happened to Dale, don't you? If I try to formally question these guys and one of them is involved in his death in some way, he'd just stonewall me. It's always possible some stranger got Dale drunk, whacked him on the head and killed him, but this group had lots of dealings with him. We know he had a financial relationship with at least two of them. Maybe there are other connections as well. So the Fathers' Club seems a good place to start. Hell, I *am* a father. I feel crummy about joining the group under false pretenses, but . . ." Willie was looking rather crummy himself. He was already up and halfway out the door, heading back to his keyboard, wanting to be somewhere else.

On a half-baked impulse I blurted, "Willie, is your father or mother alive?"

He stopped, turned back, his usual unflappable expression replaced by one of caution. "I'm adopted."

"I guess I thought it was something like that. Do you know anything about your biological parents? Are they dead?"

He looked out the window toward the parking lot. "No, my mother's alive. She lives in Summit. I tracked her down last year. It wasn't hard. I've just never met her or talked to her. Maybe I will one day." He took a swig from his Snapple, looked toward the floor.

Time to drop it. "Well, if you ever want to talk about it, I'm here." He nodded. I changed the subject, fast.

"Any news on the Jamie Gilbert case?"

"Yeah, Kit, I'm going to write up the report this morning." Willie was obviously relieved to talk about someone else's secrets. "We should probably get it over to his family quick. He's into some heavy stuff, all right; his dad was right. I trailed him to this guy Rivera's house in Paterson. Rivera has been arrested for dealing, a bunch of times. I got a picture of Jamie going into the house. then I followed him to the Random Club afterward, and he asked if I was selling. Started even to haggle about prices until I said I didn't have anything to sell."

"Good work again, Will. I appreciate it."

It was strange being a boss again, although Willie didn't require much supervision and Evelyn gave *me* orders more frequently than the reverse.

I closed the door and called Linda Lewis at home.

"Hi," she said. "You can't have news already?" Her subdued tone indicated that reality was sinking in.

"No, no news. Just checking to see how you are."

"I wouldn't say I'm okay, but I would say I'm handling it. With two kids, I don't have much choice. They need a parent who's functioning right now. I'm it. I just can't quite get past the shock."

"That's normal," I said, fishing around for words that might comfort. "I'm sorry you and your family have to endure this. I'm not saying that because you're a client. I just sense how much you wanted your marriage to work, and I was very touched by how forgiving and generous you were toward Dale. He was lucky to have you, however long you were together. I was wondering if you could use lunch tomorrow, if that might help . . . if you're tied up with the kids or something that's fine too."

"No, that would be a help," she said quickly. "I'll be around, probably on the phone half the day. We're planning a cremation, then a private funeral service for family only. Anything more open might attract the media, and I couldn't bear that. Even though we split up, I have to do this. He's still family, still the father of my kids."

Not everybody would have viewed it that way. "It's good of you to take care of all that. You don't really have to."

"Oh yes, I do. Dale deserved that much."

I heard a kid's piping voice in the background. I had no doubt Linda would manage the awful challenges in front of her, but raising two children by yourself was rough. Doing it as an artist with no real income to fall back on had to be twice as rough. Doing it while helping the kids deal with the murder of their father . . .

But I had called to tell her plainly what I was planning. I was afraid she wouldn't like it.

"Look, Linda, I just wanted to let you know I'm joining the Fathers' Club undercover, meaning I'm not telling anyone that I'm working for you or investigating Dale's death. So if and when you talk to these guys, please don't mention me or the fact that you've hired me."

There was a prolonged silence on the other end of the line. I *knew* she wouldn't like it.

"But, Kit, why? These were his friends. They meant a lot to him. Why do you have to deceive them this way? That sounds awful, infiltrating a group of men who are talking about the most personal things. That isn't easy for men, you know . . ."

Boy, did I know. My closest friend was a Cuban immigrant who had never set foot in my house.

"Linda, I know it sounds callous. But you told me yourself that

Dale had quarreled with one of the men in the club—Battelle—and owed money to at least one other. These people were somehow involved in his business and financial life, and one of them was even involved with you, briefly. Whether or not they had anything to do with Dale's death, and I'm by no means suggesting that they did, chances are they know more than anybody else about him. If there were problems, he'd have talked about them there, maybe even more than he did to you. The cops say they don't think robbery was a motive, so it had to be something personal or connected to his business dealings. I don't think some stranger just walked in there and killed him."

"Then why not just interview them?" Linda snapped. "Why not just visit each member and ask him what he knows?"

I paused. There was no *way* she was going to like this.

"Linda, only Perry Mason got people to talk themselves into prison terms because he questioned them in a tough baritone. First off, if any of these men *were* involved, which is a possibility we have to consider, they'd simply shut up and stonewall me. But if I'm just a guy in the group, that's different. Someone might know something he wouldn't pass on officially to a cop or an investigator, but he might mention it to another club member. People can even give things away in casual conversation. For all kinds of reasons, believe me, my way is more effective than a formal investigative visit."

"You don't seriously suspect that one of these men could have harmed Dale, do you? Because this makes me very uncomfortable, Kit. How am I supposed to face his friends, thank them for their support, accept their condolences when I'm sending a spy into their private meetings?"

"I can see why it troubles you, Linda, and I respect that. It troubles me too. But I'll be blunt. This is a murder investigation. Somebody murdered your husband. It's not pretty, finding out who might have done such a thing, and it's not polite. A killer violates the most basic ethic holding our civilization together. The methods you sometimes have to use to bring him to justice aren't sweet. I keep lying to a minimum. But this is well within my own ethical standards, especially when it comes to murder. If you want me to work for you, you have to let me investigate in any legal way I deem appropriate. If you're not okay with that, then I'll stop taking your money. I'm alerting you to this part of my plan as a courtesy, and so that you won't give me away. But otherwise, I intend to bring you my findings, not get your permission for the means by which I obtain them. We need to be clear on that."

We went back and forth a bit, but her resistance weakened. She clearly wanted me on the case; she had to know what had happened to Dale and why. We agreed to have lunch the next day, when we could talk this through some more if she wanted to. But I wasn't going to bend. This group was my best—and at the moment perhaps my only—wedge into a tough case.

I spent the next hour going over some reports, trying to clean up an insurance fraud case, then steeling myself to call Jamie Gilbert's father with the bad news.

Arthur Gilbert was a cardiologist and a pillar of Rochambeau's Congregationalist Church. Arthur, like any other parent, didn't want to hear that his seventeen-year-old was driving the family Jeep to Paterson to visit a drug dealer. Or that he'd asked Willie to sell him some heroin, and that we had that exchange on tape. Or that he'd stolen stuff from his parents to pay for his habit. And "I simply do not believe it," was exactly Arthur Gilbert's stiff response when I laid it out. Most parents are instinctively loyal to their kids, naturally enough. I suggested that he look at the photographs, listen to the tape, read the report, then judge for himself. I assured him I had no interest in tarring his son with false accusations.

But I understood. This isn't what parents move to the suburbs for. In my experience, they deny everything violently for fifteen minutes or so after they're confronted with the evidence, until the shocking reality breaks through and they accept what they've suspected for months, shift gears, and ask what they need to do to help their kids. I had the phone numbers all ready, thanks to Jane: the rehab facilities, therapists for follow-up, support groups for parents. I'd had this conversation more times in the past five years than I cared to.

In the overwhelming majority of cases, once the parents grasped the problem, they really got moving, propelling their kids and themselves into counseling, facing up to reality. Kids in towns like Rochambeau had enough resources, caring people and professionals behind them to deal with trouble when it hit. Kids in some other places didn't. It made all the difference. Arthur Gilbert would get it, and his kid would be in some shrink's office by sundown tomorrow, if not sooner.

I had a quick lunch with Luis at the Lightning Burger, at his suggestion trying out the new broiled chicken sandwich the chain had concocted to get with the healthier, fat-free times. As always, Luis was immaculately dressed—blue suit, crisp white shirt, tie pin—the most elegant fast-food franchise manager in America, I suspected. I had no trouble picturing him where he belonged, at the center of a packed courtroom, disemboweling some obtuse witness, dazzling a jury with his intellect. Yet we both knew he would never set foot in a courtroom again, unless, as he'd once joked, "somebody chokes to death on a french fry and sues me." Which could happen.

I told him about the Lewis case, and he agreed that joining the Fathers' Club made perfect sense. "I know it seems dishonorable," he said. "But this is murder; you must do what you must do. Murder is the ultimate sin. It takes precedence over convention, even over some forms of honor." That about summed it up.

We mulled over various puzzling aspects of the murder. Luis was particularly interested in the FBI's involvement, spinning various theories about what might be prompting it. I was glad for his input. It was like having an extra, and superior, brain at work.

I rarely asked Luis much about his own life. Aside from the sad fact that he had left most of his family behind in Havana, he had never revealed much about his past and seemed ill at ease when asked. Luis had clearly come to terms with the limits and rewards of his new life and, not being an American, wasn't into pouring his heart out about how unfairly life had treated him. I had never been invited to his Jersey City apartment, and doubted that I ever would. He had never come to my home, despite repeated invitations. I had learned to accept our friendship on his terms.

I was back upstairs looking up Charlie Montgomery's address when Evelyn buzzed me to say Ben's school was on the line. That was a call you had to take. He probably was sick. Hadn't said he felt bad that morning, but then Ben and I hadn't been talking much lately.

"Kit?"

"Yes. Nate?" This couldn't be good news. Nathan Hauser was the Rochambeau Middle School principal. He had ascended to that position under horrific circumstances—he'd been vice-principal when his boss was gunned down in her office, a case I had helped to unravel. I had a lot of respect for Hauser, who cared deeply about kids, worked like a demon and had always been honest and helpful to me. But there couldn't be a happy reason for him to be calling. Nurses, not principals, called about flu or tummy upsets.

"Kit, I'm sorry to be giving you this news. But I'll be direct. I've got your son sitting here in my office. I've just suspended him for a week. You need to come get him."

"My son? Ben?" As if I had several. Hauser was probably as accustomed to this bewildered kind of response as I was. But I had reason to be startled. Ben had never even gotten detention before. Suspended?

"He was caught smoking pot. Right in the building. He could be expelled for this, but it's a first offense and he's got a good record. They still leave us a bit of discretion. I have to notify the police, of course; you know Chief Leeming doesn't take a happy view of drugs around the school. I don't take a benign view of that either, so, depending on your son's attitude, he's suspended for at least the rest of the week effective this morning. But this doesn't have to appear on his record or become part of any criminal file or permanent administrative record. First offense is a misdemeanor here, especially if he's using, not selling. And the quantities are small. It doesn't have to be a big deal, not if he gets the message. He will have to attend some lectures on drugs and health, have a couple of sessions with the school counselor. I know you'll take whatever steps you deem appropriate at home. And then my fondest hope is that I never have to have a conversation like this with him again."

"Nate, are you sure? I just can't believe that Ben—" Lord knows I had heard too many parents perform this routine, but I was as profoundly shocked as they were.

"Kit, I'm looking at one joint I pulled out of his hand and two he gave me out of his pocket. Can't be more sure than that."

I hung up and headed for the school.

Five

IF I'D KNOWN ahead of time how much parents worry about kids, I can't swear that I'd have wanted to have one, let alone two. But how could I have known? There is almost no point in a man's life when he sits down to talk at length or in depth about the meaning of fatherhood and whether or not to embark on it. Having kids was simply what you did, even as recently as the eighties, a period my kids talk about as if it were the Civil War. ("Did you ever actually see Ronald Reagan on TV when he was President, Dad?")

I never received the booklet warning that, from birth, children will drive you crazy with worry and concern.

It began for me the instant Ben was born. He didn't seem to me to be breathing, though everyone else in the delivery room could see that he was. It was the first of countless times in my life when somebody, usually a woman, looked at me with amusement and compassion and murmured of Ben or Emily, "(S)he's just fine, Mr. DeLeeuw." I always needed somebody else to tell me so, and even then I wasn't sure they were telling the truth. It was, after all, *my* responsibility, and say what you want about men and their problems, there is hardly one functioning male on the planet who doesn't carry this gorilla called responsibility on his back.

The sense of burden is numbing, when you consider it. For twenty years and often beyond, you are responsible for the health, safety, emotional stability and future prospects of another human being. If you screw it up, the consequences are horrible to contemplate. Jane says having kids is one of those ventures you don't want to overintellectualize. "It doesn't bear a lot of scrutiny," she says. "If you *really* thought about it, would anybody do it?" But I think about it a lot, particularly when I get calls like Nathan Hauser's.

To be candid, there occasionally are times when I wish we hadn't done it, that Jane and I could still scoot up to Cape Cod for a weekend, make love at odd times and in odd places, go to late movies and worry about nothing but us. There, I've thought it and now I've said it. Sometimes I'm tired of wondering whether my children are happy or not, whether their value systems are well grounded, whether they have friends and a comfortable future. *Sometimes I just wish they would go away.*

I've fantasized about reaching a point in the process when the kid is clearly fine and sort of goes his own way, while cordially checking in with you from time to time. Alas, kids' lives seem to consist primarily of lurching from one complex phase to another, each one arriving before you've figured out how to handle the last.

A few days before my visit from Linda Lewis, Emily—one of those kids who is diligent about schoolwork without being nagged—had freaked out. She'd gotten a C on a math test and forgotten a looming science project. "Dad," she whimpered, "I feel so stupid. I feel like I'm drowning. I'm having a nervous breakdown. I can't handle this." I mumbled soothing platitudes, brought her chamomile tea and cookies, talked to her for half an hour to get her to sleep—she was weeping much of that time—then rushed to the phone to leave a message on her homeroom teacher's voice mail. The teacher always told us to let her know if her students were having any special problems and, if I remembered correctly, Emily's comments contained most, if not all, of the buzzwords and sentiments on the checklist that are supposed to send you scrambling for professional help.

The next morning, my daughter bounced downstairs for breakfast, chirping like a songbird in spring. "Hey, Dad," she greeted me, literally skipping across the kitchen. "What's up?"

"Hey," I said. "You're feeling better." It wasn't really a question, more a shocked declaration.

She stared at me with that slightly revolted what-on-earth-could-you-possibly-be-talking-about look that preadolescents specialize in.

"You were so upset last night," I explained lamely, already imagining the jokes in the teachers' lounge. "I actually called the school and left a message for Ms. Ziebarth, telling her how overwhelmed you felt." It seemed like the right move at the time. Jane wasn't around to consult; it was a battlefield call.

Emily laughed out loud. "Oh, Dad," she said, wolfing down the first spoonful of Cocoa Krispies. "You're so *cute!*"

That was the big difference between my two offspring right there. Emily found every stupid thing I did somehow endearing; my pathetic incompetence brought out her deep nurturing qualities. Ben, on the other hand, was more basic: he thought every stupid thing I did was just stupid. I kept thinking maybe there was something to this psychoanalytic notion that, deep down, the son wants to kill the father. Maybe it isn't even that deep down.

So Ben smoked a joint or two. That was bad. But how bad? Was the next step necessarily crack or heroin? Did it mean he was a troubled kid and we were bad parents? Or did it mean kids will experiment and parents have to stay steady about it? And how could we decide in the eight minutes before I had to pick him up and make some intelligent response?

"Of course we have to stay cool and steady about it," said Jane in some exasperation when I reached her at the clinic via cell phone. "We have to talk to him, see how he feels about it, how he reacts to being suspended. If he's embarrassed and humiliated, then we smother him with love, gentle reproaches and understanding, and move on. If he's sullen and hostile, then we might need to get him to a counselor. But don't lecture him, Kit, talk to him. We'll all sit down . . . well, I can't be home in time tonight. Shit. Just sit him down and tell him we're concerned. Then *listen.* I guess we'll have lots of chances to talk to him this week, since he won't be in school."

Good advice, but I didn't feel especially confident as I drove to the school and walked toward the principal's office. I shivered, and not just because of Ben. The last time I'd been in that office I'd found bloodstains on the floor.

This trip was less dramatic, but it wasn't going to be pleasant, either. I wished Jane were here with me. I didn't feel as calm as she'd advised me to be. Ben had sworn a thousand times that he had nothing to do with drugs, avoided kids who did, and understood how we felt about the dangers. So the problem wasn't only that he'd smoked marijuana. The problem was that he'd been lying to me and I'd failed to perceive that.

He was sitting in the outer office, looking both conspicuous and uncomfortable. Every kid passing in the hallway could see him through the glass wall and would know that he was being called on the carpet. By the close of school, they would all know what for. By dinnertime, so would all their parents. I wasn't on the social A list anyway, but I did fear for him a bit. The suburbs are phobic about drugs, sex, kidnapping and violence. I didn't want Ben branded an outcast in the eighth grade.

Nathan Hauser's severe-looking secretary surely was aware of what was going on. She took turns glowering at each of us.

Ben was closing in on fourteen, sprouting faster than his mental or emotional ability to absorb the growth. He was lean, gangly, but really rather sweet-looking with his wide eyes and shaggy brown hair; girls had been calling for months. He said nothing about this to us, of course, drawing from an inexhaustible repertoire of monosyllabic grunts when asked about anything involving his personal life. He wore size 12 sneakers, his jeans were too short, his face wore a dusting of mild acne, which he never referred to but I was sure made him uncomfortable. Sprawling beyond the narrow confines of the straight-backed office chair, he looked flushed, uneasy and, yes, sullen.

"Hey, Ben," I said.

"Hi, Dad." He studied the floor. His expression wasn't so much abashed as annoyed and impatient. But I could see that was a stance. He was scared. The brief glimpse he'd allowed me of his eyes gave it away. I knew the look from intense movies, high-pressure Little League games and times he'd gotten in trouble. Ben was still a kid, just a big one.

Our terse exchange was fairly typical of the dialogue between us in the past few months. Everybody told me that was what adolescents were like, but I missed talking to my kid. I didn't really understand why this was such a healthy phase of development. Why couldn't we just stay close all the way through his adolescence?

For the first eight years of my son's life, I was hardly at home during the week, but spent weekends racing around like a Divorced Dad. Then, suddenly, I was home a lot. My picture appeared in the local paper along with a story about how my firm was being shut down by the feds.

The change gave me time to build a different kind of relationship with Emily, who was too little to care how I made a living or even whether I did. But Ben and I might be struggling for a long time to fill the gaps in our own relationship. He'd had to fend off sneers and taunts from his classmates that his father was a crook. I found out only later that the fending off sometimes involved fists.

Still, we'd somehow gotten through all that—and now, without warning, the sight of me seemed to make him ill. I had the feeling he'd never quite forgiven me for not being around for so long, then suddenly appearing and expecting the two of us to be like Pa Cartwright and Hoss. Maybe he was paying me back for that now.

Hauser invited us into his office. Nate's greeting was stiffer than usual, for Ben's benefit, I suspected. I noticed a large pile of confiscated water guns and baseball caps—both verboten—in a corner of the room. Coolly Hauser repeated what he'd told me on the phone, reiterated how disappointed he was, how Ben would have to attend six lectures on substance abuse run by the school's guidance counselor. He showed me the half-smoked reefer he'd taken from Ben. He paused to let all this sink in, then calmly but forcefully warned about the next step.

"If there is any repeat of this— *one* more incident—we will have to seriously consider sending Ben to the county's special needs school." Ben looked rattled at that. I was rattled too, though I hoped it was mostly bluster designed to terrify kids, who'd all heard horror stories about the county school. I doubted Ben could be sent there without evidence of serious, sustained behavioral problems. But was there any? Had I been blind and deaf? Piously informing other people about their kids' drug problems while failing to see my own son's? I saw Ben glance at me from time to time, trying to gauge my mood.

I was trying to gauge my mood too. I'd smoked marijuana plenty of times as a kid. Though I didn't want Ben getting into drug use, experimentation was normal among smart, adventurous kids. We probably gave our suburban children too many scary advisories about the evils of everything: child-snatching strangers, sex without condoms, drunk driving, Halloween candy. Emily and her friends in the fifth grade knew more about body fluid exchange than I did when I entered college. They were taught to say no a dozen different ways to a dozen different threats. Emily knew the Heimlich maneuver before she could name the continents. It's a wonder she ever left our house.

Was this concern all for our children? Or did it serve mostly to allay our own fears? I always had this nagging sense that we were teaching them to worry more about themselves in their relatively safe suburban cocoons than about their urban counterparts a few miles away in Newark or New York, many of whose lives were every bit as perilous as all our warnings suggested.

So how mad should I get about my kid smoking a joint? And what the hell was Ben going to do at home all week? I had scribbled myself a Post-it to call Mrs. Steinitz, our humorless and Draconian baby-sitter for whom Victorian England was the golden era of child rearing. Ben would be as safe as he would be uncomfortable. A week with Mrs. Steinitz, sans friends and Nintendo privileges, would put the most hardened criminal back on the straight and narrow.

Nate Hauser asked Ben to step outside, which he did with visible relief. I was hoping Nate would break into a we-scared-the-hell-out-of-him-didn't-we-Kit chuckle, then offer me one of the Diet Cokes he stored in a tiny refrigerator behind his desk. But he just stood up and walked around to the front of the desk. He was tall and muscular and I suspected many a kid had sweated it out under that towering presence and steely gaze.

"Kit, I'm sorry to be seeing you under these circumstances. But I'm worried about Ben. I haven't caught him before, but I understand this isn't the first time. He's acting up in class, and—I was about to call you to set up a conference—his grades are dropping too. He's looking at a C in French, maybe even worse in science. When I asked him why he was smoking dope—we both know he knows better—he wouldn't answer me. He said it was his business."

I felt my face redden. I was quite aware that my first reaction to Nate's lecture was intense embarrassment. *I must be a crummy father. Otherwise I would have one of those great kids who never get called to the principal's office.* Whoa, I thought. Don't be a jerk. This is about Ben, not you.

"I'm shocked, Nate. But that's what every parent says, right?"

Hauser did, finally, smile. "No, Kit. Usually what they say is, 'How dare you suggest my child has a problem?' and they threaten to sue. *Then* they say they're shocked. Look, we're all busy. It's not easy to see problems, especially at this age when you can't always distinguish between the usual adolescent prickliness and something more serious. I am concerned about Ben. I don't want to blow things out of proportion, this stuff happens, but we have to deal with it. Is there anything going on in his life that could give us some insight? Problems at home?"

Hauser motioned me to sit down, and I did. He reached back into his refrigerator and found me a diet soda, tossing the can across the desk.

"Well," I told him, "Ben and I haven't been talking much lately. He seems exceptionally irritated around me, has a really short fuse. But there's no marital trouble, nothing like that. Jane's been awfully busy and I guess I have too, and I can't say I've been paying a lot of attention to Ben. Not enough, clearly."

Hauser waved a hand dismissively. "Skip the part where you blame yourself, Kit. It's not productive and it's not true, either. That's a popular misconception, that parents can anticipate every problem and make it go away. Can't be done. Ben's showing the classic preliminary signs that there's trouble, though. We have counselors, but I know your wife is . . . what, a psychologist? You might want to get your own referral if you can't talk it out with the boy."

"Jane's studying to be a psychologist. She knows plenty of therapists. Believe me, there'll be no hesitation about getting help if there's a problem."

"Good. 'Cause there's definitely a problem." He wasn't rubbing it in, just making sure that I got it.

I guess I was sounding a bit obtuse. "You mean a drug problem or something else?"

Nate shrugged. "A few months back, this boy is a model kid, happy, popular, butt-kissing and working his way onto the honor roll, playing in the jazz band. Today, he's still a neat kid, but he's a bit listless, a little hostile, struggling academically and showing signs of some drug involvement. We have to figure out what's going on."

Maybe Ben would just tell me what was bothering him. Maybe cows would fly.

"I'll talk to him. Jane will too, Nate. I'm glad you called. I know you're doing your job and I appreciate it." I did, too.

Ben and I walked out to the car in silence. In the car, I mentioned the weather, asked him if he were going trick-or-treating for what would almost surely be the last time. He grunted, which usually means "I don't know." He didn't appear either abashed or embarrassed, if that was what Jane had been hoping for.

So I dropped my increasingly feeble attempts at conversation, and we drove wordlessly home. At the back door, Percentage, wriggling with happiness, brought me a chew bone, then seemed to sense that the vibes weren't affable and withdrew. Ben headed for the stairs.

"Wait a minute, Ben," I said evenly and quietly. "You must know that we have to talk." I could *feel* his eyes rolling, I swear it.

"Jesus, Dad," he muttered. "Didn't Hauser talk enough?"

"Well, he's not your parent. I am, and Mom is—"

"No, really?"

"Ben, being snotty isn't going to help. Either we talk it through ourselves or you can choose to talk it through with a shrink. But you need to talk about it with someone. This isn't the end of the world, but we need to be sure you're okay. It isn't a punishment, it's just our job as parents."

"What, to make a huge deal out of nothing? So I smoked a joint, so what? I just got caught. If every kid in the school who smoked a joint was suspended, Hauser and the teachers would be there all by themselves."

I was aware of sounding pompous, angry and judgmental, the very things I had just told myself I wasn't going to sound like. Why couldn't I be like one of those TV dads who close the door, sit down on the edge of the kid's neat twin bed and come up with the key that unlocks all the pain, confusion and misunderstanding?

Far from being penitent, Ben was signaling defiance and contempt every way he could—with tone of voice, body language, smart-ass answers.

"Ben, is there something wrong? Some problem?"

"My biggest problem right now, Dad, is that I don't want to have this conversation that you're going to try to make me have."

"Well, you've got that right. I'm sure going to try. You've been suspended for a week. You can't just pretend that didn't happen and go upstairs and turn on your CD player."

He shrugged. I opened my mouth to blast him, then closed it. This conversation was heating up too rapidly and was accomplishing nothing. If I pursued it, if I forced him to talk, every word would be hand-to-hand combat. Being the older and presumably more experienced of us two, I decided to beat a strategic retreat.

"Ben, we're both getting steamed, which isn't healthy. Go ahead, go upstairs, and we'll talk about this later, maybe when Mom gets home. But here are the rules, meanwhile: you're grounded. No phone, no going out for any reason without permission. No hanging around with friends. No TV or Nintendo or computer games. You can listen to music, work on your schoolwork, of course. But you're grounded for the week of the suspension and the week after, too, when you're back in school."

I thought I heard him curse under his breath, but he turned without replying and walked upstairs, each step an angry stomp. In seconds, I heard the door to his room slam.

I sat down on the sofa. Percentage presented his head for scratching. I thought about calling Willie and asking him to start sniffing around about my own son.

The funny thing was, I didn't really have anybody to call. Luis's grown children were still in Cuba, and in any event the cultural differences were vast: I couldn't imagine Luis sitting still while his son turned his back on him. Benchley Carrolton, my gardener friend, was wise and sympathetic, but he was in his eighties and didn't have much of a feel for the contemporary world of suburban children. And Jane wouldn't be home until late.

So maybe I had a topic to bring to the Fathers' Club after all. Assuming I passed muster with Charlie Montgomery, whom I was due to meet shortly.

I thought about leaving Ben alone in the house. He would be quite free to sneak out if he wanted to and there wasn't anything I could do about it, not until tomorrow morning when I'd arrange for the eagle-eyed Mrs. Steinitz to show up. But I didn't want to treat him like a felon. I went upstairs and knocked on his door.

"Yup," I heard through the closed door.

"Ben, I've got to go back to work. You understand you're grounded, right?"

"Yeah."

"Mom won't get in until nine or ten. I need you to keep an eye on Emily. I expect to be home to make dinner but in case I get hung up, I'll leave some money downstairs to order Domino's. I trust you to stay in the house. Okay?"

I was telling the truth; I *did* trust him and wanted him to know that, however he snarled. Besides, Em would be bounding off the school bus soon, and I knew he was too responsible to leave her alone in the house for very long.

"Thanks, Dad. I'm really touched." The sarcasm was venomous. Be cooler than he is, I advised myself. You're the grown-up.

I left twenty-five dollars on the kitchen table and headed toward my audition for the Fathers' Club. Five years ago I would have found the idea of a men's group bizarre. Now I was stunned to find myself anxious to sign up.

Six

MONTGOMERY, Raskin & Jones, attorneys-at-law, occupied a filigreed old Victorian in Livingston, one of those ornate wedding-cake affairs with turrets and bay windows all iced with carved curlicues. The house was painstakingly well maintained; there wasn't a flake of paint or a patch of crabgrass in sight. Law firms, like banks, have to project an air of meticulous prosperity, else people will hesitate to entrust their money or their messy confidential affairs to them.

I drive past professional offices like this all the time and fantasize that the guys inside eat lunch together at leather-boothed steakhouses and sneak out on Wednesday afternoons for a round of golf.

Fortunately, private investigators are under no such pressure to look respectable. Thanks to novels like Raymond Chandler's and TV shows like "Columbo," clients don't avoid detectives with tacky office decor. If anything, they expect PIs to tilt toward the picturesquely seedy. I am in fashion for the first time in my life. Come to think of it, maybe I should give prospective clients a tour of my decaying house as well.

There was nothing seedy inside the quarters of Montgomery, Raskin & Jones, however. The offices weren't lavish, just tasteful and vaguely clubby, neither scaring you away by looking overdone nor unnerving you by appearing too modest. The walls were lined with shelves of lawbooks bound in leather. Every legal statute and code in the country is readily available on electronic databases or CD-ROM, but impressive-looking volumes probably reassure the people passing through for real estate closings. Even the art on the walls felt safe and conservative: horses, hunting dogs, landscapes.

I was ten minutes early. Montgomery's secretary, as proper and WASPy-looking as the decor, brought me a cup of tea and steered me toward a stack of current magazines. Like any good real estate attorney, Charlie was punctual. At 3 P.M. exactly the phone on the secretary's desk bzzzzzed discreetly and I was led in past the engraved brass plaque on the door that quietly announced, "Charles H. Montgomery."

He looked prosperous and hearty, with a warm smile beneath his mustache and a strong handshake. In his late forties, he'd held on to a full head of close-cropped blond hair. A touch chunky but still fit-looking, with a ruddy face that probably resulted from time on the courts, he wore a gabardine suit and one of those denim dress shirts that are supposed to look casual but cost $120. The shirt seemed to signal, "I'm not completely stuffy but I have to appear to be." I have never in my life seen a lawyer with scruffy shoes. (Scruff and dog hair are staples of my own wardrobe.) It must be something they emphasize in law school. Montgomery's were soft suede oxfords.

"Kit, I'm Charlie Montgomery, as you've undoubtedly surmised. Welcome. I've got a meeting in a little while, so we should get down to it, I guess. Please come in. Gemma will bring you coffee or tea if you'd . . . oh, I see she already has. Well, come in. Take a seat. I'm glad you've come by. I've had more than one man express interest in the Fathers' Club, then turn tail and never show up."

Framed photos of his wife and two daughters were propped all over the office. One looked to be a high-school kid; the other was younger. The wife was youthful-looking, always smiling for the camera. Montgomery was a jock or at least an ex-jock: basketball and golf awards lined the far wall, along with the usual array of diplomas, certificates and other well-framed bona fides. Behind his desk hung a lovely and, I was sure, fairly expensive oil painting of sand dunes and sea.

"That looks like the national seashore on Cape Cod," I offered, taking the leather chair from across his desk.

"North Carolina. Similar topography, except the Southern

beaches' dunes are gentler, with more gradual slopes." I nodded. Okay, now I knew about Southern dunes.

Montgomery glanced at his watch. He wasn't being rude, just reminding both of us that he was busy. I understood; five years earlier, I was one of the people with secretaries and full appointment calendars.

He leaned back in his chair and quickly took me in, from head to toe: chinos, blue blazer, never a tie, well-worn L.L. Bean mocs which had almost as many miles on them as my Volvo.

"So. Glad you came by. Please call me Charlie—or some people prefer Chuck. Either is fine with me. You know, we have a Fathers' Club meeting tonight."

No, I said, I hadn't known.

I wasn't sure how to proceed. I liked to think I was reasonably evolved for a male, but I guess all that stuff about drums and sharing feelings made me uneasy. Plus, to put myself in Montgomery's oxfords, I would have thought someone who called to join a group the morning after one of its members had tragically died was a clod, if not a downright creep. I'd be thinking: Do we really want a boor like this in a group where sensitivity matters a fair amount?

What I couldn't tell him was that I had no choice but to move quickly. The more intensely I investigated the case, the more likely it was that someone in the group could figure out who I really was. The longer I waited, the more likely the police were to get wind of the men's group, too and start asking their own questions. I should have told the Rochambeau PD about the group myself; I didn't usually hold out on Danielle Peterson, who would not be a happy cop when she found out. But I was hoping to attend at least a few meetings before she did.

"Charlie, I feel awkward about having called you so soon after Dale's death," I said. "I'm being intrusive at what I'm sure is a difficult time, and I'm sorry for that." He nodded noncommittally, folded his hands on the oak desktop. He did think my approach a bit unseemly, I was sure. Time for some directness. The best way to lie is to tell what you really feel, if you can.

"To tell the truth, I wasn't completely at ease with the idea of a men's group. I'm not into thumping drums or group confessions. I don't believe that what men need most are Native American rituals. Plus, to be blunt, I still have no idea what *Iron John* is actually about."

He smiled indulgently, probably as tired of cracks about drum beating as Dale had apparently been. "It's tough for men to talk to each other. I don't really know why: maybe because we spend so much time beating one another up. So we get a lot of 'deer' here, our nickname for men who sniff and circle the group for months sometimes, then skitter away. Skepticism is understandable, Kit. But we don't use drums or have rituals, at least not yet. And believe it or not, *Iron John* has never come up.

"Mostly what we do is sit around and talk—about our kids, our wives, work, whatever problems or difficulties we're having. We just bring bottled water, soda—no beer in the church—and some pretzels and shoot the breeze for a couple of hours. It's not like those movies about women where we form these great supportive relationships that transform one another's lives—that hasn't happened yet—but we've helped one another through some sticky problems. Or tried to. We have failed, too, sometimes pretty seriously." He looked grim at that. I wondered if Dale Lewis was on his mind. "But given how you feel, Kit, what is it that *has* brought you here—especially at this sad time? I understand what your concerns are, but what's drawing you? You mentioned some problems regarding your son?"

I sat back and sipped my tea, considering the way grim reality had just supplied me with a better motivation than deception ever could have. "I apologize if I sound smug about men's groups, Charlie. It's just that this is hard for me. The thing is, I'm having this problem with my son. He's almost fourteen, and . . . well, he's been suspended from school for smoking dope. The school officials say he's behaving erratically. He's certainly not talking to me much; it seems we can't even open our mouths around each other without World War III breaking out. And Linda had mentioned how helpful Dale found your group . . ." I paused, as if for encouragement.

Montgomery nodded reassuringly. Another skill required of lawyers, no doubt.

"So that's the pressure I'm feeling. My son might need some help, and I don't even know how to find out what kind. Every time I say two words he gets furious and disgusted. I don't quite know where to turn. It's opened up all sorts of other questions, too, naturally. I wouldn't even have contacted you at a time like this, otherwise."

Montgomery nodded again and laced his hands together, clearly having decided something. "That's why we started the group, Kit. We all wanted to be better fathers, and we all felt we needed help learning how. It's nothing to be embarrassed about. In fact, you should feel proud of the fact that you came here. I understand now why you felt you had to move quickly. I've seen a fair number of men come in here, and you belong." He glanced again at his watch. Montgomery's busy schedule was in my favor. He didn't have time to probe all that deeply.

I realized that what he was saying was complimentary, but I've rarely felt lower about being praised. If Montgomery had been a bit less understanding, I would have felt less slimy.

Actually, I hadn't intended to be so specific about Ben and his problems. But sure enough, just like the shrinks were always saying, it helped to talk about it. I felt better. And I appreciated Montgomery's sensible, supportive, nonsquishy response to my blurted-out problem. Normally, I'd never unburden myself to a stranger. Or to anyone, really, except Jane. I hoped these guys didn't turn out to be *too* nice, because then I would feel even worse about betraying them than I already did. But remember, I told myself, you're investigating a murder.

He glanced at the lined yellow legal pad on his desk. "Kit, you say you're a security consultant? Just out of curiosity, what does that kind of work entail?"

I only had a second or two to frame an answer. I hoped he just wanted to feel comfortable that he knew what my work was. What would a criminal want with a Fathers' Club anyway?

"Mostly, I advise companies on how to maintain or upgrade their security. You know, to guard against burglary, in-house theft, embezzlement. I suggest how to monitor inventory, run background checks on personnel. I evaluate internal and external security procedures, prepare a report and help them implement my recommendations. Some clients I work with regularly. For others, I do spot evaluations." I had, at various times, actually done all these things. I was skirting dangerously close to the truth. It was opportunistic, maybe, but safer—fewer lies to remember.

Montgomery allowed himself another glance at his watch. "Here's how we usually proceed, Kit. We invite a potential new member to come sit in on a meeting. If anybody feels uncomfortable—the newcomer or the members—then by advance agreement we just part company, no questions asked. If everybody feels okay, which is what happens most frequently, then you're in. I have a feeling you'll feel good about the group. Besides me, there's Hal Etheridge, Ricky Melman, Jim Rheems and David Battelle. Frank Dougherty, who's a schoolteacher, drops in from time to time. But he's got a part-time job at night, so he can't be regular, and we all feel that, for the group to work, most of the members need to come pretty faithfully. We each kick in five bucks a month to buy pretzels and soda."

His phone buzzed. "Yes, Gemma. Sure. Right, I understand. Just give me a minute." Time to go.

Not entirely consciously, I've sort of picked up this habit of reading upside down. The files on Montgomery's desk, I noticed as he murmured to his secretary, were labeled "Burns," "Grove Properties," and "Interstate Housing, Inc." Might mean nothing, might matter. When I got outside, I'd jot the names down on Post-its and, if I could remember, give them to Evelyn. There were thousands of Post-its in some drawer recording the details of my cases.

Montgomery hung up, then stood up. "We meet in the library of the Methodist Church in Springdale, about half an hour from here. No set format—we go once around the table, people tell what's new in their lives, then it's free-form. Whoever has the most pressing problem gets the floor and our attention. Tonight, we'll probably talk some about Dale. It's a pretty heavy thing for us. Some of us got fairly involved with him—" He stopped, the lawyer's reticence kicking in just as I waited for more details. "Well, anyway, hope to see you at eight. If you need directions, my secretary has them."

He walked me to the door, then offered his hand. "I hope this works out for you, Kit. I have a good feeling about it." I nodded and tried to smile. The feeling I had, somewhere in the depths of my abdomen, wasn't good at all.

Seven

I DROVE from Montgomery's law office directly to the supermarket across the street, mixing a few domestic chores with my undercover work. I also, prompted by the beeper I had taken to carrying in my blazer pocket (when I remembered), checked in with the office. Evelyn said there were no messages that couldn't wait until the next morning. "A Mr. James Stonebrook asked to speak with you. Quite belligerently." Foolish man, I thought. Mr. James Stonebrook had offended Evelyn. And those who offend Evelyn disappear into voice mail, never to be retrieved.

"Something about your following his girlfriend around to see if she's being faithful," she continued. "Shall I . . . ?"

"Please," I said. "Feel free to steer him elsewhere." She would enjoy that. Even at my most desperate, I never took those kinds of cases. Well, not after the first year or so.

That case would probably be simpler than the one I had, though. I felt the slightly panicky feeling I get when I see work building up and the kids not really being taken care of. I was off balance, upset not only by Ben's suspension but even more by the fact that we couldn't even discuss it. Withholding is one of the major weapons any kid has; the smart ones wield it ruthlessly. You want badly to know how they feel about the big issues in their lives. Mostly, you content yourself with blank stares, shrugs, I dunnos and maybes.

I couldn't afford to hover over my kids like the SuperMoms

did—Jane and I were both too busy for that—but they did come first. You couldn't disconnect when you knew they were having problems. At times, that was a huge pain in the ass. With Jane closing in on her degree, I was the one who had to be paying real attention. Ben *needed* attention. And I wasn't consistently providing enough of it, certainly not this week.

Sometimes it seemed too complicated; sometimes I just got too tired. And sometimes, like now, I wanted to be focusing on something else.

When they were little, it was simpler. They loved you, you loved them. The sight of a dog would send them into fits of ecstasy. Taking them to the zoo was a transcendent experience. Parenting adolescents was something else, however, like walking through a rice paddy filled with land mines. Five inches in the wrong direction, and bam!

"Now you know what women have always felt," was Jane's blunt response when I whined to her. "Pulled this way and that. 'Should I work, should I be at home?' I'm sorry you're going through it, Kit, but what can I say? I've been there. In fact, I'm there now. I understand how uncomfortable it is. But you'll rise to it."

Sensitivity was tiring, and I was getting impatient with it. If you were a man who worked all day and got home at 8 P.M., you were an insensitive lout. If you took care of the kids and worked and struggled over how to do both well, then you were only learning how tough women had it.

Mrs. Steinitz couldn't come until the next morning. She would provide supervision, but not much parenting. So I had a troubled, seething adolescent boy at home with no adult, while Emily was probably cheerfully doing her homework. And I had another murder case that was sure to take a lot of my time. Had it been a mistake to accept it? I could call Linda up, tell her I had too much going on in my life, and refer her to somebody else. She'd understand. But this wasn't just another Deadbeat Dad case anymore. Kids came first, but murder was a pretty compelling competitor.

On the other hand, what about tonight's dinner? Things had gotten a little sloppy the past few days. Ben, Emily and I had had Chinese takeout last night, on the late side, too, and pizza the night before that. Two hit-and-run meals in a row was my limit. I was determined that tonight we'd have an actual balanced, nutritious meal.

I usually went to considerable pains to cook solid if uninspired meals, relying heavily on meat loaf, burgers, pasta, and flounder filets. I was also a devoted patron of Pluck You, Rochambeau's upscale takeout chicken emporium, the working mom's—or dad's—best pal. Sometimes I sneaked the bags in and just warmed and served the meal as if it were my own. I think Ben was wise to this, but not Emily, who lavishly praised my cooking. I wasn't getting many compliments on anything from Ben these days.

We'd sit down together anyhow, even if two of us were barely speaking. The process of being together, talking, even fighting, was therapeutic in ways I didn't quite understand, as if being a family was healing in itself. Or so I told myself.

So I grabbed a cart and dashed into Fresh 'n Tasty. I now actually get a bit of a kick out of shopping. It has taken me years to learn to shop without a list and not end up pouring gallons of spoiled milk down the drain and tossing limp lettuce into the trash. It's no small triumph to remember the exact kind of cookies Em likes—chocolate *chunk*, not chocolate chip—to get the brown sugar that pours and doesn't harden into useless granite chunks, to secure the yogurt with *90*, not 110, calories for Jane—and no banana or blueberry, please.

Tonight, knowing I'd have to drive to Springdale to share my feelings and spy on my fellow dads, I made do with two barbecued chickens, some precooked stuffed potatoes requiring only unwrapping and warming, a giant honeydew melon and some green beans.

I passed "She's Not Ready" McGann as I drove into Rochambeau; she was going the other way with her captive daughter. Ellen McGann was an anthropologist in some former life. In her current one, she drove her daughter around.

Alison was a friend of Emily's whenever it was possible to pry the former out of Ellen's fearful grip. It seemed Alison "wasn't ready" for sleepovers even as she approached middle school. Alison wasn't ready to go for walks alone with Emily or anybody else, or to cross Main Street by herself. She wasn't ready to go on fast rides at amusement parks. She certainly wasn't ready for sleepaway camp. What she was mostly ready for was to ride all over the state with Ellen, prowling through malls, exclaiming at museums, buying crafts projects to build together. When Alison *was* liberated, she came with more instructions than a power mower—what she liked to eat, what she didn't, what movies scared her, how to approach bedtime. God help "She's Not Ready" McGann and her kid both when adolescence arrived.

I was out of the Fresh 'n' Tasty and back in my kitchen in an hour. Dinner was hot and on the table in an hour and a quarter.

Emily chattered like a jaybird; Ben stayed sour-faced and silent.

"Dad, I got 102 on my French test today," Em said. I offered the usual declarations of amazement and pride. "But, Em, how did you get more than 100?" I knew the answer, but she loved my shock and delight.

"Extra credit," she announced. She told me about her class trip to the Morris County Museum to look at an iguana and, incidentally, some art. She prattled on about her current events discussion of homelessness and her Family Life discussion of sexual harassment. Each week they warned her about a different dreadful danger. Jane sometimes extended opportunities like this into serious talks, but tonight I didn't have the heart or the skill. No matter how you tried, you sounded like an old fart when you broached this stuff with your kids.

"How about you, Ben? How are you passing your lonely hours?"

He shrugged, staring down at his plate, moving his food from one side to the other. He wasn't giving a thing away. I couldn't tell if he was distracted or angry or both.

"What are you doing?"

He shrugged. "Not much. I guess. I dunno." He flushed, as if the questions themselves were offensive and unanswerable.

"Mrs. Steinitz is going to be here tomorrow," I announced, bracing myself for the chorus of protests and complaints that the appearance of this hardheaded woman usually triggers.

"Shit," said Ben. "Why? I don't need a goddamn baby-sitter. I'm not a fucking child."

"Ben!" Emily scolded before I could open my mouth. "Do you have to curse all that much in one single sentence?" Ben and Em were close and rarely quarreled, especially in recent years. He was fiercely protective and tolerant of her. If he ticked her off or was behaving badly, she'd usually be the first to point it out, and he'd usually take it. I'd decided to consult Jane before blurting out to Em that her adored elder brother had been suspended for D-R-U-G-S. Instead I explained to Emily that I needed Mrs. Steinitz around because I would be especially busy for a while.

"I've got an important case," I said. "I'll tell you a bit about it when we're farther along. I can tell you it's a murder, though. Somebody was killed." Emily loved to hear about my murder cases.

"What can you tell me?" she asked, wide-eyed.

"Just this. A man was found dead in his office. Someone gave him too much to drink, then hit him on the head."

"Wow," she said. "Do you know who did it?"

"Not yet," I said. "But I'll keep you posted."

Em cleared the table, which was her job. Ben's was to rinse the plates and run the dishwasher. He would usually wait to be reminded. One feature of adolescents is their knack of turning you into a scold even when you don't want to be one, so you can become a suitable target for their contempt.

I checked the mail, put the bills in one pile, threw out the junk fliers, fed Percentage and took him for a short walk. Then I yelled upstairs to both kids that I was leaving, that I'd be home in a couple of hours. Em yelled goodbye. Nothing from Ben. He knew the drill. He was grounded: no phone, no going out, no TV or computers. The schools hadn't quite faced up to the kids' new reality—being suspended and forced to spend hours at their electronic home entertainment complexes was no punishment, not in suburbia. They could yak online with their e-mail buddies in California, fire up the Nintendo, troll through fifty TV channels or program the VCR. Being home for a week was great.

Percentage looked at me balefully as I headed for the back door. Labs are so unfailingly generous and affectionate that they always seem puzzled and disappointed when anybody leaves them.

I thought briefly of taking him along. Percentage was, technically, a hunting dog, a macho guy's dog, a perfect candidate for a men's group. Come to think of it, he'd probably make a better member than I would.

Eight

THE STRANGE THING wasn't that I was anxious; it was *why*. Infiltrating this group under totally false pretenses, even the fact that there might be a murder among the group's members—the ultimate irony for a support group—didn't faze me. It was the male stuff. Would somebody offer healing massages? Minister to my inner child?

I'd be doing something I'd never done before: talking to a group of men about the personal parts of my life and theirs. I just hoped things didn't get too squishy.

I was only slightly reassured by my brief meeting with Charlie Montgomery: he, at least, didn't appear to be the touchy-feely type.

Now that I thought about it, what, precisely, was a men's group, anyway? What were men after? Being more sensitive? Not me. If I were any more sensitive, I'd melt. Was sensitivity supposed to help me be more successful? It seemed to me that the challenge of being a man these days was to learn how to get used to being *less* successful, graciously.

Women, I figured, had common goals, more or less centered around getting an equal shot at things and elbowing Neanderthals aside. But what exactly did men want?

Evelyn had pulled a couple of articles about men's groups out of the library for me—all from women's magazines, naturally. Now I was on the cell phone with Benchley, who'd been trying unsuccessfully for several years to get me to join the men's group which met weekly in the basement of his Quaker Meeting House.

"It's a nice bunch," Benchley was saying. "You don't get very macho or belligerent fellows in a men's group. You tend to get men who want to talk, even if they find it difficult at first. As in five or six years."

His group never grew larger than eight or smaller than five, Benchley said, but it had proven difficult to keep it stable. "Men will put almost everything in their lives ahead of the group, ahead of talking to other men," he informed me. "Work, kids, social events . . . even home repairs. And of course everybody's working hard these days, too. Members tend to show only if nothing else comes up. I'll bet it's just the opposite with women." I bet he was right. Jane had dinner with three of her fellow Rutgers students (all women studying to be psychologists) every Tuesday night, and only crippling injury or massive blizzards kept her from going.

Benchley sighed. "And these days, of course, men who admit to joining a men's group are constantly ridiculed as chanters or drumbeaters. It doesn't seem to matter that the men's movement was always a media myth. But as you can see, it's not easy, Kit. Why don't you come and see for yourself?" I told him I was going to get a look at such a group tonight, under circumstances I really couldn't discuss. But as I hung up, I felt a twinge of guilt. I knew that I'd gotten his hopes up.

I skimmed the articles Evelyn had given me. They talked about men's group members being mostly middle class and well educated. Members were often drawn to the company of other men by some trauma: childhood abuse, alcoholism, divorce, unemployment. Ironically, powerful men who hadn't been through any of these experiences—maybe the ones who most needed to go?—hardly ever did. According to one article, members veered off at key transitional points in their lives—when they got married, had a kid, suffered an illness. How like men to abandon their groups, just when they most needed them. Which was, Linda Lewis had told me, exactly what Dale seemed to have done.

When I wasn't feeling anxious about the meeting I was speeding toward, I was halfway looking forward to it. I could have dearly used a men's group when my Wall Street career fell apart. I could still use one: I had lingering money problems; I felt overwhelmed at all the domestic work I was doing; and my son and I seemed to be suddenly at war. Would this happen with Emily, too, once she hit adolescence?

The Methodist Church was enormous and Gothic, built of pale stone and flanked by floodlit outcroppings, marble statues and an immaculately tended lawn and garden. Following the directions Montgomery's secretary had provided, I veered toward the annex, right off the main building. Nobody was around. There was no mention of a Fathers' Club on the bulletin board, which posted notices of potluck suppers and canned-food drives. In the suburbs, churches are common meeting grounds used for almost everything from dance classes to AA meetings. The hallway lights were on, but most of the rooms on either side of the hall were dark. I saw a sign that said LIBRARY, with an arrow pointing left, and followed that.

As I turned the corner I nearly collided with a lanky, curly-haired man.

"Kit?" he asked, offering his hand. "Sorry, but I'm stumped on pronouncing the last name. . . ."

"De-loo," I said, smiling. I wish I had a dime for every time I pronounce it for people.

"Hal Etheridge," he said, pumping my hand. "Sorry. I was deputized to serve as a one-man hospitality committee. I should have been here to meet you. But you're early . . ." He glanced up at the clock on the wall. "Anyway, welcome. It's good to see you. We'll be talking tonight about some sort of Fathers' Club memorial for Dale Lewis . . . you know all about that, right? Charlie said he'd discussed it with you . . ."

I instinctively liked Etheridge's manner—he had the straightness of an insurance executive, but warmth and ease too. And some sorrow in there as well.

"Yes, I know. That's how I learned about the group, from Dale." My first Fathers' Club lie. Not an auspicious beginning. Not worthy of Etheridge's gracious welcome, either.

"Well, sorry for you to come in on so sad a note, Kit. But I sort of like the fact that our group is meeting. Seems right, somehow. I'm a life-goes-on man, I guess. Though, to be honest, I'm reeling. A part of me hopes Dale's death was suicide, and another part actually hopes he was murdered. You see, we've been talking as a group for some time now. And if one of us went out and killed himself and none of the others suspected anything, well, what the hell kind of men's group is that?"

I nodded, though suicide was not likely, from what the homicide investigators had found so far. We walked in silence the rest of the way to the church library, down the portrait-lined hallway.

The library was a lovely room, paneled in dark wood with a small fire burning in the big stone fireplace and a brass clock on the mantel. Books lined the walls, and in the center of the room an antique oak table was ringed by carved chairs, all of them empty.

Four men were standing off to one side puttering with a coffee maker, putting pretzels and cookies onto paper plates and chatting easily, if somberly. I wondered if these men would be at all like me. And I braced myself not to get too close. However friendly these men seemed now, they would never forgive me when they learned I had lied about my real reason for being here.

"Hey," said Montgomery, "you're right on time. I see our welcoming committee performed admirably." The men moved over to shake my hand.

"Ricky Melman," said the shortest man in the room and—I thought, scanning the others—probably the youngest. Willie's research had put Melman, the social worker, at thirty-four. I hadn't expected to encounter a guy in frayed jeans, rimless spectacles and a gold stud in one ear. "I didn't greet you myself because I figured out that, given half a chance, Hal eats all the good cookies."

"Well, screw you," Etheridge shot back, laughing. "That's because I buy 'em, you cheap son of a bitch." Ah, macho banter here, too. Men do have a universal language.

"Ricky's our hippie, sort of," explained Montgomery affectionately. "Note the earring. We don't want any surprises for you, Kit. Full disclosure."

I laughed. "Well, if an earring is your biggest surprise, I guess I can handle this group fine.

"My son has been bugging me for a pierced ear," I added.

"Let the kid go for it," Melman protested. "It's no big deal anymore. Half the boys in my kids' school have earrings. So do a lot of the male teachers."

"I don't think I'm quite ready for that," said Etheridge.

I was surprised to find myself jumping in. "I'm inclined to say yes. It's a trap, to play the reactionary dad blocking his personal expression. I think we should only fight with our kids when we really need to, and then we should fight to the death."

There was an awkward silence, but Melman flashed me a thumbs-up.

Montgomery grinned. "Well, you see already what we're about here, Kit. We try to help each other avoid the traps. Glad you're here."

Except for Melman, it seemed a pretty straight crowd. But then, suburban New Jersey is a straight place. There are pockets of poverty, like Newark and Paterson, where Jane's clinic was, and islands of great wealth like Summit and Short Hills, where bankers and traders ensconce their families in huge, sprawling houses which could easily accommodate dozens. And then there are all these vast stretches of ordinariness in between.

"Now, tattoos are trickier, because you can't take them off," Melman went on, upping the ante.

Montgomery held his hand up. I was right: he was clearly a leader here. "Wait, guys. Why don't we check in so Kit here can meet everybody? Kit, check-in is how we start our get-togethers. We go around the table, give every guy a chance to talk briefly about his week. If there's something heavy going on, we come back to it. You can always pass if you don't feel like talking or whatever . . . No pressure. We're formally informal here."

"And no drumbeating," chortled somebody down at the end of the table.

Montgomery grinned. "I'll go first. I'm Charlie Montgomery. Kit and I have already met. I'm a lawyer, specializing in probate and real estate. I'm forty-six. I live in Livingston, my daughters are twelve and sixteen. I'm going to pass on talking about Dale for now. That doesn't mean everybody else should, I'm just not ready to speak about it yet. Sort of want to see what happens and think about it." He reached for a pretzel and nodded at Etheridge, on his left.

"Hal Etheridge," he said. "I live in Mountain Lakes. Got a boy and a girl, he's eight, she's twelve. I'm an insurance executive— what's straighter than that, right? My wife Gina is a biologist, she teaches at Rutgers. I'm outvoted, but I would love to beat drums. And yes, even dance naked in the woods. I'm the resident ritualist here." He stopped and took a breath before continuing. "Dale and I have had our differences, but I am grieving for him. He was an important part of this group. I look forward to our being able to talk about him. I don't want to do our he-man thing and only mention a year from now how torn up we all were, okay?"

I liked Etheridge's dry humor. I didn't see any traces of a killer there. But then, you can't always see any traces at all.

Melman went next. "I'm Ricky. A social worker. About to turn thirty-five. I belong to this church, along with Charlie, which is how I got into this group. My wife is at home because we have three young children. I live in Greenbriar and do a lot of addiction counseling. I'm trying to set up a private practice. I should tell you that I do have a pretty hot temper, but I'm really sweet, loveable and harmless—"

"Quick to anger, quicker to forgive," interrupted Etheridge. Useful to know.

Melman smiled. "Maybe that's why I've had three jobs in five years. Shirley thinks I've calmed down since I started coming here and have somebody else to shout at besides my family. I didn't know Dale well, but I'm terribly sad about his death. I agree with Hal—we have to confront it."

A tall, tan and noticeably fit man came loping in, slightly out of breath, and slid into the empty chair next to Melman. He raised an eyebrow when he noticed me. Montgomery quickly filled him in, and the newcomer gave me a cool, appraising stare. Unlike the others, this guy wasn't pleased to encounter an interloper. And unlike the others, he was almost elegant—navy blazer, custom-made shirt with discreet monogram, crisp slacks, salt-and-pepper hair slicked back.

"I'm David Battelle," he said, eyes on me. "I'm divorced and haven't remarried. No kids. Nor do I want any. Listening to all of you yammer about your brats is the price I pay for belonging to this group. I drive a Land Rover, which I mention, Kit, because I get a lot of shit about it here." He seemed done with me and turned to the others. "Have we talked about Dale? Do we want to? I wasn't the only one here dumb enough to go into business with him. It lasted—what, three months? But I did protect myself. He lost his shirt, but I had created a separate holding company, so I didn't lose mine. Dale and I had a partnership in a low-income family housing project . . ." This he tossed in, apparently for my benefit. He continued, "But despite the bad blood, I wouldn't wish this kind of death on anybody." He scowled and fell silent. No one said anything.

Battelle got up and fiddled with the coffee machine. He looked ill at ease, the most fidgety man in the room. I wondered whether the normal mood of the Fathers' Club had been thrown off by Dale's death or by how much.

Linda thought things had gotten "intense" between David Battelle and Dale, but businesses went under all the time. A business failure wasn't necessarily a motive for murder. Looking over this group, wondering if one of them was a murderer, I suddenly felt ridiculous. This was a support group, for God's sake. You didn't join a men's group, kill one of its members, then show up to share intimacies with the others a day later. Coming here had seemed like so savvy a move; now it just seemed like an especially dumb one.

"I live in Clayton," Battelle continued, resuming his seat at the table. "Divorced, like I said. Several girlfriends. I don't have a lot in common with anybody here, but here I am." He frowned. He was done. He came off as arrogant and smart, and he clearly had money. If I had to guess, I would say he didn't want to be here. He wasn't even a father. So why *was* he here?

There were two more members. Jim Rheems, the only African-American in the group, introduced himself as a stockbroker, father of two sons, also divorced. I knew Rheems had been one of Linda and Dale's most devoted friends. He'd even taken out a second mortgage on his house to help Dale's business venture, and, according to Linda (and Willie), had taken a dreadful bath when Battelle and Lewis's business collapsed. His face was gray and there were deep shadows under his eyes.

"About Dale," he said, his voice a bit shaky. "Shit, this is just about the worst thing that's ever happened . . . it feels worse than my family's falling apart. At least they're all still around."

Frank Dougherty was the last member to check in. Dougherty, a twinkly elf in a work shirt and jeans, couldn't seem to open his mouth without bragging about his two teenage girls. Or without saying "fuck." I don't think I'd ever heard anybody outside the military curse quite as much as Dougherty did. "Fuck" seemed to be his favorite noun, verb, adverb and adjective. Surprisingly for one so foul-mouthed, he was a high school teacher in working-class Lincoln Township. He must have to work awfully hard to keep his vocabulary in check on the job, I thought. Furthermore, he was in AA.

"I can go very melancholic in the blink of a fucking eye," he told me, "and be laughing out loud five minutes later. Some people would call that manic, but I like to think of it as being fucking Irish." He chuckled. "The fucking Irish," he said, as if that explained everything. "I have a quotation by W. B. Yeats above my desk at school. It reads, 'Being Irish, he had an abiding sense of tragedy which sustained him through temporary periods of joy.' "

He grinned. "We had a game for a few years where my girls were trying to get me to clean up my language. Every time I said the F word I had to give each of them a quarter. I stopped when Valerie bought herself a CD player and Jody got a Walkman. I couldn't fucking afford it!"

Dougherty absolutely beamed when he talked about his daughters; he seemed to be equally enthusiastic about teaching. I found myself liking him instantly and cautioned myself just as quickly. I wasn't joining the damned group; I was infiltrating it. It didn't matter if I liked Dougherty or not.

Rheems was clearing his throat in the way people do when they have something important to say and need to prime themselves to say it.

"Look, I know we all have different ideas about how to handle Dale's death, but I need to talk about it, at least a bit. I get creeped out when I pretend everything is normal. I have a couple of things I'd just feel better saying."

I, for one, was anxious to hear them.

"Just let me get this off my chest." Rheems reached for his glass of mineral water. "Dale and I . . . we had our ups and downs. And you all know how smart he was. Funny. And what a dreamer he was . . . And you all know how irresponsible he could be. I sure found out about that. Kit, I apologize, because some of this is going over your head, I'm sure. I'll be happy to walk you through it if you want."

He took a drink, maybe to steady himself. The others watched him intently, without interrupting. "I loved Dale," he continued. "And came to hate him, too, you all know that. Unlike David here, I lost a lot of what I owned helping him. Dale knew the deal was risky but he didn't tell me. Now most of the money for my boys' college fund is gone. I'm in shock. I never forgave him for that. I wish I had. But how was I to know he'd end up dead? He was the kind that gave everybody around him coronaries but always landed on his feet. But, boy, was he ambitious and enthusiastic about his dreams. That's the part I loved. . . ." Rheems shook his head, unable to go on. Dougherty reached over and patted him on the shoulder.

"That's all, I guess," blurted Rheems. "I loved Dale and hated him. Sounds dumb, but I just felt I needed to say it."

Montgomery nodded. "I respect your saying that, Jim. I think we all had some of those ambivalent feelings for Dale, though you paid more dearly for them than the rest of us. I wouldn't touch that deal when he came to me, and I warned him to stay away from those people. I guess I know too much about real estate schemes. The lawyer in me sounded the alarm. The friend in you supported him and took a chance."

"The absence of brains in me, you mean," said Rheems grimly. "You warned me, Charlie. You told me his partners were smelly and unreliable. All I had to do was listen." He groaned. "I'll be paying this off for years. Years. So how can I mourn him? But . . ."

Dougherty shoved his glass aside. "Look, Jim," he said impatiently, his elfin mode vanished, "this fucking bullshit doesn't help you. You were a great friend and you took a gamble on a pal. Dale screwed you, is what he did. Would've screwed David, too, except David knew more about risky real estate than you did. You don't need to be ashamed of being angry, believe me. Both emotions are valid. You cared a lot about him and he did something really shitty to you. He fucked you, and good. All you can do is be honest about it, right? I mean, what the fuck?"

Right. There was a fairly long spell of silence. Nobody else really wanted to talk about Dale right then, it seemed. Montgomery was looking at me. It was my turn.

"I'm Kit Deleeuw, from Rochambeau. A security consultant. My kids are ten and almost fourteen. And my wife Jane is a therapist who's studying to be a psychologist. I'm glad to meet you all." I was hoping to get away with this simple self-description.

Montgomery wasn't about to let me. "Kit, when you came to my office this afternoon you said you were having problems with your son. Do you need help with that? Some of us have been through it, too." There was considerable nodding, chuckling and eye-rolling at the mention of adolescent children.

Looking around the table gave me a strange sensation. I had never been much of a joiner. Being inept at sports and uninterested in talking business or politics tended to leave me outside the pale of most male discussion. Yet here were a group of strangers, all watching me intently, waiting to hear what I had to say. I couldn't tell if that was merely because they were curious about the new guy or if they made a point of listening carefully to what any member of the group said. There hadn't been much of an initiation rite. They simply seemed to take it for granted that I was there for good, one of the guys.

This was, I suddenly realized, sort of a business meeting, except the business wasn't commerce, but the strange task of being a modern American male. Women always say they can't win no matter what they do, but that is true of men too. If you are hard-headed and successful, it always comes at the expense of your family. If you are sensitive, you're a wimp, and probably broke to boot. You are still expected to bring home the bacon, but now you have to be too sensitive to kill the pig.

Well, in for a dime, in for a dollar. "I do have a problem," I said. I told them about Ben, his suspension for dope. About the sullen stares. About how I reflexively turned into my father when things got tense, adopting a windy, pompous, hectoring voice that made both Ben and me feel worse. About all the conversations that left me feeling like an out-of-it jerk, usually concluding with Ben's giving me a hateful look and storming out of the room. Some people could be philosophical about those kinds of scenes, I said, but I couldn't. They hurt. And somehow, I knew, I was hurting Ben. I couldn't seem to strike the right balance. No matter how many times I went through things in my mind, I always felt like an asshole.

I had this notion that I had failed Ben. I told the group briefly about the insider trading scandal that had cost me my career, embarrassed my family and led to this new life. I hadn't actually planned on confiding quite so much.

"Maybe I was a bit oblivious," I added, "about how the scandal seeped into Ben's life." I told them about all the fistfights and shoving matches he got into, in response to his buddies suggesting I was a thief who ought to be in jail. I had talked with Jane about all this, of course, but listening to myself now I realized I hadn't really explored the toll my actions had taken on my boy. I was conscious, even as I said it, of how self-serving the term "a bit oblivious" sounded. Maybe something a bit stronger would have worked better . . . like "completely blind."

I was flabbergasted to glance up at the clock and realize I'd been talking for nearly twenty minutes. "I guess I don't know what to do," I said quickly, not wanting to hog the whole night. "I can't pretend my son didn't smoke dope. I know if I just come across as a hard-ass he'll turn off. And I'm not much of a hard-ass, anyway. I know I'm not serving him well in some basic human way, but the only model I have is my father. He delivered speeches by my bedside all the time, and I just learned to pretend to be asleep. Ben has more freedom; he walks away. But that's not helping him much."

Frank Dougherty fiddled with his key chain. "Kit, we don't have a lot of time here, so we tend to be honest. You raised it, so I'll give you my point of view. I'm no fucking shrink, but I've been through some stuff and here's how this strikes me. Nobody wants to have a kid in trouble. But you're dumping all your own shit onto this kid, I think. Leave him the fuck alone. No speeches. No monitoring. Ben's not dealing or cutting people with knives, right? He's basically a good kid who's pushing the envelope right now, testing and experimenting. Let him find his way. You've got your life to lead; he's got his. Let him know you're there if he needs you—let him know this every single day—but that you trust him. He reacts to you as if you were a fucking asshole because you *act* like one. You can step back and let him reach his own conclusions about what's right or wrong, or you can keep crowding and force him in directions neither one of you wants him to go. I hope you understand that I'm not meaning to attack you, just telling how I feel. You did ask."

I felt myself flushing, as if I'd been scolded. And I guess I had been. It was straight talk, okay. It was also disorienting. I don't think anybody had ever talked to me like that about my parenting, other than Jane. And she never called me a fucking asshole.

"But you're telling me to back off when Ben might be involved in drugs and won't talk to me? I find that a little hard to—"

"You and fifty million other parents," Etheridge chimed in. "Look, Kit. I'm with Frank. We all worry about our kids. We think we have all the answers for every problem and situation. We suffocate them with our awareness and interest and concern. What Frank said—back off. Yes, there's some risk. You can't protect your son from everything. But don't use this drug shit as a license to invade his life—"

"Unless," Montgomery interrupted, "you've done all the work sorting out your own issues."

My own issues? Therapy talk. I'd heard it from Jane. People don't have problems these days, they have "issues."

"Look," I said, "I appreciate your candor, but I'll tell you what my *issue* is. My kid is depressed, angry and fooling around with drugs in the eighth grade, and I can't talk to him about any of this. It's as if I'm the enemy. I haven't had a chance to explore my other *issues* 'cause I'm running all over town all day shopping, rushing the kids to lessons and trying to make a living. So I don't have time and I don't have the money."

The room was still. I didn't need to be told that I sounded defensive. That I wasn't listening. That I was pissed at a bunch of strange men pointing out my inadequacies as a father.

"So what do you sound like to you, Kit?" asked Ricky Melman, smiling. The social worker.

"I sound whiny and defensive," I replied. "Because I'm pissed off. At you, at Ben and at myself."

"Fuckin' right," Dougherty chimed in.

Etheridge leaned over in his chair. "Gee, Frank, I don't think you're saying 'fuck' enough. You okay?" Both of them laughed. "But seriously," he added, "I think you're being a bit rough on Kit here. *Drugs* . . . that isn't like throwing a ball through the neighbor's window. That's serious stuff. I'm not sure I'd go for the 'you've got your life to lead' stance myself, in that case. If your faith is misplaced, your kid will pay for it the rest of his life." He looked at me sympathetically.

With quiet authority, Montgomery once again stepped in. "That's why we're all here, to throw problems and questions out and to get honest responses. Even ones we don't want to hear," he said in my general direction. "In general, we try not to get offended. But I have to say, Frank, I'm sort of with Hal. Drug use is a pretty serious matter these days. Kit's boy gets caught with drugs and he can do some serious time and have a screwed-up record to boot."

Etheridge nodded. "But Charlie's made a good point, Kit. It's a good idea to hear everybody out without losing it. Because if people think you're touchy they won't talk. And that's why you're here, right? We might have just met you, but believe me, this isn't the first time we've discussed this issue."

Montgomery was nodding vigorously. "Every one of us with kids has discussed this issue. Your dilemma is very familiar to us. We grew up lonely, so we want our kid to have friends. We were lousy at sports so we want him to be Michael Jordan . . ."

"We got crummy grades," Dougherty interjected, "so he has to be Einstein. We keep these pains and disappointments with us all of our lives, and when we have kids we relive them. Did you get into some sort of a muddle when you were a kid?"

I blinked, then nodded.

"So you have a kid who is pushing you, testing the rules. He isn't a perfect kid and it makes you crazy, right?"

"Well, it is making me crazy," I conceded. "But I'm not sure why yet."

"But you hear what you're saying?" Etheridge put in. "This is your problem as much as Ben's. He's having to deal with your shit as well as his. And when you do the authoritarian male thing, puffing yourself up and issuing warnings, well . . . if it ever cut much ice, it doesn't in the nineties, does it?"

Everybody laughed, including David Battelle, who hadn't spoken in some time.

"I get what you're saying," I said. "But it does, if you don't mind my being frank, seem a bit pat. I just don't think it's realistic to respond to your kid's smoking dope in school by giving him more space. Maybe he has too much space. Maybe I'm not paying enough attention."

By now I was wishing the conversation would move on. Didn't anyone else have an issue to discuss tonight? I was profoundly uncomfortable.

Battelle yawned elaborately. "Moments like this make me glad I don't have any kids. Everybody who does seems to have nothing but trouble."

I thought I saw a flash of genuine hostility in Charlie Montgomery's gray eyes. "Sometimes I wonder why you're in a men's group at all, David. You seem to find it beneath you." It was an excellent question, given the way Battelle communicated his dislike in words, sneers and body language.

Battelle shrugged and said nothing. Montgomery turned to me. "Kit, let me ask you a direct question. Have you ever smoked dope?"

"Sure, in college," I said. Hadn't everybody? "*And* I inhaled. But," I added quickly, "not when I was Ben's age. Not in eighth grade."

Ricky Melman reached over and grabbed more cookies than he probably should have eaten. "At moments like this, it's probably worthwhile having an addictions counselor on hand, right?" He crunched a cookie, mulling the situation. The others waited.

"I don't know Ben at all and I hardly know you, other than to see that you seem to be a nice guy," he said. "But here are my thoughts. I assume Ben's not a chronic troublemaker, never been arrested or anything . . . ?"

No, no, I quickly assured everybody. Absolutely not.

"So what's interesting about what he did wasn't that he smoked dope. Most kids will take a puff sooner or later, it's a natural part of exploring, being curious, even rebellious. Few make it a serious habit. Parents who think their kids are too sane to get into drugs are often right. Trying dope doesn't make Ben an addict any more than it made you one—"

"I believe my daughter tried it a few times," Montgomery said. "It wasn't the end of the world."

Dougherty leaned forward. "We're always warning our kids about things, from the minute they can walk. When they experiment a bit, stretch their legs, we freak the fuck out. We can't seem to find the middle ground."

"But speaking of Kit's situation," said Melman, smiling, steering the talk back again, "because he's got an immediate problem to deal with—it seems to me, Kit, that Ben's smoking dope in school and getting caught, as opposed to taking a safe puff in the back of somebody's garage where he'd never get caught, is a message to you. You know what the message probably is?"

" 'I hate your guts'?" I suggested.

The whole room cracked up.

"Probably not," said Melman, still smiling. "Probably the message is 'Back off, give me some air.' " I wondered if he gave this speech often. "A kid like this who gets in trouble this way is almost always sending a message; the trick is figuring out what that message is. You want him to give up the drugs, sure, but you also want to make sure you know what he's really trying to say to you. Sometimes I think we might just be the most intrusive parents in world history. We're well meaning, for sure. But we've produced the most scrutinized generation ever. Your son has been through a lot. There was a time he would have wanted your attention, you concede that, right? When misbehaving might have been some kind of cry for help. But that was a while ago."

Melman's summary was deadly. The memory of those awful days wondering if there was an indictment in my future nearly brought tears to my eyes.

I never discussed it much with Jane, certainly never with Ben or Emily. The only person who saw me blubber night after night while federal prosecutors debated whether or not to charge me with insider trading if I didn't turn in my friends was Benchley Carrolton. My upper lip was stiff as a board for everybody else. But Ben, of course, had to have been enduring some torment of his own on my account.

"So then, on top of all that, here comes Mr. Mom, the stay-at-home Dad squiring his kids around, scoring points for being nurturing while the other guys are on the seven twenty-five to Penn Station. Before he deals with being pissed at you for being gone or being pissed 'cause you got into trouble, now you're sitting there at dinner every night saying, 'So tell me, Ben, how was history class today? What did you eat for lunch? What homework do you have? Did you eat all of your spinach?' Shit, Kit, I'm pissed off at you *myself*, and I don't even know you."

Another round of laughter. I joined in, weakly. I was the detective, but it felt as if Ricky Melman and these other guys had been spying on me. He had just recounted, verbatim, my dinner conversation with Ben most nights.

Melman took a swig of water. "So Ben grunts and gives you a lot of 'Uh-huhs,' and 'I dunnos,' and you're pissed 'cause he's uncommunicative to a father who's running his ass off all day trying to be a good dad. You don't respect the fact that he doesn't want to discuss this stuff, am I right? You don't fully accept that he's entitled to his own life. Meanwhile, what the hell have you told him about you? About your life and work and your disappointments?"

As the cliché goes, I was speechless. I did have the presence of mind to nod, however. Melman wasn't being cruel or hostile. He was clearly concerned about my problem and was, as directly as he could, giving me something to think about.

"But in any case," said Etheridge stubbornly, "he has to give up drugs." Melman shrugged.

To my relief, the conversation moved on. The members of the Fathers' Club seemed to agree by some silent signal not to push me any further that night. I didn't speak again, and had a hard time concentrating on what the others were saying.

I did expect Ben to be totally forthcoming with me, while I told him little or nothing. I had trouble accepting that he was entitled to have a life distinct from mine. And I had been totally lug-headed about what his life must have been like while Jane and I were making all of our transitions.

These guys had not only given me things to think about, but things that made sense. Maybe things that would help. But now I was in an even weirder situation. I was in the group, okay. Maybe I even *liked* being in the group.

But I didn't feel one fact closer to understanding Dale Lewis's murder. What was I supposed to tell Linda? That I'd gotten good advice on dealing with my kid but not a clue as to why her husband and the father of her children was dead.

Nine

PRIMARY CARETAKERS of small children tend to be light sleepers. It used to take a high-decibel blast from the alarm clock to rouse me, but since I'm watching over the kids more, it takes amazingly little to pop me out of bed—a whimper from a bad dream, the sound of bare feet charging toward the bathroom (which invariably means vomit, fever, day at home to follow, a scramble for child care), sometimes even a weak "Mommy? Daddy? Are you there?" surely one of the most primal calls among life forms.

After my first Fathers' Club meeting, though, I seemed to toss and turn in bed without any outside stimulus. Jane had been asleep when I got home and was now, four hours later, curled up against the far side of the bed. Perhaps my thrashing had driven her there. Tuesdays and Wednesdays were brutal for her. She had to be in her office at the clinic by 8:30 A.M. and spent the evenings at NYU, typing up notes and case reports and taking emergency phone calls in between. She generally slogged home at ten or eleven and passed out. It was understood that she was a boarder those nights, using the house to sleep, giving us all hugs and squeezes as she rushed in or out. "Those days," she'd say, "I can't really be a part of things; I don't even want to pretend." So she didn't. Sometimes she even stayed at a fellow student's apartment in the Village, too exhausted to drive back home. Like a fifties housewife, I would mutter to myself about all the tasks I had to do by myself and how little help I got. It was small comfort on those days that Jane cleared most of Saturday and Sunday for us (she had studying and filing to attend to, even then).

Ben wasn't into quality time with Mom or Dad at this point in his life, anyway, though we all tried to have at least one meal together. Ricky Melman's exhortation to "give him space" seemed to ring true, even though "space," like "issues," was a word that gave me hives. Still, if Ben didn't want to talk, maybe I should just accept that and leave him alone. Why did that seem like such a radical notion? Our friends' homes were adolescent battlegrounds, with eternal squabbling over unresolvable issues, the most potent being the parents' hammering at the door to their children's emotional lives while the kids were busy piling up sandbags on the other side. Why didn't we get it?

Weekends, Jane and Emily always went off on a "girl trip," either shopping or a movie, sometimes a show in the city. Ben was not interested in any "boy" trip, and I don't know what we would have done if he were. I was permitted to go to the mall once in a while—credit card at the ready—when styles changed abruptly and some variety of hat, shirt or jeans was approaching uncoolness and needed to be replaced.

Which might have been the only detail of life with Ben I hadn't spilled during my supposed infiltration the previous evening. How had I wandered into such a highly personal discussion about my son, anyway? So provocative a talk I couldn't sleep?

I had been accepted into the Fathers' Club, I guess. The men had welcomed me, listened to my parental angst, and moved in to help. In exchange for this, I had lied about my reasons for being there and was now planning to surreptitiously interrogate them, one by one. I had already asked Battelle, as the meeting broke up, if we could "talk" more. We were having lunch today. Maybe I'd find out what a nondad was doing in a Fathers' Club.

I made a mental note to move Emily's two-thirty piano lesson back a half hour to give me time to get back from the restaurant where I was meeting Battelle. Fortunately, nobody in the group lived near Rochambeau, which would at least postpone the inevitable discovery of who I was and why I had joined, a moment I was already dreading.

Awake and roiling, I took Percentage for a 6 A.M. walk. A couple of automatic sprinklers were spitting away. On a neighbor's lawn, ignored by Percentage, a brown rabbit nibbled peacefully at a bed of mums. In about two hours the school buses would come skittering along like fat, yellow, flashing beetles. I thought I heard a phone ringing behind me. Was it mine? But it abruptly stopped.

For the first time in years, I thought of my long-estranged father. Most of the time, I had no reason to think of him. Our relationship had been cold and distant. If you'd put a .9mm to his head, he couldn't have told you who his children's friends or teachers were, what his kids liked to snack on, what they did most of the day, whether they were happy. On weekends, he grimly puttered, hammering away in the garage, driving his big old Buick out for a wash. Eating and driving to family functions were the only things we all did together—until he left, and we were no longer together at all. I always suspected he disapproved of me, though I have no idea if he really did. He was a sour man, I thought, defeated in almost everything he tried. What gnawed away at me now was the growing realization that Ben might view me in much the same way as I did my father. That was pretty depressing.

I hadn't gotten more than two hundred yards from the house when my beeper went off, a summons rare at any hour but especially at this one. I looked at the illuminated number on the screen and recognized it as Danielle Peterson's. Hmmm.

I scurried back inside, tugging a baffled Percentage with me. Jane was downstairs in her bathrobe, looking disheveled and drained.

"What are you doing up?" I asked her.

"Danielle Peterson called. She told me it was urgent. I said you were out walking the dog and that you usually had the beeper attached to your belt. If I saw you first, I was to tell you to call *her* beeper right away."

She came over and threw her arms around me, gave me a warm, sweet kiss. "Morning," she said. "Didn't I used to talk to you a lot?"

"In the old days," I said, squeezing her back—briefly. Then I hurried to the phone, dialed Danielle's number and waited for her callback. "I went to this men's group last night, the one Dale Lewis used to belong to," I told Jane.

"And?" she asked. "How was it?"

"Pretty wild. Different than I expected. We had a long talk about Ben."

"Ben?" She frowned. "How'd Ben come up?"

"I don't know exactly. They told me he was sending me a message—to get out of his face. The whole thing left me feeling like my own father."

She raised her eyebrows. "Well, well. Smart guys. Maybe only a murder could have gotten you into a men's group, but we'll take it. Let's talk about it . . . er, what's today . . . tomorrow night? Or on Friday? I mean, it's good advice, but don't you have a bit of an ethical problem sharing your most intimate details with these people while putting them under surveillance in case one of them is a murderer?"

"I do," I replied gloomily. "I have a huge ethical problem."

"Well, if you're interested in my—"

"The key word," I interrupted, blowing her a kiss as the phone twittered, "is *my* ethical problem. Get back to bed. Looks like something's up, anyway."

Jane kissed me again, then shuffled upstairs. Percentage watched me mournfully as I scooped up the phone.

It sounded like Danielle was calling from her cell phone. I was right. Something *was* up.

"Hey, Kit. Look, I'm on my way over to pick you up. Be outside of your house, okay? We're going to Totowa. If you're through walking that fat, crippled dog." One thing about Danielle, she wasn't long on protocol. And then she added, soberly, "It's your client, Linda Lewis."

"What? What about her?"

"It's bad news, Kit. Possible carjacking attempt, QuickTime convenience store, just on the border between Rochambeau and Totowa. Jurisdiction, Passaic County. About eleven last night, as close as we can figure. Lewis's kids were at home with her mom. Guy came up just as she was taking one of those heavy steering wheel locks off her Toyota. We're not sure of the chain of events, understand. We've only got one eyewitness so far."

"What did you get out of the witness?" I dreaded asking if Linda were okay.

"Not much. She was inside the store waiting to buy a pack of cigarettes. She glanced out the window—she was at least fifty feet away—and saw a man approach the car. She got a quick glimpse of him walking up to the car just as Lewis was about to get out. The woman thought the guy might be with Lewis. Anyway, she bought her cigarettes and didn't look at the car again. She described a middle-aged man in a dark windbreaker. She never saw his face, couldn't ID a photo. All we got was that she had the impression he was stocky and muscular. We found the steering wheel lock outside the car on the ground."

"God," I said. "Is Linda all right?" I was struggling to put this together.

"No, Kit." Danielle's voice dropped. "We think—actually we know—this guy had a gun." My heart sank. There was only one way she could know that. "We think he forced Lewis out of the car, maybe told her he'd kill her if she moved or called for help."

In the background, I heard a police radio squawking. "But what on earth was she doing at the QuickTime anyway? She said her mother was coming, and she had friends. She was in mourning. Why would she go to a convenience store at 11 P.M.? That's odd."

More squawking. "The mother's hysterical. But she told us Linda got a phone call around eleven. Linda said it was just a friend checking in, but the mother thought she seemed upset. A few minutes later, she checked to see that the kids were asleep, then told her mother she had to get out of the house for a couple of minutes and she needed a few things for breakfast. The store was only a few minutes away, she said. The mother objected, said it was late and dark, that a dozen people had called offering to help, so why not call one of them? But Linda just said this wasn't Harlem or Watts, there was no reason to worry, she just really needed some fresh air. And she didn't hang around to discuss it. She just went out.

"Totawa PD saw the Toyota sitting in the lot this morning. They ran a check, then called us. We connected the name right away."

"And Linda?"

"They found her, out back of the parking lot. About one hundred yards into the bushes. She was shot once in the face, right above the left eye. The doctor said he has to test to be sure, but he doesn't think she was raped, which makes it even weirder. If the perp didn't take the car and didn't rape her, what the hell did he shoot her for? Unless she attacked him or ran or something. But it doesn't add up."

I was still slow to get it. "She's in the hospital?"

"Kit, she's in critical condition." Danielle's voice was sympathetic but urgent. "Wake up, man. The guy nearly killed her. She's in a coma. I'm sorry to tell you this way, I know how attached you become to your clients. But I'm just three blocks away and we need to get out there fast."

"He never took the car," I said.

"I just didn't want you to hear it on the news, okay? And maybe you can help us talk to her, when she comes out of it. If she does. If this is linked to her ex-husband's killing, the state police will come in on it. Maybe they will anyway. This isn't really in Totowa's league. Be at your house in a second."

"Danielle—"

But she'd hung up. When I turned around, Jane was already standing there with her arms outstretched, a tissue handy to wipe the tears off my face.

I barely had time to tell her what had happened when I heard a car pull up in front of our house. One impatient beep sounded. I gave Jane a hug goodbye and blew my nose. I'd have to go into shock later. Now wasn't the time.

The car's lights were flashing, and as I dashed outside I saw blinds being pulled up, doors opening a crack and the day's first commuters pausing to stare at the Rochambeau squad car outside our door. I even thought I saw Ben peer out from his bedroom window. What the hell, they would all be wondering, had this madman gotten himself into now?

Danielle patted me on the arm. "Sorry, Kit." As the car jerked forward, further conversation was mercifully impossible. The driver switched on the siren as soon as we left the neighborhood; the noise was deafening.

A carjacking? It's a statistically rare crime in suburbia, yet nothing except kidnapping strikes more deeply at people's sense of security. Next to homes, cars are our individual sanctuaries, our fannies in them much of the time shuttling to and from work, ferrying the kids around. If memory served, there'd been a rash of carjackings around Totowa. Malls were beefing up lighting and other security.

The American Way had hired some guy to sit in a car painted to look like a police cruiser, though it wasn't, with roof lights that were constantly flashing. It was hard to know if this second-rate solution worked at all; our second-rate mall had never had a carjacking. I guess the idea was to make customers feel safe.

We moved quickly, darting in and out of lanes and around traffic, lights and sirens going full tilt. I was trying not to think about what Linda's face, those terrific eyes, might look like right now.

I had a lot of feeling for Linda, but what kind? I'd hardly had a chance to decide. I liked her instinctively, all my internal alarms clanging after our very first meeting. But I knew the rules: never get emotionally involved with a client, even if you don't act on it. It clouds your judgment, affects your work; it's unprofessional. And I was absolutely *not*—on pain of death—going to be one of those men whose mid-life foibles bust up their families. Jane could have me as long as she could stand me, and that was that. Still, there was an ache in my chest as I watched the towering oaks and old clapboard houses of Rochambeau recede en route to Totowa. Somehow meeting Linda Lewis had made me realize I was a bit lonely, with Jane so seldom around, and what poor substitutes kids were for soul mates. Maybe because Linda felt lonely that way too.

Danielle was reading from some notes on a pad and rifling through a manila folder. The file on Dale's killing, I supposed. She would naturally be rushing to the scene in case there was any link. But was there? With Dale dead, who would have a reason to hurt Linda? I fought off the urge to bury my face in my hands.

God, let her come through this okay. She'd suffered enough. And there were two little kids who'd already lost a father and needed a functioning mother. What kind of society had we become, where people shot people in the face over cars? And why had *this* person not taken the car?

We passed a long series of small strip malls. I saw the "H" signs about three blocks before we got to Totowa General and charged up to the emergency entrance.

Danielle flashed her shield at the security guard in the lobby and we pushed inside. Up ahead, amid a gaggle of men in suits who were probably detectives and some uniformed cops, I recognized Lieutenant Tagg of the state police, a sort of pal and sometime source. I had fed Tagg a couple of drug rings once when we were both in the process of extricating Rochambeau's wayward rich kids from the greedy lure of nearby dealers. He helped me when he could, if it wasn't too much trouble and he was sure his ass was covered.

It would definitely be a break if Tagg were on this case. He knew he could trust me to be discreet. And he did owe me, something cops took very seriously. You did them a turn, they did you a turn. Part of the code.

I looked around, leery of press photographers or TV crews. If my picture was taken, that would surely blow my membership in the Fathers' Club. No media yet. They'd be here soon. Rare though they were, carjackings were big news. Ten city kids a week could get blown away in shootouts and drive-bys and you didn't hear much about it, but every carjacking was treated like the Lindbergh case. What had happened to Linda Lewis would probably get the same kind of headline coverage.

Tagg nodded at me, as if I'd been expected. "Hey, Deleeuw, I understand we have your client here." He looked both grim and bored. It was true about veteran cops: they saw too much. Leeming had the same dead eyes. "Give us a minute, will you?" he said. "Cop talk."

He and Danielle ducked into a private room for a minute or two, then Danielle motioned me to join them. It was a storage closet, its shelves stacked with bandages, linens, bottles of alcohol. It reeked of disinfectant.

"Probably the most germ-free place here," said Tagg, wrinkling his nose. "Any self-respecting bacteria would get away from the smell." It was tough to imagine Tagg as anything but a cop. Immaculate white shirt, gray slacks, polyester blue blazer, crew cut. Gun bulging toward the rear on his left side.

"Kit," Danielle said quietly, ignoring him and putting a hand on my arm. "I'm sorry. But Linda Lewis is dead."

The closet was very, very quiet. I closed my eyes, felt a brief surge of tears, but only for a moment. This was a time to be very professional, I reminded myself. This was my client; I owed it to her to remain her investigator. This was business. Business only. Especially now.

"She's been dead for half an hour," Tagg said. "They talked to her mother and pulled life support. She never had a chance. The bullet lodged right in the front of her brain; she was only technically alive since the shooting. I'm sorry."

I nodded. "I'm staying on the case. You both know that."

Tagg pulled over a carton of paper towels and sat down. I declined a similar seat, preferring to stand. Danielle kept her eyes on me.

"I want to warn you not to take this case personally," Tagg said. "I mean it, Kit. Leave the investigating to us—"

"Let's move on," I said curtly. "She was my client. I'll be on the case working it as hard as I can. Period." The coldness of my tone surprised even me. Danielle shrugged at Tagg in a conciliatory, see-I-told-you-so gesture. Tagg just looked at me sadly.

"If you stray from the straight and narrow, friend or not, the state licensing board is right across the hall from our offices in Trenton, Kit. Literally twenty yards. I won't hesitate to have your shield pulled if you withhold information, break off on your own, take risks without informing us." I've already done all that, I thought. "I'm serious, Kit. I wouldn't like it, but I'd do it." He sipped from a Styrofoam cup of black coffee. God knows how many cups he'd consumed since last night.

Danielle didn't wait for me to respond. "Kit, this is a very odd case. It creeps me out on lots of levels. There are things I don't understand and don't like. There's nothing to link Dale's death and Linda's. Witnesses say some guy appeared to be canvassing cars in the QuickTime lot. Thirties or forties, stocky, with a Jersey Devils cap. I don't understand why he picked her car. It wasn't new or in demand in chop shops. I don't understand why he didn't take it or how he got away after he shot her."

"And," Tagg added, "you don't understand why she doesn't appear to have been robbed. Or raped."

"Lieutenant," I interrupted, "I seem to recall some publicity about carjackings around here. Am I right?"

Tagg looked at Danielle. He shook his head.

My temper snapped. "Look, let's not start off with this bullshit. I can go back to my office and get on-line and have every newspaper story about carjackings in the last six months up on the screen before you finish your coffee. You talk about cooperating, but your notion of it is to suck me dry, then wink at each other when I ask a routine question. That's just crap. If you want to play it that way . . ."

Peterson gently rapped me on the head with her police radio. "Easy there, cowboy. Let's not go busting a blood vessel. We are just trained to be cautious, okay? Chill. Tagg, tell the man, or I will."

Tagg shrugged. "There have been three carjackings within a three-mile radius of the convenience store in the past two months.

Twice the perp just threw the woman out of the car. Once he raped her for good measure, then took the car. This is the first killing. If it's the same guy—and the descriptions are kinda vague, so it's hard to say—he never used the gun before. I need you to be discreet about this, Deleeuw. The media haven't connected them. Two different counties, and no deaths till now." Tagg and the local police weren't anxious for the taxpayers to know there was a serial carjacker running around northern New Jersey, let alone a murderous one.

Tagg shrugged. "Look, I don't really want to go into more detail about what we do or don't know, Kit. What I'd like to know from you is, do you know of anything or anyone who might tell me something about the Lewises' relationship that I don't already know? Who might give me some reason why these murders could be linked? Because it seems to me that this is a tragic coincidence—a bizarre one, but still a coincidence."

I blinked. "Lieutenant," I said, "you really think that these two killings were just happenstance? How many times has a spouse been murdered one day, and the other killed in a different place for some unconnected reason a day later? Has that *ever* happened?"

This time Tagg yawned *and* shrugged. "You read the papers, Kit? How many times has a one-year-old baby been machine-gunned in her stroller, until it happened in Newark this year? How many times has a kid committed suicide by running over two cops and gunning for a roadblock until some jerk did it in Trenton this month? And how many times has some shithead blown up twenty kids in a day care center, before Oklahoma City? We rewrite history every day in this fucking country, pal. Nothing is impossible." He reached into his pocket and pulled out a pack of Camels. I decided if he lit up now I'd probably have to kill him myself.

"I suppose it's possible somebody followed her to the store," Peterson mused. "But it seems a strange sort of premeditation. Too much you don't know; too much that can go wrong. This looks like a classic crackhead carjacking gone bad. Picked a bad car, panicked maybe, shot Lewis, took off. We don't have any motive for her husband's getting killed, Kit, so you have to admit it's tough to link her death to his."

Tagg lit his cigarette, took a deep drag. "But we're not ruling it out, Kit. I don't know what the fuck happened. You start with a working hypothesis, then you go where the evidence goes. Right now I have a carjack that turned nasty. You have something that ought to take me someplace else, let's have it."

Danielle put on her Sergeant Peterson look, which was formidable. I'd seen her anger, and didn't take it lightly. "What *have* you found so far, Kit? I know you. You've probably got your little network going on this one, right?" She was referring to a group of women who called themselves the Rochambeau Harpies, a diverse lot who were wired into every coach, teacher and block association in town. The Harpies had been invaluable in helping me break my last case. So far, I doubted they could help me with this one, but maybe I ought to give them a try.

"We found a neighbor and friend who told us Dale Lewis belonged to some group in town, but that he wouldn't talk much about it. He was sort of embarrassed. Some men's group, maybe one of those where guys beat drums and run around naked? You know about that?"

This was tricky ground. Withholding information in a murder investigation meant losing a license. Best not to get too cute. On the other hand, the group met in Springdale, far away, and Dale had obviously not spread the word about it. The only other person who probably knew much about it would have been Linda. I had no doubt Danielle would dig it out soon enough, but as I had a couple of days head start, I decided to use it. I don't know why exactly. Let's say I felt I owed it to Linda. This was one case I wanted to break myself.

"Linda told me Dale was in a men's group, but that he didn't talk about it much, as I'm sure he wouldn't to his ex. That was probably where he went to trash her," I said. Danielle seemed to buy my response for now. When she learned more, she'd feel betrayed. She'd consider how to respond. Leeming, on the other hand, wouldn't hesitate for thirty seconds. He'd see my license yanked.

I asked if I could make a telephone call, and Tagg waved his cigarette toward a phone booth down the hall. I said I had to call home, which was a lie. Fortunately, I remembered the number.

A young woman's voice answered. "Yes?"

"Look, this is urgent," I said. "My name is Kit Deleeuw. I was hired by Linda Lewis. I'm at Totowa General. I'm sure you know by now what's happened." I didn't know for sure that the police had told them at home that Linda was dead. If not, I didn't want to be the one to break the news. "Who is this, please?"

"This is Marge Bacon. I live down the street. I'm Linda's closest friend. She told me about you. God, this is so horrible. Her mother's under sedation. We're going to tell the kids later. . . . How is she?" So she didn't know.

"Look, Marge, I just have a few minutes. And I really need your help. Is that a portable phone you're using?"

"Yes, it is. I spent the night on the couch."

"Marge, do me and Linda a huge favor. Walk to the kitchen. Tell me when you get there."

"I'm there," she said, sounding puzzled.

"Okay. Linda told her mother she was going out last night to get food for breakfast. We're going to quickly tour the kitchen and see if this is true, okay? I know you're upset, but I really need you to be sharp and help me."

She seemed to snap to. "I'm sharp," she said. "I've got three kids. I know about breakfast. What do you need?"

I, too, knew about breakfast. "Look for milk," I said. "Skim and low-fat, okay?"

There was a half gallon of each, full to the top, she reported.

"Eggo waffles?" Plenty in the freezer.

"Cereal?" Wheaties, Fruit Loops and Cheerios.

"Mr. Deleeuw," Marge said, "there's plenty of breakfast food, all kinds. I should know—I went to the market with a list Linda gave me yesterday afternoon. I spent $150 stocking up for the week, so she wouldn't have to worry about it. She was very grateful. There's no food shortage here."

What was she after, then?

"Does she smoke?" I hadn't seen her light up, but maybe Marge had.

"No, never. Linda is a fitness nut. She runs every morning."

"Does she drink?"

"A beer, once in a while. But there are two six-packs here."

"Pardon the indelicacy," I said. "But might she have needed sanitary napkins? Was she having her period?"

"I don't know about that, Mr. Deleeuw, but they were on the list. I bought two boxes. I bought two of *everything* so she wouldn't have to deal with shopping for a while."

"Did she need pantyhose? Run out of makeup?"

Marge ran up to Linda's bedroom to check. "She hardly ever wears pantyhose, and there's plenty here in her dresser. She doesn't care for makeup. She sure wouldn't have worried about makeup at a time like this. She didn't want to leave the children. That was the whole point of my shopping. I can't figure what might have made her go out. She got that phone call—"

I thanked Marge and hung up. Danielle Peterson was watching me closely from down the hall. She knew I wasn't calling home.

So the breakfast-items story was bogus. There had to be something urgent Linda needed that we hadn't thought of, or somebody had made a phone call that lured her out. Nothing else made sense.

Ten

IDENTIFIED Linda Lewis's body for the Totowa police and the Passaic County Medical Examiner's Office. A "preliminary" ID, the police called it. Her mother would provide the official identification. I wish I could have spared her that. No parent should have to see what I'd just seen.

Linda was lying on a gurney in a curtained-off corner of the emergency room, her face curiously peaceful given the circumstances of her death. At our previous encounter, Linda had been a lively, strong, concerned woman worried about her ex and determined to care for her kids. Now she was cold, her skin blue-gray, with bruises around the face, and her left eye blackened. There was one small, neat bullet hole just above her right eye and puncture marks from the tubes that had been inserted to try to save her. Danielle and Tagg vanished to confer with other investigators and talk with the medical examiner's office about an autopsy. I went into the men's room and splashed cold water on my face. I'd lost not only a client but somebody I had real feeling for, somebody who touched me briefly but in a powerful way. I wasn't unaware of the current of anger that ran through me either. I had to get the hell out of here. I left a note for Danielle at the desk and called Luis Hebron at the Lightning Burger.

"Good morning, Kit," he said, courteous even in the midst of the breakfast rush. "How are you this morning? How can I help you?" Calls from me were unusual at this hour. I made it a point to stay away during busy mealtimes when Luis was graciously explaining that the numbers of fries in every bag was about the same, or exhorting his motley crew of teenagers to be polite, neaten up and move briskly.

"Not so good, Luis. I need a huge favor. A client of mine has been murdered in Totowa. I'm kind of shaken up about it, but more to the point, I need a ride home. I'm at the emergency-room entrance at Totowa General. I need to get away from these people. But I came in a police car, and I don't want to go back that way. It would take forever to get a cab. I know you're busy . . ."

"I'm on my way, my friend," he said, as I'd known he would. He knew I'd do the same for him, if he ever let me. I walked toward the exit to wait for him.

Pacing at the entrance ramp in front of the emergency room, I felt shaky in the knees and tight in the throat. My philosophy is, you fall apart when the case is over. But this killing had gotten to me ahead of schedule. It was obvious, even to me, that I'd nursed a mild crush on Linda Lewis, the healthy kind, the sort you don't do anything about. Nonetheless it made her death cruelly painful, even though I barely knew her. It was as if an idea, a promise, the possibility of something had died along with the thing itself.

Luis's big black Buick glided up. The car was spotless, of course, with no debris or adornments of any kind except for a faded photograph in a plastic case affixed to the sunshade on the driver's side. I could make out a man and a woman and some children on a beach somewhere, palm trees in the background.

"Good morning, Kit," Luis said softly as I got in, strapped in the seat belt and nodded. We circled back onto the highway, heading toward Rochambeau. True to form, Luis didn't ask about the murder or my feelings about it. He understood privacy and distance. Nor did he chitchat or fill the silence with words.

In fifteen minutes the Buick was idling in front of my house. I watched him take in the tree-lined street, the bike-strewn lawns, the few Halloween decorations beginning to appear, and my home—a barn of a Victorian, with a white porch curving all around. It was a solid old house, but sorely in need of upkeep. The lawns were weedy and paint was flecking off the clapboard. I invited Luis in for coffee, knowing he wouldn't come.

"Thank you, but I've got to return, Kit. I'm pleased you called me. You seem deeply troubled. I'm very sorry. Perhaps you'd care to tell me what you know."

I leaned over and patted him on the arm. As I did, I got a closer look at the snapshot—a younger Luis with his wife and family.

I filled him in on what Peterson had told me about the killing. "Linda was unusual, maybe a bit more than a client to me." I was fumbling to explain. "We weren't romantically involved or anything, she just was very courageous and generous. Decent. I'm stunned to think she's dead. That both of them are dead."

Luis sat quietly as I stumbled on. "The police are leaning away from linking the two killings. The state police lieutenant, a guy named Tagg I know who's pretty sharp, says you have to go with the evidence and the evidence in this case leads toward a bungled carjacking. Thing is, Linda drove a not very desirable Toyota. Which the killer just left sitting there. And even though he led her out to a deserted area behind the store, she wasn't raped or robbed. Why take Linda out back and shoot her? How can that not be connected to the murder of her husband two days ago?"

All this sort of came spilling out, a mixture of grief and frustration, and none of it made any sense. Luis was taking it all in.

"In some countries, you could rule out a lot of possibilities," he said when I had finished. "But here, people are killed for no reason at all, every day. Even in a squalid dictatorship in Latin America you usually must *do* something to get killed—criticize the regime, sleep with the wrong general's wife, something. In America, all you have to do is stop at the wrong convenience store. So many sick people, so many guns . . . anything is possible. Maybe the killer was on drugs? Or walked out of a psychiatric institution? Perhaps he was already a murderer, freed on parole, who started killing again the day he was released." He shook his head. America made little sense to him. I wondered if he liked much about it.

He turned to me soberly and continued. "Kit, I will be candid with you, as I know you would want me to be. I think this lieutenant may be toying with you. You are a fine investigator, Kit, but you do prefer to believe the best about people, sometimes in the face of powerful evidence to the contrary." I nodded, to show that he hadn't offended me. Over the past years Luis had given me strength in my new work, generously guiding me toward solutions of some daunting cases. And he'd provided me innumerable cups of coffee, too. But I wasn't sure where he was going this time.

"What do you mean, Luis? I'm not following."

"I think your friend Lieutenant Tagg is not being totally candid with you, Kit. I'm sure he wants to follow the evidence. But I would wager that he is also very suspicious of your deceased client, that at this very moment he is probing into her affairs. It is what I would do if I were he. Perhaps her interest in her ex-husband was not, as she presented it to you, simply a matter of concern. Perhaps they shared some business enterprise or other venture together. Perhaps they both did something that got them killed. Don't forget that, for reasons we have not yet identified, the FBI is also paying attention."

I said nothing, just worked that one over.

"It's merely a possibility, Kit, but one the police will surely consider. You must too. Linda Lewis may not have been the innocent she seemed to be. That might explain why she and her husband were killed within a day of each other."

That was a tough thing for me to swallow, Luis knew. But what he was saying was possible. My logic was certainly clouded by sentimentality—the great enemy of investigative work—in this case. What if Linda had manipulated me into investigating her husband for reasons she was never truthful about? What if she wasn't the sympathetic mother and artist she so skillfully had presented herself to be? Was I that naive?

"Luis, I appreciate what you're saying. I'm sure Tagg is already considering these possibilities. But it's always been my cardinal rule—my clients are innocent and I have to presume they're in the right—"

"So long as your eyes are open to the possibility that they are not," he said bluntly, looking me square in the face. "That is probably what the police now believe, and you must take it into account." Luis must have been a murderous attorney.

"Let me play devil's advocate, Luis," I said. His calmness and focus were helping me settle down, too. "A husband and a wife are killed within days. You logically think there has to be a connection. But they had already filed for divorce. They weren't in business together, that we know of. She had no money, lived in a modest place, drove a modest car. She sure didn't strike me as a player."

He gave me a quizzical look. "Perhaps it was a carjacking," he acknowledged. "And perhaps something went wrong. Somebody interrupted it. Something happened to frighten the man. Somebody came along . . .''

I had learned to take Luis's instincts very seriously. If this wasn't a random carjacking gone sour, then somebody had a reason to kill both Linda and Dale. I wondered if the media would go berserk over these killings. I wondered how long my cover would last at the Fathers' Club.

I thanked Luis again, then went up the walk and into the house. Jane would be off to the city, Em off to school. My suspended son, however, would be home. In fact, I already heard the familiar beeps of the verboten Nintendo.

Rebecca Steinitz, the iron-fisted baby-sitter I'd hired to monitor Ben while he was home, startled me by looming up as soon as I was in the front hall. Mrs. Steinitz had to be in her seventies. A violent opponent of almost everything kids liked—candy, TV, video games and computers—she believed the only real recreational options were to play in the backyard or to read books, and not comic books, either. Comparative libertarians, we'd gotten Mrs. S. to loosen up some, but grudgingly. The kids would do almost anything to avoid her, but she was punctual, tough, reliable and fiercely protective.

And our kids were always thrilled to see us return and relieve her of her duties. I guess in the back of my mind I'd hoped leaving Ben in the house with her for a few days would encourage him to think long and hard about his pot-smoking episode.

But Mrs. S. looked flushed and angry today, as opposed to merely stern. "Mr. Deleeuw," she began, "I'm afraid you'll have to have a long talk with Benjamin. I told him he couldn't play Nintendo, as you'd instructed. He just told me to 'butt out' of his business, that he would do whatever he wanted. He used words I won't repeat and his attitude—well, it was beyond disrespectful. Ben used to be so sweet a young boy." My stomach knotted. I hadn't had a chance to brief her about how delicate I thought Ben was at the moment.

"I'm afraid I can't work under these conditions," she continued. "I'll stay through the day, as I said I would, but I won't come back tomorrow unless I can be sure my instructions will be followed. Please let me know when your household is under control." Then she bustled upstairs, murmuring something about the laundry, clearly leaving the errant child alone for the talking-to from Dad.

I didn't need this. I walked into the playroom where a barefoot Ben, in tattered jeans and a cotton sweater, was sprawled in front of the TV, his Knicks cap turned backward.

"Ben," I said, over the singsong cadence of the game, "turn that off, please." He ignored me. It was as if I weren't even in the room. I waited a few seconds, walked over to the wall and yanked the plug.

He sat staring at the screen for a few seconds, then turned to me. "I'll just put it on again the second you leave," he said coolly.

Maybe, on a different morning, I would have handled it differently. I reached down, ripped the Super Nintendo control box from the plug that attached it to the TV and smashed it against the wall. It shattered.

"No, you won't," I told my son. "Not today. I just came from identifying the body of a murdered friend. Mrs. Steinitz tells me you've been rude and obnoxious, and neither she nor I want to take any more of your shit. This isn't a vacation, a pleasant few days to lie around and play games, you understand? You've been booted out of school, remember?" I almost never yell, but I was shouting now. How dare he screw up so badly, take no responsibility for it, lounge around playing Nintendo first thing in the morning while being abusive to an elderly woman? I wasn't the least bit in the mood for reasonable, deliberate parenting techniques. So much for the sage advice of the Fathers' Club.

"The idea is not that you'll sit on your ass being rude and snotty, Ben, goddamnit. The idea is that you'll use this time to think a bit about what you did, realize that you shouldn't do it again and then get back to school with a healthier attitude. Otherwise, things are just going to escalate. You'll end up in therapy, maybe even in some special school. Maybe you'll have to deal with the police. But one way or another, buddy, you'll have to get serious."

He crossed his arms, his expression a frozen leer, his anger encasing him like an impenetrable wall. I had obviously not succeeded in awakening or even frightening him. Would the men in the Fathers' Club approve? Was I invading his space? Should I leave him alone to play Nintendo for a week and be nasty to his gray-haired baby-sitter? And to his father? Mostly, I wanted to brain him. I was furious—at whoever had killed Linda, at Jane for vanishing and sticking me with two kids and a double murder case, and at this creep I was supposed to love but at the moment didn't even like.

He didn't speak. It was clear he wasn't going to, no matter what I said.

"Ben, look," I said, with effort lowering my voice. "I'm sorry you're so unhappy. I'm sorry I wasn't around when you were a kid. I'm sorry you were embarrassed by what happened to me on Wall Street. I'm sorry if I've crowded you. But this is not going to work. We can't have this kind of civil war going on in this house. We have to figure out how to talk to each other . . ."

At that, I saw the index finger of his right hand extend over his folded arms. A millisecond later my fist shot out. It stopped within an inch or two of Ben's face. He didn't speak, but he did blanch, and I saw the flicker of fear in his eyes.

I had kept intact—by inches—my record of never having struck the kids. The leer was off his face now. But besides that, I didn't know that I'd accomplished a thing.

Eleven

WHEN YOU START raising a hand in anger, it's time to stop and recognize that the situation is beyond you. Aside from the very rare swat to a toddler's fanny, there is never an excuse for it. It never makes things better. And it had never happened before, I told myself as the waves of guilt began to crest. But I'd been sorely, probably willfully, provoked. I needed to get out of the house for a while and cool off. And I also needed to pursue my now dual investigation.

"Ben, this is no good," I said softly. "We have to find a way to talk. Just stay here for a while, okay? I'll be back later."

I didn't want to leave this way, though. I turned back. "I love you, Ben. A lot. That's what this is really all about, you know, figuring out how to love you."

He sat staring at me as I called for the dog and headed for the back door. I didn't know how to reach him and I wasn't really in the mood for help.

I wasn't in the mood for Jessica Gurwitt-Owens either, who was standing by our back door in her flowered shirt and denim jumper, pretending she hadn't heard me screaming at my son.

It was Emily who had christened Gurwitt-Owens "the Petition Lady." Jane saw her as a potent symbol of what can happen to women who stop working to take care of their kids, if they're not careful. Jessica had practiced law once, with a public interest firm in the city. Now, in her late thirties, several years of intense full-time child rearing and round-the-clock fighting for justice had grayed her hair, broadened her hips and thinned her lips into a perpetual frown.

Her Chrysler minivan wore pro-choice, anti-death-penalty and "Fight Racism" stickers. Good causes all, but the effect was to create the near impossible: a self-righteous automobile.

It fit its driver. Jessica was a regular at school board meetings, erupting in weekly outrage at the racism, sexism, homophobia and Eurocentrism that permeated the curriculum, texts and classrooms of our schools. She haunted the neighborhood too, bearing petitions demanding municipal workshops on diversity, high school seminars on acquaintance rape and mandatory educational programs for those convicted of failure to recycle.

"Everything she wants is *right*," Jane would groan when the doorbell rang. "So why do I want to kill her?"

Maybe it was the fact that my day hadn't started off well and was rapidly getting worse, but I didn't have much heart for her latest— which, I knew before she said a word, was banning leaf-blowers. Her recent stream of letters to the editor of the local paper had already alerted me to their evils.

September was, in fact, something of a dread time around Rochambeau. By 9 A.M.—sometimes even earlier—it sounded as though a giant horde of killer bees had descended on the town. Leaf-blowers roared on every block to keep those lawns pristine. I didn't especially like the racket, but worried about all the guys named Vinnie who manned the blowers. Gurwitt-Owens wanted them silenced. Now.

"Kit, I need your support for this ordinance," she began as soon as Percentage and I were within earshot. "These noisy landscapers intrude on our privacy and damage the environment. They—"

I held up a hand. "Jessica," I said, "I'm in a postpolitics mood today. I'm out of outrage. Maybe some other time." I waved to Percentage to follow me and kept walking.

Mrs. Steinitz was in the house; she'd at least keep an eye on things. I doubted even Ben had the stomach for more confrontation. Whatever his demeanor, he had to be upset about the things going on in his life.

Percentage seemed happy to escape the tension of the house and hopped into the shotgun seat of the Volvo. But before I could turn the ignition key the cell phone I keep in the glove compartment warbled. God, I thought. Not even nine-thirty yet. What else can be happening?

Evelyn was calling from the mall. She'd heard the news about Linda on the radio. And Luis had thoughtfully called to alert her to watch out for me. "Kit, this is just awful, awful. I know how upsetting this must be. Should I call Willie in?"

I backed out of the garage. My son was staring out the playroom window as I pulled away. It broke my heart to see his miserable, angry look. What could I do to help him through this?

"Sure, give him a call," I told Evelyn. "Tell him we need to add Linda Lewis to the list of people to check out, on foot as well as on line. We have to figure out if there's a connection between these two murders. The police say they doubt it, but they may be fudging. I was certain there must be some link, but now I'm not so sure."

Evelyn delivered a message. "A lawyer named Charles Montgomery called," she said. I'd given him my private office line, the one where the answering machine simply said, "You've reached Kit Deleeuw." Evelyn checked it when I wasn't in. He'd heard the news about Linda Lewis, Evelyn reported in a neutral tone, and was calling a special meeting of the Fathers' Club at 9:00 P.M. at the church. Heaven knows what she thought of *that*. I asked Evelyn to call his office back and say I'd be there, then to call David Battelle and—being careful not to discuss my work—see if he'd agree to move our lunch up. I suggested twelve-thirty today at Miele's, a modestly priced Italian restaurant in Verona, roughly between our offices. I needed to start gathering some data, and Battelle had indicated his willingness to talk. Here was at least one person with a connection to both of the dead.

"I'll call, Kit, but remember, you have insurance reports to fill out on those accident claims, and tonight is Emily's Back-to-School Night at six-thirty . . ." Shit, that had completely slipped my mind. But I couldn't miss my only chance to get to meet her new fifth-grade teachers. I'd stay for most of it, then rush out to Springdale.

I put in a call to Jane at the Paterson clinic, but she was in an urgent meeting. It was therapist time for the Leon/Deleeuw family. I saw troubled families almost every day in my work. Jane saw far worse. There were people who faced up to their problems and got help and there were people who didn't. Ben was in trouble, and

I couldn't seem to help him, so I had to get to somebody who could.

In the rearview mirror I could see Percentage's baleful expression. Labradors always look as if they understand that the world is a complex place.

I got to the American Way, waved to Luis—who was overseeing the postbreakfast cleanup—and to Murray Grobstein. Percentage climbed up the back stairs with me and scooted over to a raggedy old quilt I kept in the corner of my office. He was asleep instantly.

Willie came bounding in seconds later. I wondered if he had a half dozen Pearl Jam T-shirts or simply wore the same one every day.

"Evelyn called you in?" I asked.

"No, Chief, I spent the night here, actually. I'm sorry about Linda Lewis. That's horrible, man. The security guy here told me about it this morning. He didn't know she was our client."

I nodded glumly. "You were here all night?"

"Gathering stuff on-line about your men's group buddies. I even went out for some actual field work. Visited Mr. Battelle's office complex, talked to a couple of the neighbors at his apartment in Clayton. Came up with some interesting stuff on our man Dale's business dealings. Talked to one of the Lewises' neighbors, too." Willie used to call me Kit but had started watching old TV reruns of "Superman" and, in homage to Perry White, had taken to calling me Chief. Much of Willie's worldview was shaped by sixties and seventies reruns on Nickelodeon.

I told Willie to come in and close the door. He had been busy, apparently. Perhaps he had come up with some scrap of information which would make the recent violent turn of events even remotely comprehensible.

He gave the dozing Percentage a pat, lowered himself sideways into his usual chair, and with a certain pride began reeling off his latest findings.

"First off, Dale was cheating on Linda when they were still together. It seems she found out. I got this from the person you taught me to look for first—the retiree out puttering in her garden all day, missing nothing and anxious for somebody to share it with. Mrs. Juniper. She says the other woman was one Bev Cadawaller. Linda came over to see Mrs. Juniper one morning and just burst into tears and blurted it out. It wasn't easy to get this out of her,"

Willie added, a trifle smugly. "I had to let her give me milk and a half dozen cookies. But she was so upset about Linda, she needed to unburden herself."

I sat slack-jawed. "What? What are you saying?" This was too much to grasp. And then, of course, there was more. Evelyn buzzed to say that Mrs. Steinitz was on the line and had to talk to me. Mrs. Steinitz did not hit the panic button easily.

"Mr. Deleeuw, I'm sorry to bother you," she said. "But Ben just left the house. The boy simply walked out. I couldn't stop him and he wouldn't tell me where he was going or when he would be back. I'm sorry, but I'm not a policeman. What do you want me to do?"

I wanted her to go home for a bit, then come back before two-thirty so that she could be there when Emily got back from school. Then I wanted to crawl under my desk and stay there.

She was upset and concerned. "He's such a nice boy. I don't know what's gotten into him." Welcome to the club.

I put in another call to Jane, but she wasn't in her office. I left a voice-mail message briefly describing my argument with Ben and Mrs. Steinitz's news, emphasizing that the last thing I'd said to Ben was to stay in the house. I also told her that my case was heating up and that perhaps she could plead flu and manage a day or two at home.

My head was whirling. "Wait, Willie, you're telling me that Dale had an affair and Linda knew about it? She never mentioned that to me! Why would she have stayed with him under those circumstances?"

Willie, who found the whole idea of marriage exotic and un-fathomable anyway, held up his palms. "Who knows? Maybe he groveled. Maybe he wanted her assets . . ."

I snorted. "What assets? She was an artist, for God's sake. She came to me in the first place at least partly because he wasn't meeting his child support . . ."

Willie tossed some printouts onto my desk, then pulled a choco-late doughnut out of—where? His jeans pocket? Thin air? "Maybe she didn't have great cash flow, Chief, but she had assets. Blue-chip stocks from her parents, plus she owned undeveloped land near Bar Harbor, Maine. A gift from her grandfather, it seems. The stocks are worth $250,000 or so; the property is worth another $250,000. It was all listed as collateral for one of Dale's loan applications to the feds."

Before I could say anything meaningful, like "Holy shit," Evelyn stuck her head in the door. She looked uncharacteristically unnerved. "Kit, there's a TV crew outside. Channel 4 from New York. They say they got your name from the medical examiner and want to interview you. You are aware, I guess, that this story is all over the radio, too."

This crew would have to be especially enterprising to have squeezed the name of the preliminary identifier out of the ME's office. "Goddamnit," I muttered, "I should have let someone else ID the body."

"Well, you could hardly refuse," offered Willie politely.

If I even popped my head out of my office, there was always the chance the cameraman would tape me and throughly blow my cover with the men's group. Showing up with the cops to identify Linda's corpse would reveal my involvement and screw up everything. I had to get more time. Between Danielle Peterson, Lieutenant Tagg and the men's group, I was in for it when this all finally broke, as it was certain to do. But no other reporters had called, or Evelyn would have told me, so there was at least a chance Channel 4 was the only news organization that had my name.

"Willie," I ordered, "get into your office. Stay out of sight. Evelyn, go back out there and tell the producer to come in. Alone. No reporter and *no* camera." I stood back from the door just in case.

In seconds, a young woman in jeans and a black leather jacket came in wearing a cell phone holder on one shoulder like a holster and a briefcase over the other. Percentage looked briefly skeptical, then rolled over and went back to sleep.

"Debbie Silverman," the woman said, meeting my gaze, her hand outstretched. "We understand you ID'd the body. We want to talk with you about the Lewis murders. You're sometimes called the Suburban Detective, am I right? You're in our tape library, I think. I could just call that up if I need to." She looked like she wasn't about to mumble apologies and leave merely because I asked her to. This was a combat-ready New York TV producer. Underestimating her would be a major mistake.

"Ms. Silverman, I know you're just doing your job, but I can't be quoted or taped about this. I'm investigating something that isn't related to this killing"—technically that was true; I'd been hired to find out what had happened to Dale. "I'd met the deceased, so I ID'd her as a favor to the police until her mother arrived. But I wasn't an intimate of hers and I'd like to be left out of this, at least for now.

"So how about this? How about I slip you the name of some-body who really does know what the hell is going on, a Rocham-beau police detective? I'll give you her private number. I can't promise she'll talk to you, but that's your problem. And I promise that if and when I have any more information relating to this case you'll get it first. I'd take this deal, Ms. Silverman, because I don't know a thing yet. But there's a good chance that I soon will. And you'll have it first. In exchange, you leave now and keep my name out of this."

She looked at her watch. I had a sudden inspiration. From my journalistic encounters on previous cases, I knew that a producer always worries, first and foremost, about taking videotape back to New York. The cardinal sin was to return without pictures. With-out pictures, a story dies. All I had to do was to steer her to a better picture than me.

"Let me give you another tip," I added before she could re-spond. "A few of Linda Lewis's paintings are on exhibit at the Rochambeau Art Museum. That could be a very touching, visual element to your piece. I bet no one else knows about it."

I had her and she knew it. A dead artist's work would be much better than some bland-looking investigator saying no comment. She was gone in a flash, yelling over her shoulder, "You better not go back on your word when this breaks." I doubt she was still close enough to hear me yell back that I wouldn't.

Willie and Evelyn came back into the room. "How'd you do that?" asked Evelyn respectfully. "She came in here swinging. I thought we'd have to call security to get her out."

"Just charm." I smiled. But there was no time to gloat. I'd yet to absorb what Willie had been telling me.

"Okay, Will. Let's get back to business here. So Dale Lewis tries to build some low-income housing, with Battelle in some kind of partnership. Rheems takes a second mortgage out on his house to help them, right? The project goes bust. Dale and Rheems lose their shirts. Battelle structured the arrangement to protect himself, somehow. Then Dale wants to take another shot at being a devel-oper and Linda allows him to put up her stocks and property as collateral for some government loan? After she found out he was having an affair with this Cadawaller woman? And what do we know about her?"

Willie leafed through a notebook, couldn't find what he wanted there, shuffled the printouts. "Bev Cadawaller is an architect," he announced. "Several interesting things about her. For instance, her mailing address is the same office where you found Dale's body. Credit card records for the two of them a few months back show several meals at the same restaurant, which means Dale and Bev might have taken turns taking each other out for rendezvous. She has another office listed in Paramus. I called; she apparently works there part time. Some architects move from firm to firm, depending on the project. If she's working on one development, she'll give that development office as her business address for a while. I'll find out where she is working today. I'm going to try to find out if she was involved in any of this housing stuff Dale was into. . . . And, Kit, I've found something that might be even more important."

The number of important things was getting out of hand. I held up my hand and picked up the phone. I dialed Danielle Peterson's private line at police headquarters. She picked it up on the first ring.

"Kit, you son of a bitch. Did you give my number to some fucking TV reporter? You know the county cops and state police are handling this—they would kill me if I talked. Bad enough looking at that body and watching the mother fall apart. I don't need reporters on my ass, too."

"Danielle, I have no time to be abused. Does the name Bev Cadawaller mean anything to you?"

Silence on the other end. Danielle might, on occasion, be persuaded to give stuff away, but she always wanted to know exactly where it was going and why. "Why do you ask?" she said, on cue.

"Just bear with me, Danielle, and I'll tell you why. Promise."

I heard her sorting through her notes. "Yeah, I knew I'd heard it. Cadawaller had some mail and files at the office where Dale was found. She was a part-time business associate of his. But one of the other detectives called her the night of the murder and she said she hadn't been there for weeks. She's on our interview list, but not high priority. Didn't seem to have anything crucial to tell us. What do you have?"

Hmmm. If I gave Danielle the information about Dale and Cadawaller she might be slightly less enraged when she learned about the existence of the Fathers' Club and my membership in it. I couldn't withhold much longer without risking my license. Tonight might even be my last meeting.

"Look, Danielle, I don't know if you care or if it matters, but I think this Cadawaller woman and Dale Lewis had some sort of personal relationship."

"Big fucking deal, Kit. So what? He was a single guy. Why shouldn't he get laid?"

"Apparently he was getting laid *before* he was a single guy. That might be even why he *was* a single guy."

She whistled. "Oh, one of *those* personal relationships. Well, well. We'll just have to move her up a little higher on the list, won't we? Thanks, Deleeuw. You actually told me something I didn't know. I guess that was inevitable, sooner or later. But it doesn't make Cadawaller a suspect. Unless you've got something else."

"I don't."

"Well, I don't like what we have, at this point. Pretty paltry. And now with the state police on the case, I don't know how much more we're going to get. They're like the FBI—takers, not givers. Tagg still thinks that, statistically freaky though it is, this was a busted carjacking. What about you?"

"I don't know, Danielle. That's hard for me to believe. A husband and wife killed within forty-eight hours of one another? A friend of mine pointed out to me that no kind of violence is really impossible in America. But I'm looking for a connection."

"Well, if you find one, pal, your first call better be here. I hate surprises, and you know the chief hates them even more than I do." I made the usual obsequious promises, and Danielle told me again she was sorry. She said it was obvious that I was fond of Linda, and she left it at that, mercifully, and hung up.

I was skating pretty far out, and had just glided a bit farther, withholding evidence about Dale's group, and now hiding information about Linda as well. Willie might have uncovered an innocent business arrangement—or a link that could help explain why both of these people were dead and their two kids were orphans.

All traces of a family and their life in Rochambeau would soon be gone: the mother and father dead, the kids living with relatives somewhere, the pets given away. They would endure for a few weeks or months in the clip files of reporters and the memories of a few teachers, coaches and friends. Then there'd be little record that they were ever here at all. My job was to at least discover whoever was responsible for the death of the family, to see that this story had an ending.

Evelyn buzzed me again. I was starting to hate that sound. But this was a person I wanted to hear from: Jane. I waved Willie out of my office and picked up the phone. "Finally," I said. "Jeez, all hell has been breaking loose. I'm sure glad to hear from you."

She sounded exhausted. "Sorry, Kit. Evelyn told me about Linda. That's rotten, Kit. I know how you feel about your clients. Do you know anything?"

"No, Willie and I are just getting started. My gut tells me the two deaths are linked. The police aren't so sure, and they have a point. There's no concrete evidence that one death had anything to do with the other. But I'm feeling a bit overwhelmed. I miss your steady hand. Part of me feels like a fifties wife whining 'cause Hubby isn't home. Part of me feels like shit because I'm screwing things up, I'm handling it wrong."

I walked her through the drama with Ben—the defiance of Mrs. Steinitz, the rage at me. I told her I thought we needed help.

"Kit, that's always an option. If you think we need it, we should get it. It's only a phone call away. Jennie Cote is supposed to be great with adolescents."

We agreed to thrash it through this weekend. Talking to Jane was soothing and reassuring. "You don't think we should call right away?"

"I don't know, Kit. I think Ben is furious with you. You want to be close, now that you're around more, but it takes time, work, patience. A lot of taking guff, a lot of looking the other way. I know you suspect there's a murderer in the men's group, but I like their advice to you. Sounds like they've been there. I do have an instinct that Ben's acting out in response to you, in some way. . . . But this should be coming from somebody outside the family, not from me." She sighed.

"I'm sorry I'm not around more, Kit. But I shouldn't really apologize for that. I was around for years when you weren't. I'm sorry this is falling on you, but it fell on me before and probably will again." All that was true. For years, I had trooped into the financial district at dawn and dragged home at sunset, and I never questioned that Jane took care of everything.

We talked for another five minutes, until Evelyn came in to

remind me that I had barely enough time to get to Miele's and meet Battelle.

Miele's was an unassuming family-run Italian restaurant twenty-five minutes from Rochambeau, not too far from Clayton, the almost rural Morris County town where Battelle lived. It was a good place to talk, rarely so crowded that you couldn't hear, never so empty that others could hear what you were saying.

He was on time. Despite the autumn chill, Battelle was in summer country club gear: green polo shirt, khakis, tasseled loafers and a blazer. He'd slicked back his thick, salt-and-pepper hair. He sat ramrod straight, his ruddy complexion suggesting hours of running or biking, his stomach flat as a computer screen. His late-model blue Land Rover was parked in front. He looked every inch the successful developer Willie assured me he was.

"More male bonding, eh, Kit? You enjoyed getting roughed up the other night so much you came back for more? I presume Charlie called you about the meeting tonight. Horrible news about Linda." His handshake was, of course, firm. But my first impression was off: up close, Battelle looked haggard, with dark circles around his bloodshot eyes. His hair was unwashed and his khaki pants wrinkled. David Battelle hadn't slept the night before, it appeared.

"The beating you guys gave me turned out to be timely," I told him. "I almost slugged my kid this morning, for the first time." I made sure my handshake was firm too. "I'm sorry about Linda. I know you were friends."

Battelle shook his head. "Well, Deleeuw, as you undoubtedly noticed, I'm the only member of the Fathers' Club who isn't a father. Dale's fault. We were working on a project and he told me there was a group of nice guys who met every week to talk. I had never encountered a lot of nice guys, so I jumped at it even though I was a nonfather. The group let me in. It's a little goody-two-shoes for me, but I've liked it. I won't be at tonight's meeting, though. I'm just not up for it." I could see that. He was a wreck. I was surprised he hadn't begged off our lunch too.

"You knew Linda well?"

"Yes," he said, without elaboration. The best possible answer: not lying, but not telling me anything either.

A good interrogator has to acknowledge the truth: I didn't like him. He didn't seem to belong in the Fathers' Club, not because he was childless but because the other men wanted to make an effort to talk to one another. Battelle had made it clear right away that he *didn't* particularly want to talk. So why was he there?

I didn't want to seem overeager on the subject. "I'd be interested to know a little more about Dale Lewis. I've been curious."

He laughed and leaned back, eyes glinting with humor and skepticism. He didn't trust me either. That was why *he* was here. "Yes, I noticed. I've been curious about your being curious. The one person who barely knew Dale, who has been to a men's group only once, naturally is the only one in said men's group who wants to discuss a deceased member of the group everybody else knew quite well. Odd, don't you think?"

We ordered pasta and salads, though I doubted he would eat much. He'd barely glanced at the menu, and he barely took his eyes off me, even to order.

"And what do you make of that, David?" I asked.

"It's probably rational behavior for a private investigator," he replied, smiling thinly, taking a piece of bread from the basket.

I put my butter knife down and sat back. His move.

He just smiled some more.

"I told Charlie I was a security consultant," I said evenly.

"Yes, but you didn't tell him—or us—that you were a private eye. Is that what a security consultant means? You gave your mission away, Deleeuw, with the look on your face when I was talking about Dale. Nobody else was as interested as you were, yet we all knew him. I found that intriguing."

"I am interested in him," I said. "Is that how you knew what I do?" There was no point in bluffing now. I'd just look dumber than I already did.

The food came. Neither of us touched it.

"No," Battelle said. "Linda told me. She told me she was going to hire you to find out what was going on with Dale. In fact, I was going to advance her the money to hire you. I had plenty of reasons for wanting to know what was going on with Dale myself."

I took out my notebook, trying to show no emotion while scrambling to put things together. Linda had told him about me? And he was going to pay my fees?

"It was several weeks ago," he continued. "Linda and I were having dinner. As you may or may not know, I was very much in love with her, Deleeuw. Alas, she was not very much in love with me, although I hoped that would change. Mostly what we talked about on our few dates was Dale, whom she still cared for deeply. She wanted her family back together. She couldn't understand what had happened. She was close to obsessed about it. She couldn't get past it. . . ."

I speared a circle of cucumber from my salad.

"Not an easy situation for you, I bet."

"Not on any level. Especially since Dale had taken more than half a million dollars of my money and misrepresented how much other financing he had for a mixed-income housing project in Parsippany."

"Is that illegal?"

"You bet. I just had to screw up the courage to call the FBI, which I couldn't bring myself to do. The project did have some federal funding, but not half as much private investment as Dale told his investors he had. He was 'kiting,' a term we use in development. He was getting five bucks, then going to another investor and saying, 'I have ten bucks, give me twenty.' Then 'I've got fifty, give me a hundred.' And so on." Battelle sipped from a glass of mineral water. When he leaned forward, I got a closeup of just how red those eyes were. He'd been crying. This was somebody far more devastated by Linda Lewis's death than I was.

"Sometimes they get lucky and pull together enough money. Usually, as with Dale, it all falls apart, and they move on to some other scheme. It would take the government sixty years to catch up with all these people."

"If you knew all about kiting, why'd you sink your money into Dale's deal?" I wondered.

"Mostly for Linda's sake," he said, looking uncomfortable. "I thought this business might help him get on his feet again. I didn't know he was simultaneously soaking Jim Rheems. That was really inexcusable. I'm a developer; I know how to structure a business arrangement to protect my money. But Jim took a second mortgage. We don't talk business at the men's group, alas. I could've warned him, if I'd known." He called for a whiskey and soda. I bet it wasn't the first drink he'd had today.

"Is that why you didn't call in the authorities? Because of Linda?"

He smiled. "Linda had this notion of Dale as a dreamer, who sometimes got in trouble, sometimes even shortchanged his own kids, but was never malevolent. No, he was a guy who gazed at the stars and wanted too much. Christ, there's nothing sadder than a smart woman falling so hard for a worthless jerk. Dale was a liar and a cheat. He *hurt* people." Battelle's voice was tightening along with his fists. "And before you ask, I thought often enough about suing or ruining him, but it never occurred to me to kill him. I'm not the type to spend my life in prison for that scum."

I leaned forward. "Are you the type to get so angry or obsessed that you couldn't bear the thought of Linda being with anybody else, especially that scum?" I was as close to his face as I could get. The script called for him to lunge forward and slug me. He did. I fell backward, chair and all. The bread dish and one water glass got knocked to the floor. From the carpet, looking up at the ceiling, I saw Battelle standing over me.

Tony Miele came rushing out from the back. I scrambled up off the floor, threw some money on the table. I told Tony that everything was all right, that we were leaving. There was no reason to call the police, I assured him. The last thing I needed today was another encounter with the law.

My jaw, already beginning to swell, felt sore and hot. I rubbed it with my left hand. With my right I walked Battelle out the door.

We stood outside on the sidewalk. Battelle was ashen, but still angry. I was ticked off myself. "You had reasons to hurt both of those people, whether you would or not," I told him stiffly. "Hit me again, and I'll have you arrested. I can make your life plenty miserable if I bring certain nagging concerns to the state police."

"I'm sorry, Deleeuw," he said, not meeting my gaze. "I loved that woman. For you to suggest that I could kill her, shoot her like that—Jesus—" The anguish beneath the control was painful to see. This man was broken up.

"Good Lord," he said, wiping his forehead with a monogrammed handkerchief. "That's not how I thought this conversation would go."

I rubbed my jaw. "How did you think it would go?"

"I was going to hire you, Deleeuw. I wanted to ask you to continue to investigate. I presumed you'd be dropping the case, now that you didn't have a client."

"I've got a client," I said. "Linda is my client."

"Linda's not writing any checks now. I'm offering to pay you what she wanted to pay you, to keep the investigation going." He might have been sincere. Or he might have wanted to co-opt my investigation by funding it.

I stepped away. "Battelle, I just asked you if you might have murdered one of two people who died this week, both of whom you might conceivably have had strong motives to kill. You respond by slugging me, and then by offering to hire me? Doesn't that strike you as a bit on the dubious side?"

People inside Miele's were still peering out at us. A Verona patrol car cruised by but glided on past. Battelle looked less belligerent, more bewildered at the turn things had taken. My guess was that, having learned I was a private investigator, he figured me for somebody happy to pocket some money, even if my client was lying in a refrigerator in the morgue.

"I'm sorry," he said. "I've been hit hard by Linda's death. I thought maybe with Dale gone she'd let go of this attachment to him. That might make me look like a murderer in your book—"

"Good, Battelle. Then where were you Monday afternoon?" A ridiculous question, because I had no idea if the medical examiner had pinpointed a time of death or not. But vague questions get vague answers.

"How the fuck would I know?" he said, pissed off all over again. "This isn't cute anymore, Deleeuw. Keep this up and I'll have the best lawyer in the state right on your ass."

To be afraid of lawsuits, you have to have enough resources to worry about losing them. If Battelle took my house, I'd be thrilled. "My advice is to refresh your memory," I told him. "The police are going to find out all the stuff I know and they will be at your door asking you exactly the same questions. Puff up like a blowfish and slug a cop, he'll beat the shit out of you and toss your behind in jail. Now I want you to think hard about where you were on Monday. Take your time, but let me know, okay?"

You had to bluster back, I guess.

"Deleeuw, here's the truth. I was supposed to be in Rochambeau. Dale and I were supposed to have a face-to-face over the money he'd lost. I had to decide what to do. I wasn't prepared to go to the police, but I sure as hell was prepared to pressure him into thinking about repaying me. I called all afternoon and got no answer—"

"Starting when?"

"Starting about one or two. Home and office. Dale never answered the phone himself, probably because of bill collectors. The machine always picked up the calls, and he would screen them. But he didn't pick up on Monday. So I figured he was going to weasel out of our meeting. And not for the first time. This wasn't a person who took responsibility for his shortcomings. So after a couple of hours, I ordered takeout pizza, watched some football and went to bed. Didn't talk to anybody all night."

It occurred to me that Battelle wasn't the type to order pizza. His waistline was much too trim.

"Do you know a woman named Bev Cadawaller?"

"Sure, she worked with Dale. An architect. Drew up the plans for my housing development with Dale. If I'm not mistaken, Dale was sleeping with her, even before his marriage broke up. Certainly he was afterward. Bev's beautiful and tough as nails. And a hell of an architect, I think. Really topnotch."

The wind was picking up. I pulled my jacket closer and eyed the Volvo longingly. Percentage was sitting in the back seat looking mournfully at me—but then, he always looked mournful.

"How do you know about her and Dale?"

He looked surprised. "Linda, obviously," he replied, slightly disgusted at the stupidity of the question. And then, in a completely different tone, without menace or bluster, he told me what a creep I was. "Deleeuw, I know I can be arrogant and abrasive," he said calmly, "but I care about that group of men."

"So?"

"So what you're doing is really crummy," he said. "Infiltrating the group like that, hiding what you want. You could well destroy it. Dale broke their trust; that was bad enough. It will devastate them to discover somebody they've taken in and talked to and tried to help is . . . well . . . is a liar. People might dislike me, but they're going to hate your guts. I ought to tell them, but I know I'm in a difficult position here. It could look like I'm blocking a murder investigation, interfering with the search for Dale's, and maybe Linda's, killer. I don't want to do that. I don't really care much about Dale, but if somebody in that group had anything to do with Linda's death, I want to see him on Death Row. You understand me?"

All too well. He'd said his piece. I didn't like hearing it.

My clients had a sacred bond with me once they signed that contract. I was their advocate; I saw things through to the extent possible. Linda had come to me for help, and the next day she'd been shot to death. I felt responsible.

Without replying, I turned toward my car. I wasn't in a good mood. I didn't like Battelle; I felt guilty about Linda; and I'd discovered nothing of much use. I felt lost about how to handle my son, scummy about the men's group whose members had tried to help me while I was scarfing around for incriminating evidence against them. And my jaw ached like hell.

"Look, here's what's going to happen, okay?" I said quietly. "You're not going to tell anybody, at the Fathers' Club or elsewhere, about me or about this conversation. You're going to go home and write down exactly what you did Monday afternoon, then fax it to my office. You decline to do that, my best advice is to get a lawyer."

He looked miserable, but nodded.

"And here's another thing you're never going to do again. Hit me. Don't hit people. Hitting is out. Nurturing is in." I got into the Volvo and headed for home.

Twelve

I SHOULD get organized. No, I *had* to get organized. There was no other way to survive this day. I called Evelyn, whose job it was to organize me. I'm not proud.

"Evelyn, this is among the most brutal days of my adult life. I am engulfed in crises and responsibilities. I have more stuff to confront than I can possibly deal with rationally or well. Help!"

I couldn't ignore the case, which was careening in a whole new direction. I couldn't ignore my son, the harsh way we'd parted that morning, or all the cries for help he was sounding. And I had to be careful not to ignore Emily; I didn't relish the notion of her parents' being among the few unrepresented at Back-to-School Night. Was that more important than murder? No. Maybe.

What an inspired move I'd made in hiring Evelyn, the yin understanding that it needed the yang to survive. She scribbled some notes, asked a few questions, and in short order announced: "At the moment, Kit, you have three priorities. Ben. The case. Em.

"Here's how we'll proceed. Go home. Talk to your son. See what happens. Then stop by here and dictate those two insurance fraud reports. The case is going to court. Give Willie and me whatever instructions you have. Have a cup of coffee with Luis, talk about the case—that always gets you thinking in the right direction. Then head for the school, stay as long as you can before you have to go to the men's group. Afterward, you can always meet

back here with Willie if you need to. Oh, and you want to meet
with this Cadawaller person"—I could tell she was already in disfa-
vor with Evelyn—"who's going to be in Rochambeau tomorrow
morning meeting with a client. Willie tracked her down. The two
of you are having coffee together at the Roadway Diner at eight; I
set it up. She was very curious to know what the meeting was
about, but I, of course, said nothing."

Translation: Cadawaller had gotten testy with Evelyn and
smacked right into the iron wall.

Sounded like a good plan, if you didn't mind compressing three
days' work into one. I drove home. Percentage bounded out of the
car. I walked him briefly, but had forgotten to bring the pooper
scooper. Naturally Percentage immediately dropped a large load in
front of the Rosettos', and Mrs. Rosetto (naturally) was on the way
back from her midday walk. Mrs. Rosetto had chaired the committee that had successfully lobbied the town to adopt one of the most
stringent canine waste laws in the state. I have no love for people
who don't clean up after their dogs, but it isn't high on my list of
social outrages either. I'm willing to look the other way if they are.
Mrs. Rosetto isn't.

"Morning, Mrs. Rosetto. I forgot the scooper," I blurted, the
courageous detective fearlessly facing the head of the League of
Women Voters. "I'll come back and clean it up, promise."

"Good," she said.

When I went into the house, I blinked. It was as if Ben hadn't
moved from the spot where I'd last seen him that morning. Draped
over the couch, baseball cap on backward, he was now watching
"Ricki Lake."

"Hey, Ben," I said.

"Hey, Dad." There was no rancor in either of our voices. Maybe
he didn't want to fight either. I picked up the size 10½, four-pound
Nike Airs he'd left in the middle of the playroom. He caught them
without looking away from the TV screen.

"Turn it off," I said. He did.

"Put your shoes on," I barked. He did. Maybe there was something to this authoritarian stuff.

"Let's go," I said, in a voice I hadn't used since my two-year
stint in the military, where I'd worked as a criminal investigator
and thus gotten the desperate inspiration for what to do with my
life after being run out of Wall Street.

"Where are we going?" Ben asked.

"Out. Just come on. It's important."

He loped outside after me, an expectant, slightly nervous expression on his face. We drove six blocks in silence. His nervous expression was replaced by one of surprise when we pulled into Parkside Ice Cream Store.

It had turned into a sparkling, breezy fall day. New Jersey winters are messy and unpleasant, summers often sticky and uncomfortable, but for a week or so in the spring and fall the air is clear Plexiglas, the temperature actually pleasant.

I ordered a soft vanilla and Ben had a double mocha fudge, his favorite. We walked over to a bench by the parking lot.

He slurped away at his cone the way kids do, licking carefully around the sides, taking large gulps out of the top, miraculously managing to keep the ice cream from spilling down the cone or toppling off or becoming a squishy mess.

"So," I said. "Are we at war?"

"Sort of," he said.

"About anything in particular?"

He offered a shrug, the first of what I assumed would be many.

"Would you like a truce?"

"Kind of."

"Do you know what we're fighting about?"

Shrug.

Ben seemed to sense that this wasn't going to suffice. The only thing worse than a heart-to-heart talk with your father was the prospect of a series of them; it was his only motive for trying to get this one working.

"I don't know." He licked at his cone, looking away from me. "You just seem to get on my nerves lately. All these lectures, all this stuff about how I should behave. I don't think you have the right to give me all this advice."

I knew I should shut up, but I was puzzled. "Ben, I'm not aware of giving you a lot of lectures. I don't mean to. I know lectures don't work. It's just that I got into a lot of trouble when I was your age—"

"That was you, not me."

I gave us both a few seconds to eat our ice cream. My own experiences didn't mean squat to him, but I'd had them and I couldn't pretend otherwise.

"Ben, I can see some of our problems. I wasn't around much when you were little, when you might have needed me. Now I'm always around. When I came home, that was a difficult time for you. I went from absent dad to interfering dad, and there was all that stuff over my leaving the industry. I know you got in more than one fight over that."

He watched me sideways, licking his cone. I didn't know why, but he seemed less angry. Maybe I was approaching him differently, not as a ticked-off parent but as somebody willing to hear him out. I was keenly aware that I could very easily blow it, so I picked my next words carefully.

"When I was in high school, I started smoking a lot of dope," I told him. "I took some pills, too. Got suspended twice. Then, in college, I got arrested and almost thrown out of Columbia. I was in jail for two days. It all had seemed like a lark to me, I guess, I don't know. And I rarely talked to my father at all. If you think I'm a pain in the ass, well, it's all relative. He was an angry guy, pretty free with his hands and his belt. When I raised my hand to you . . ." I choked. My own childhood didn't bear thinking about.

"You got kicked out of school?" Ben asked, wide-eyed. I sure had his attention.

"Yes, and almost sentenced to a jail term. I lucked out. A dean at the school interceded for me, went to the judge with recommendations. The judge talked to the prosecutor, they ordered me to do some community service—I worked in a day care center—and expunged my record. The school gave me a semester off to think about my life, then took me back. Of course my father would no longer pay for my college, not for a 'drug addict,' he said. I had to borrow a lot of money in order to continue. Paid off the last loans a few years ago, actually." I smiled at the memory, though nothing about it was funny.

"So *I* go and smoke pot, and get kicked out of school, then *you* almost *slug* me," Ben observed. The insight rattled me. It was right on the money.

"So this drug thing, it shook me up. I thought, Here we go again. And I thought it was all my fault, that it wouldn't have happened if I'd been home when you were younger, and if I'd handled everything more sensitively."

Ben finished his ice cream. I tossed mine in the trash. I wasn't hungry.

"Dad." He paused, as if rehearsing his speech. "I didn't know about all that. It sounds rough. But I *am* pissed off. A lot. I'm sorry about what you just said, but it's not my life. You're not your dad; I'm not some kind of junkie. Yeah, I've been suspended, but you can get suspended at my school for throwing food in the cafeteria. I've had trouble with your being talked about like some kind of crook. And lately, with Mom gone so much, you're trying too hard to be a Mom yourself. Fussing over food. Telling me to wear sweaters. Jesus. It's obnoxious, Dad. You're always in my face. A bunch of kids have tried dope. I didn't even like it, if you want to know the truth. I just wanted to try it. I only took two drags, then my friend saw Mr. Hauser coming. I'm not planning to repeat this. I'm not going to let myself get in real trouble. The worst part of it is you hovering around like some nanny. . . ."

He put his head in his hands. That was it; that was the speech. More words strung together than I'd heard from him in ages. The Fathers' Club advice echoed in my head.

"Okay, Ben. I hear you. You need a dad, not a nanny. I'll try to back off some. You're not me: my life isn't your life. I get it. You know it's hard for a parent these days to have a kid suspended for smoking dope and not get rattled. But the point is, as long as we're talking, I think we both can handle this. My problem is when you stop talking to me and I have no idea what the hell is going on. Let's come halfway here. You talk to me a bit more so that I can see you're okay, I'll bug you a bit less. Deal?"

He offered his hand. No intense hug and swell of music like in the movies, but something good had happened. I'd had a real conversation with my son for the first time in months. I could see that he was all right—grounded, thoughtful, clearheaded. I didn't think he'd get hooked on drugs, thrown out of school, face jail. I didn't think he needed therapy. I didn't even think I was such a bad father, at least not for the moment. I felt an immense surge of relief. Talking to your son can be great. Even if it only happens twice a year.

I looked at the Post-it I'd used to jot down what Evelyn had advised. The first item said *Ben*. The second said *murder*. I dropped Ben off at home, asked him to make supper for himself and his sister, and headed for the mall.

Thirteen

O NE BREAK, if you could call it that, was
that media attention was abruptly and violently diverted from Rochambeau and its two murders. Three
members of an apocalyptic cult that believed the end of the world
was near had seized control of a mothballed warship in New York
Harbor, the radio reported as I steered the Volvo toward my office.
The pier had been turned into a war zone, complete with tanks,
hundreds of cops in flashy designer windbreakers and a massive
encampment of reporters and camera crews. Hundreds of boaters
were ignoring Coast Guard warnings and cruising as close as they
could get with their videocams, perhaps hoping for some tabloid
TV money.

Meanwhile, the media-savvy cultists transmitted live commen-
tary from a portable satellite station they'd brought aboard, and
had set up a toll-free 800 number and a home page on the World
Wide Web to answer questions and field media inquiries. They
hadn't killed anybody yet.

So the murders of Dale and Linda Lewis were yesterday's news
as far as the headline-hungry media or the public were concerned.

Back in my office after quickly dispatching the two reports Evelyn had been after for days, I summoned a Deleeuw Investigations
council. Willie and Evelyn convened with their notebooks and
printouts. Luis not only agreed to help out but brought a complimentary tray of soda, coffee and burgers. Despite Luis's heroic

efforts, the burgers taste like seasoned carpeting. Lightning Burger is, after all, a franchise, and Luis doesn't raise the cattle. Still, I was glad to see the food. I hadn't eaten much at my tense standoff with David Battelle. Nor had I learned much.

We all squeezed into my inner sanctum. The hum from the highway outside the mall was nearly continuous, but when it quieted, you could hear the mall music drifting up from below, a series of uplifting show tunes and old ballads, intended to put everybody in a buying mood.

On complicated cases, I'd learned to sit down with trusted friends and sort through the evidence. Benchley Carrolton's nursery at the edge of town was often the site of these explorations, the two of us sipping iced tea or cider and musing about human nature. Benchley was a Quaker whose family dated back to colonial times in Rochambeau, and a wonderful sounding board. But he was not very familiar with the dark side of human nature. Whereas Luis, for all his gentility, saw quite deeply into that realm. To a surprising degree, so did Evelyn and Willie. She brought a steely eye to everyone and everything, and Willie had the guileless person's keen awareness of falsehood and manipulation. Suburban murders almost never proved to be random killings by strangers, the kind police find hardest to solve. There is almost always a reason when somebody gets killed out here. Sometimes it's over money. Usually it has to do with family. So far, I've been lucky: I've looked for the logic behind the killings I've handled, and with the help of my friends, I've usually been able to follow it.

I think Evelyn was worried that I was about to be overwhelmed by the convergence of work and personal concerns. She'd called in the cavalry. I was grateful. I *was* flirting with peril. My false entry into the Fathers' Club would be seen for what it was—a painful, even destructive, betrayal of a group of men struggling to do what most men don't: confide in one another. Withholding the group's existence from the police, sure to be discovered momentarily by Tagg's thorough minions, would land me in the kind of trouble Chief Leeming continuously predicted. I didn't want to lose my license. I couldn't afford to. Jane was at a critical point in her education; Ben had clearly been through quite enough change; the house was crumbling around us as it was. I owed my clients, but I owed my family too. Percentage still went to weekly canine physical therapy for his gimpy leg.

And there was Linda. Meeting her had touched off a brief burst of self-pity and attraction. I was prepared to mourn her, until I thought of all she had hidden from me. Was I risking a lot, according to some honor code, for a client who had lied, possibly used me for reasons I might never understand?

But in the meantime she was still my client, entitled to the presumption of innocence and entitled to have her murderer brought to justice.

Evelyn had wedged an extra chair into my office and arranged the Lightning Burger tray on my desk. I picked out a cheeseburger, small fries and a Diet Coke. Evelyn took a soda. Luis never ate junk food. Willie would eat everything everybody else didn't, and probably pull out a bag of potato chips too. Junk only made him leaner, taller and better-looking.

God knows I could use some help. Before the meeting, I'd made a quick phone call or two, scanned a couple of police reports. Thinking ahead, I'd put in a call to the next Fathers' Club member I planned to deceive and betray, one on one. Frank Dougherty had seemed like an open, friendly guy, so I called the school where he taught, hoping to connect with him before the end of the school day.

"Lincoln Township High," a receptionist had announced.

"I'm trying to reach Frank Dougherty, please."

"I'm sorry, Mr. Dougherty is no longer on the faculty."

I was momentarily tongue-tied. "He was as of a couple of days ago."

"No, sir," the woman said firmly. "Mr. Dougherty hasn't taught here in two years."

Two years? "He's moved to another school? Another district?"

"I wouldn't think so."

And what the hell did *that* mean? "I'm afraid I don't understand. How can I get in touch with him?" She had to be one of those prim, topknotted battle-axes with scrunched-up mouths.

She dug in. "I'm sorry, sir. All I can tell you is that Mr. Dougherty's no longer teaching here, and so far as I know he's not teaching anywhere nearby. Good afternoon."

Great. More questions instead of answers. This confab wasn't taking place a minute too soon.

"So," I began, glancing down at my notes. "Here's what we know. Dale Lewis was probably drugged and suffocated sometime around midday on Monday. No witnesses, no robbery, no signs of a struggle. Possibly because he was pretty blotto—his blood alcohol level was three times the legal limit. He was in no condition to fight. No evidence of drugs, says Danielle. He might have gotten drunk elsewhere and then been attacked in his office, although the police can't seem to find a bar or restaurant where anybody remembers serving him."

Luis cleared his throat. "Possibly," he said, "he was killed as a punishment or to prevent him from doing something—"

"Like going to the police," Willie put in. Luis nodded.

I riffled through my notes. "Two people in the men's group lost a lot of money because of Dale. Jim Rheems took a second mortgage out on his home to help. David Battelle lost money but is too smart to have risked his personal assets. Complications: Dale had a girlfriend even while he was married to Linda, an architect named Bev Cadawaller. I'm going to talk to her in the morning. But what's disturbing is that Linda apparently knew about the affair and didn't tell me, which makes me wonder how truthful she was in general. . . ."

"That would trouble me, Kit," Evelyn interjected. "It seems like the first thing you'd tell a private detective if you were making inquiries about your husband or ex-husband."

Willie raised his hand, as if he were in high school. "And don't forget, Chief, that she didn't mention she was willing to risk half a million dollars so Dale could get a loan. Whatever that means." Maybe she was protecting him, as usual, thinking he'd look even worse if it were known that he'd siphoned off his wife's money as well as everybody else's.

Evelyn had a thought: "Maybe she wasn't hiring you just out of concern for her ex. Maybe she wanted that money back." And maybe she realized she'd have to get in a long line for a refund. David Battelle had mentioned Dale's debts to him and Rheems— and there had to be others.

"This must have been one charming man," mused Luis. "He seems to have had a gift for getting people to give him lots of money, yet no record of ever having done anything successful with it. I find that curious. Weren't these people suspicious?"

I took a bite from my burger. "Sure, I bet they all were. Speculators fail more than they score. But when they score, they score big. And maybe that wasn't so farfetched in this case. Local communities are under intense pressure from the feds to build low- and mixed-income housing. None of them want to, of course. Developers snag government grants, then local zoning boards run them batty with restrictions, hearings and delays. Neighborhood people file lawsuits and battle them every step of the way. People don't move to the suburbs to live near poor people; they can do that in the city. So they get here, sink all they own into the perfect house, and when some developer comes along with a plan for garden apartments, the locals immediately imagine an invasion of gangs, drugs and crime. A lot of the developments never get built. But planning grants keep flowing and where there's government money . . ."

"Right," sighed Luis. He understood only too well. Willie, sucking on his ballpoint pen, looked interested, perhaps a bit smug.

I went on. "So we jump to the next day. Linda got pulled out of her car around eleven at the convenience store. Witnesses saw a middle-aged guy in a windbreaker. There have been a series of carjackings and carjacking attempts in the area. But she was the only victim taken out behind a building and shot." I winced at the image. "The police aren't clear about a possible link. . . ." I waited for some input. For enlightenment. For anything.

Luis had some. "Kit, I've been thinking a lot about this killing. Evelyn showed me the police reports, and I've read the accounts in the media." He sipped from the black coffee he always drank and leaned back, gazing through the window behind me at the thickening stream of traffic on the highway. He glanced at his watch. He never left his teenage staff alone for the dinner crowd. But it was still early.

"I think this was an execution," he said flatly. We all sort of froze, mid-motion, me with my mouth open to chomp on a burger, Willie reaching for a fry.

"It's the only scenario that is sensible," Luis continued. "I discount completely the carjacking theory. I don't think even the police believe it. Professionals who want a car for money would have no interest in an old Toyota. And kids . . . well, that is possible, but there are so many cars to steal with nobody inside them. And in any event, no one took the car. Somebody looking to rape a woman, then? But if so, why didn't he assault her?" Luis's eyes flared in a way that was unusual for him. Considerable anger simmered just below those fine Latin manners.

"Why? Because he wanted this incident to look like a carjacking or some other random crime. He didn't want it connected to her husband's murder. Not the most sophisticated diversion, perhaps, but it does muddy the waters. Someone used the carjacking scares as a pretext, but he killed Linda Lewis for other reasons."

"What reasons?" I asked. "We have no motive for any execution, unless she was up to her neck in her husband's shady business—or lied completely about her life."

Luis nodded. "We have no clear motive *yet*," he agreed. "But we will. Let the police do their work, Kit. This is what they do well, digging up the details of somebody's life. What you do well is talk. Ask questions, get a sense of the people involved. Then outthink them, as you always do. That's what the police are not necessarily good at.

"Consider the possibilities. She was involved in her husband's failing business. She wanted that money back. Or somebody might have not understood that she and her husband were separated. Somebody might have wanted revenge for something he had done. Possibly she was not who she appeared to be. I believe somebody followed her to that store and improvised a carjacking. This somebody dragged Linda out back, then murdered her. To understand, we need to know more about the dead woman. There's something about her, or about her husband, that she was hiding. We need to know what that is."

I agreed. "And, Willie, let's see if there's a will filed anywhere. Find out who her lawyer is. I'd like to know where those half a million dollars in assets were to go in the event of her death—especially if they go anywhere but to her two kids."

Most nonrandom murders have a certain logic, if you can take hold of the right thread. With Dale, the thread seemed to be business dealings that had gone sour. But the thread that led to Linda's murder eluded me.

Willie ahemed, then shuffled papers from a folder. He was trying to appear sober and reflective. He was failing. "I found out something real interesting," he announced. "This guy owed a lot more money than anybody realized. Some of it was to people you don't want to owe a lot of money to." He fished out a credit agency report, plopped it on my desk.

"Dale had a piece of a trash-hauling business," he went on. "State Waste Disposal. According to papers of incorporation and his credit reports, he was planning a company that would build the mixed-income housing in the suburbs the government is always screaming about, then provide other services too, like collecting garbage. He needed a partner with experience and the know-how to deal with all the government paperwork. He picked Jacob Logovitz. You know the name?"

I shook my head. Nobody else in the room knew it either. "Who is he, Will?" I asked.

"Logovitz's an immigrant. From Russia. Named by the FBI and the state police as a leader in the Russian mafia, Jersey City division. Worked in Brooklyn for a while, according to a story in the *Star-Ledger*. Then the family split up the territory, just like the old mob used to do, and Jacob got promoted to Jersey. Or demoted, depending on how you look at it. According to the stories, he's big in waste disposal, trash hauling and construction. He put up $300,000 to start this waste-disposal thing with Dale. Dale put up nothing. But the business was not exactly thriving, since there wasn't any housing to service."

He had a right to look proud. Willie and the right password had once again worked miracles.

"If Dale wasn't putting up money, then what *was* he putting up?" I wondered. "He had to be fronting for stuff Logovitz can't do on his own. I can't think of anything else."

My colleagues agreed. I reached for the phone, dialed Lieutenant Tagg, got his voice mail. "Tagg, this is Kit Deleeuw. Hope you're okay. Presumably you are aware that Dale Lewis was a bit mobbed up, that he was in a couple of business ventures—a legitimate front, I would guess—for a Jersey City guy named Jacob Logovitz. I'm sure you recognize the name. You probably have this, but you will note for the record that I'm fulfilling my licensing obligations just in case."

Unlike fictional tough guys, we modern gumshoes cover our butts. My license was already in peril on this case, and I needed as solid a trail of cooperation as I could possibly put down. I was flattering Tagg, of course. As I'd learned the hard way, Willie often discovered things well ahead of the police.

This put a whole new spin on things. "So, unlike Rheems and Battelle, Jacob Logovitz probably didn't roll over for bad debts or write them off as one of life's bad experiences," I said, trying to piece it together. "I bet he wanted his money."

I had to go talk to this guy. "Add Logovitz to my list, Evelyn. See if he'll make an appointment to see me." She nodded and made a note. She wouldn't like my having anything to do with this individual, and neither would Jane, but there wasn't much choice. Logovitz probably wouldn't tell me anything, anyway. But I had a better shot than real cops would at getting something out of him.

"Oh, and this just in." I disclosed my recent intelligence about Dougherty, the no-longer-teacher, who clearly had gotten into some sort of trouble, the sort that keeps you from teaching school for good. The sort you lie about.

"I'll run a check of newspaper stories and felony arrests," Willie volunteered. "It'll run $150 for the latter, okay?" I nodded. We now subscribed to an on-line investigative service that looked up criminal records, among other things, for a fee. Some files I didn't think it was wise for Willie to just go rooting around in.

"Oh, and the last thing, Chief. You know about Montgomery and Battelle."

Oh, Jeez. "What?"

"Well, they renovated and own the building that Montgomery's law firm is in. They're in the county computer as titleholders." Misinterpreting my look, he quickly offered, "Hey, I got it legally. On-line title search, five dollars. Kosher."

"It isn't that, Willie, it just seems that every person in this case is in business with everyone else. It's all one big fucking deal. Excuse me, Evelyn." She nodded, on her way out. Evelyn thought cursing was unnecessary.

"Not so unusual, Kit," said Luis. "These are business people, doing business with their friends. Lawyers and developers cooperate this way all the time. Doctors build offices with other doctors, you know."

My head ached. How the hell were we going to untangle all this? I tried to cling to Luis's advice: to do what I do best. But at the moment, I wasn't so certain what that was.

Evelyn came back in. "Nine William Street, Jersey City, at eleven tonight, Kit. Mr. Logovitz came on the phone himself and when I explained who you were and why you wanted to talk to him, he said in this heavy Russian accent, 'All right. Eleven.' That was that," she said, bewildered. She was probably expecting something different from a gangster. At least the imperious summons gave me time to fit in the men's group. "Maybe," Evelyn suggested, "you should leave this interview to the police."

I shook my head. "I have to know that I touched all the bases myself."

There was no more time for brainstorming. I congratulated Willie on a hell of a day's work. But he'd complicated my already overloaded life with this growing list of suspects. David Battelle was an angry emotional basket case, head over heels in love with Linda and seething about Dale. Rheems had been betrayed and nearly bankrupted. Logovitz was almost certainly capable of killing somebody—or having him killed. And now Dougherty had joined my list, right after Bev Cadawaller.

Willie scribbled some notes for me on a yellow legal pad. "Here's what you might need to know about the deal Dale made with these people. He was a front, but the business itself wasn't illegal. Because Dale was the head of the company, Logovitz's criminal record didn't matter. But this is a fast crowd, Chief. This crowd, well, they wouldn't hesitate to take care of you if you screwed them."

I told Luis I'd help carry the tray back down to the Lightning Burger. "Kit," he asked, "who punched you?" He was taking in my slightly swollen jaw, something no one else had noticed. I told him briefly about the confrontation with Battelle.

"An unstable man," he said, absorbing it. "Unstable, enamored of Linda, enraged at Dale."

"But if he killed either or both of them, he's a great actor, because he sure didn't behave guiltily. Just torn up about Linda's death. It hit him pretty hard."

Luis shrugged. "Kit, you often take people at face value, a nice trait in a human being but not so useful in a detective. Who knows how this man reacts to things? How much of an actor he is? Whether grief and guilt look the same in him?" Point taken.

"Are you certain you wish to see this Logovitz by yourself?" he went on. "He could be dangerous and, as we know, the rough stuff—the John Wayne routine, as you call it—is not . . . uh . . . your specialty." Kindly Luis, trying to sugarcoat the obvious fact that I was a wimp Jacob Logovitz could purée if he wanted to. But although I didn't like to court danger, I felt I had to see him alone. I usually got people to deal rationally with me by dealing rationally with them. I hoped it would work this time.

Willie walked down the stairs with Luis and me, kicking it around some more. Luis was frowning; some new piece of the puzzle sliding into place. "Dale's murder—it was quite professional, was it not? No blood, no noise. Little evidence." That was true: this wasn't any passion killing. No signs of rage or struggle. Dale had been dispatched in a workmanlike way.

We walked out into the mall, where the population of plastic spooks seemed to increase daily.

"But what about Linda?"

"It could have been a pro hit designed to look like something else," Willie said. "Don't those mob guys seek retribution sometimes when something goes wrong? Look, it's not a bad working theory we've got here. Dale gets desperate for money, fronts for some guys way out of his league. The deal stalls, goes bad, and they're out a lot of money. So they kill him, but they don't want it to look like a mob hit. So then they kill his wife. Chief, I'm coming to see Logovitz with you tonight."

"Absolutely not," I said, turning toward the exit. "You—"

"Kit, it's part of my job. If you're serious about my role here, I've got to be there. I know more about the deal than you do. And it's crazy to go to Jersey City by yourself. I don't really think there's any danger, but I'm coming—"

I opened my mouth to speak.

"—or I'm quitting."

We went a few more rounds but he was adamant. And Luis pointed out that he had a point. Willie had a right to turn off the computer and learn the business. There was no reason to assume the meeting would get nasty. Logovitz had agreed to see me, and he knew what I wanted.

I started to tell Willie that I'd meet him at the mall later, but he insisted on sticking with me, even though I pointed out he'd have to wait outside in the Volvo during "Back-to-School Night" and the men's group session.

"Don't even think about meeting me anywhere," he warned. "Because then you'll be a hero and think you're doing me a favor by leaving me behind. I'm sticking with you, Chief." I grumped and fussed, but I was glad to have a partner. It felt good.

Fourteen

IT WOULD PROBABLY take a skilled anthropologist to fully appreciate the suburban ritual called Back-to-School Night, the annual contact between the local educational structure and anxious, taxpaying parents.

In towns like Rochambeau, parents send their kids off to other people they don't really know but implicitly trust to give these celestial beings the educational and social tools necessary to survive. This is not a trust given lightly. Those adults at the other end of the bus route have, in some ways, more control and influence over our darlings' lives than we do. It can be traumatic. Jane tells me her therapist friends are busier in September than lifeguards on a sunny July Fourth. Back-to-School Night is meant to keep these traumatized parents at bay, at least for a few months.

I got there just in time. True to his word, Willie stayed in the Volvo, armed with a Walkman and his laptop. He'd rigged up some sort of wireless modem that allowed him to go on-line from his favorite Burger King, or anywhere. "I'll be working while you're in there," he told me.

At the Lucretia Mott Elementary School, arriving parents were promptly herded into the auditorium for the principal's welcome.

In Rochambeau, principals lasted about as long as New York Yankees managers, coming to town full of enthusiasm and bright plans and usually fleeing within a year or two, haggard and drained. Samantha Snell was in her second year and had the slightly stunned look of a person whose day generally began in the school parking lot, with someone like Jessica Gurwitt-Owens sharing her many concerns about Johnny's math skills. And ended with someone like Jessica howling that Jimmy would never have thrown his chocolate pudding at the cafeteria monitor if he'd been more challenged in Language Arts. Ms. Snell definitely lacked the cheery bounciness of the previous year. By now, she was probably mailing out applications to some working-class district where the parents still had a modicum of respect for educators and were too busy working to give her all this shit.

She appeared, stage right, and embarked on more or less the same talk every principal gave each year: "Parents, welcome. I won't take up the far too little time we have here at Lucretia Mott with long speeches. We are excited about entering into a partnership to educate your child. We will ask a lot of you—help in seeing that your children get here on time, do their homework and interact well with the other children." This always turned out to be bullshit. The schools ask virtually nothing of parents. In fact, they quite wisely structure things so that they see as little of parents as possible, except as chaperones for field trips and Halloween parties. "And of course, you'll ask a lot of us too, and we intend to deliver," Ms. Snell continued doggedly.

"All of this will be explained to you in more detail when you report to your children's homerooms to get your schedules. The teachers are very much looking forward to matching the faces they look at all day with their parents. But first, a special treat. We're proud to present a brief presentation of the Lucretia Mott Elementary School Thunder Drums." She walked off the stage and, probably, straight out the rear door and into her car.

Forty boys and half a dozen or so girls marched out onto the stage in forest-green blazers, slacks and sneakers. Snare and bass drums protruded from their waists.

The Thunder Drums were a brilliant inspiration, and just what I needed to take my mind off all the things causing it to spin. What better idea for ten-year-olds than to hand them all drumsticks and give them permission to pound away furiously for ten full minutes? The noise was chaotic, deafening. But the kids loved it and the parents went wild, as if they were listening to Seiji Ozawa conducting the New York Philharmonic. The music teacher, Mrs. Boardman, normally a pearls-and-cardigan type, had brought the house down the first year when she broke into a Michael Jackson-style moonwalk across the stage as her charges blasted away. My ears were still ringing from that concert. Now here she went again, gliding across the stage in her purple wool skirt and silk blouse buttoned up to the neck. The crowd went berserk.

It was never clear if the Thunder Drums were attempting any particular song or coordinated musical effort. They seemed merely to be banging away as hard as they could for as long as their arms held out. As she strutted offstage, Mrs. Boardman kicked up her heels, made a chopping gesture to stop the "music," and took her bows. Pandemonium. Shouts. A standing ovation. The Thunder Drums had of course become much in demand all over town at ribbon cuttings, dedications, and holiday celebrations.

Afterward, we reported to our kids' homerooms for our five-minute orientations on Life at Lucretia Mott—what our kids do at the start of the day, how any problems are spotted and immediately responded to, how nutritious and wholesome meals (remnants of which were visible via multicolored stains on the cafeteria ceiling) are served, how much homework there is, etc.

After that we traveled in herds, constantly moving. Each teacher's presentation ended about thirty seconds short of the bell, leaving time for no more than one question. "Oh, dear," they'd say. "I'm so sorry. I just get so excited talking about the children that I lose track of time. You have to get to your next class—we don't want to be late, do we?—but please feel free to call me *any* time."

And then we were off. Emily's schedule ran: Homeroom, Language Arts, Mathematics, Physical Education, Family Life, History/Geography and Art. The art teacher gamely held up splotches of fingerpaint and sculptures straight out of a horror film and gushed over the "many interesting statements the children are making in their work."

We heard about the rocks and minerals the class could study in Earth Science, the poetry they'd be exploring in Language Arts, the Chicago math they'd be taking up. We heard that we should keep an eye on homework, but be careful not to do it for them. (Right. Rochambeau's parents start worrying about SATs and GPAs in the fifth grade.)

Willie was lucky to be sitting out in the Volvo, listening to the Cranberries on his portable CD player. I was crammed into a classroom with fifty other adults, scrunched into tiny chairs over which our bellies bulged while our knees jammed into our chins. Out in the hallways were stacks of midget paper cups, a few bottles of apple juice and trays of cookies provided by the PTA.

From the few questions they were able to squeeze in before being hurried along to the next class, you could recognize most of the parents as basically good citizens, intimidated by authority, anxious to learn about their kids, careful not to give offense. Their questions focused on how to be even *better* educational citizens. How much TV should their kids be permitted to watch, if any? How much time on the phone for their girls? Should they be concerned if they heard nothing but monosyllabic grunts from their sons?

But some parents, recognizable as recent émigrés from New York City, behaved as though they knew the system was out to screw their kids; they wanted to make it clear from the outset that they would be vigilant and unyielding on behalf of their charges. Why wasn't the literature assigned more challenging? Why did the children sit and play cards after lunch when they could be learning? Shouldn't they be improving their test-taking skills? The teachers, tenured civil servants who couldn't be punished or removed unless they machine-gunned a student in broad daylight in full view of hundreds of witnesses, took this sort in stride.

"That's a good question, Mr. Wolf. Let me think about that and we'll talk next week." Usually the bell had already rung.

Sometimes, too, the questioners stood revealed as those for whom having children was an unremitting succession of anxieties. Were the children encouraged to be supportive with one another? Were they getting quality time from the teacher? Being noticed enough? Being recognized for their special gifts? To the fearful, the answers invariably were no. The teachers seemed to know that these fears were not resolvable and responded with a store of soothing, well-worn platitudes.

I actually felt badly for the parents—intelligent, well-educated people, some of them even therapists, who didn't seem to know that they were bringing their own problems into their children's lives. As I had been, I noted guiltily, with Ben. They invaded almost every part of their children's lives, knew too much about them, were enmeshed in too many details. Their children fought no battles of their own, solved no problems by themselves. You could see the damage begin to spread as the children's phobias piled up like a stack of overdue bills. Anxious about sleepovers. Afraid to go away to camp. Terrified of gym. Unwilling to eat slimy or green foods. Rigid about rules. Angry at their parents.

Benchley liked to say that few kids suffer from too much love, but this wasn't love, it was fear. And this fear wasn't about the kids. It was about the grown-ups.

I knew I wouldn't last an hour teaching in our schools. And I understood very well why Back-to-School Nights were structured like visits to a minimum security prison.

As religiously as everyone attended, and no matter what degree of neuroses we brought with us, almost everybody left feeling vaguely unsatisfied. Some teachers tried to match the adult names with the children they taught, and passed on good words—"Oh, you're Emily's father! She's such a good student." But their cheerfulness seemed false. They kept glancing at the clocks, giving vague, nonspecific answers to almost everything. The parents were potentially enemies, not partners, and the teachers knew it. Mostly, it was a sort of Disney-staged event. Let the hordes in, give them a peek, contain them so they can't do too much harm, then shuffle them out.

But you never left with the sense that you understood much about what went on there all day, what the teacher really thought about your kid. I signed Jane and me up for a couple of tasks— driving kids to the science center in Jersey City and helping to chaperone the June beach trip. This involved traveling in a boiling-hot, noisy, smelly school bus, returning with fifty kids who had been lying in the sun, ingesting salt water and junk food for five hours, then accompanying them to an amusement park. Last year, Emily reported, one of the parents had established a Barf Contest, with winners for distance, consistency and frequency. The distance winner by a wide margin was Philip O'Brien, who threw up during an upside-down spin on the five-story-high Screamer.

Mission more or less accomplished. I had seen the teachers Emily talked about every night. I had seen her drawings on the wall. I'd demonstrated that I cared enough about her to come.

But I left early, unable to cheer for the closing blasts from the Thunder Drums. I had to wade back into the lives of two dead people.

Fifteen

I WAS ONLY about fifteen minutes late to the Fathers' Club. No reception committee this time—I was already one of the boys. When I got to the library, Hal Etheridge quietly motioned me to sit. The feeling in the room was off—not cheerful, not funereal, but definitely tense. Something was up. My first thought was that they'd found me out.

Then I noticed that Ricky Melman, sitting at the end of the table and the focus of everybody's attention, was in tears.

Montgomery held up a hand. "Kit, we wanted to mark Linda Lewis's death in some way tonight. So much loss to deal with so suddenly. We had a few minutes of silence, then Ricky here . . ." Montgomery looked ill at ease. He didn't even want to say it.

"Broke down," offered Melman, clearing his throat. "I just broke down and bawled. First time in my adult life." The others looked a bit uncomfortable, especially Montgomery—this may have been a men's group, but its members weren't into histrionics. They'd evolved to the point of sitting down to talk with one another, but there were still plenty of boundaries. Nobody wanted to look *too* New Age.

But Melman wasn't kidding; he was a wreck. He'd taken his hippie specs off to wipe his eyes with a red bandanna. I was surprised to see him laid open this way.

He looked over at me with a pleading expression. "Didn't see me as the crying type?" he said, reading my mind. "Let me bring you up to speed. I just told the guys I'm thinking of leaving my wife. Tonight. The usual cliché—I'm in love, with an intern at my clinic. She's here for six months from Harvard Public Health, wants to work in drug rehabilitation. Yes, she's younger—she's twenty-two, okay?" He announced her age defiantly, daring any of us to make something of it. Jeez, I thought.

"She asked my help in preparing a research paper for school. We spent a lot of time on that, and we work together in a weekly group therapy session I run. We really connect." Melman knew exactly how that sounded. He shrugged. "What can I say? You've heard it before. Seen it in movies, read it in books. Shirley and I, we've had three kids together, a solid marriage. But I don't feel about her the way I feel about Amy. I realize that I never have. Amy loves movies like I do, and books. It's as if we see the world exactly the same way. My lifelong fantasy woman, she just walked into my life. It's been exhilarating and horrible. All day long I yo-yo from joy and excitement to guilt and terror. I'm not casual about doing this. But I've made up my mind. I'm just letting you all know. It would seem hypocritical to be in this group and not mention it. And I'm hoping for some support. What's killing me is that Shirley is a great wife and a terrific person. And we've built this life together. Our house. A cabin in the Poconos. And the biggest thing is, our three kids . . . I love them dearly. The thought of them living without me . . ." His eyes teared up again.

What, I wondered, had these other fathers been advising? When I'd walked in, the men around the table looked like kids who want to see the lion in the zoo safely behind bars, but find themselves nose-to-nose with the carnivore instead. However evolved they are, most men find emotional displays and confrontations inherently frightening.

Montgomery cleared his throat. "Well, Ricky, you know I make it a point not to interfere with other people's personal lives." As if everybody hadn't felt perfectly comfortable telling a stranger how to handle his dope-smoking son, I thought. "But this is an extreme step, this has real ramifications." Well, that's helpful, I thought. Barely. Montgomery's equivocation was odd; I'd viewed him as the group's leader. He had to have stronger feelings than that. Maybe he just thought this was beyond the purview of the group.

Would Shirley Melman walk into my office one day and ask my help in tracking down Ricky? I could understand the pull: Melman, in his jeans and earring, viewed himself as offbeat, intellectual. And he'd sidestepped the corporate world for, as Jane would say, the helping professions. Who among us hadn't daydreamed about being a potter on Cape Cod, an organic farmer in Vermont or living some other romantic fantasy? We need fantasies. They're an antidote to the reality that engulfs us. But most of us understand that they are just fantasies. Most of us have come too far in life, and have made too many commitments, signed too many papers, worried too much over the lives of our children. And there could be happiness and satisfaction in that, too, at least for me.

I looked around the table. True to his word, David Battelle wasn't there. Jim Rheems and Dougherty looked grim. Etheridge appeared particularly squirmy. I sensed he was struggling to control his own feelings.

"Ricky, you said you came here for support," he began, fidgeting. "You aren't getting that from me, not at this point. You said you'd made up your mind. *Un*make it. You said you were leaving your family tonight. Hold on. We aren't about rubber-stamping your lifestyle choices. We're not here just to offer back pats for the dreadful mistakes we see one another about to make. That isn't friendship." He scanned the others' faces, seeking affirmation. "We are supposed to be talking to each other, not just okaying like dummies. We bring big decisions here. I feel obligated to say what I think."

He took a deep breath. We all knew Ricky wasn't going to like what followed. "This is nuts, Ricky, just nuts. Do you mean to say you're going to humiliate your wife, abandon three kids, destroy your family for some hackneyed affair with a college kid? No wonder you're crying! Are you having problems with Shirley? You've never mentioned any here. I mean what's going on, man? Were you hiding that from us too?"

Montgomery looked startled at Etheridge's bluntness, but Melman seemed almost to welcome it, as if he'd been expecting it or even thought he deserved it. Etheridge was red-cheeked; he had a strong sense of commitment to the group: he wanted it to work, to be more than an occasion for male chitchat, but a place where crises like Ricky Melman's could be discussed openly and thrashed out. Was that feeling what had caused his unspecified problems with Dale, I wondered. He obviously thought Melman was betraying the club ethic by concealing his affair and announcing his ready-made decision to blow his family to kingdom come.

Etheridge's passion surprised me. Most men probably would have nodded sympathetically and said something bland like, "Well, pal, it's sad but you've got to do what you've got to do." But Melman had come here, put this mess on the table and hadn't walked out. He must have wanted to hear what everybody had to say and Etheridge was more than willing to say it. Maybe Melman even wanted to be dissuaded.

"You can't control your heart," Melman told him defensively. "And Amy's not a child. She's a graduate student. This pisses me off, Hal. This isn't easy for me. My idea of support is understanding, not attack. I'm being honest with you. I never thought I'd feel this stuff again. I love my children, and I love my wife, but I can't help the way I feel."

Maybe it was because I'm married to a therapist, or because of my own work, but phrases like "disconnected from reality" were on the tip of my tongue. As a private eye, I'd cleaned up after messes like this all the time, but I rarely saw one in the embryonic stage. I understood some of what Melman was wrestling with. He was heading toward forty. Three kids were a lot of work and a lot of pressure, personally and financially. His wife stayed home and handled most of the daily family stuff, but I could at least see why he felt that much of his remaining life would be cruelly proscribed by responsibility, obligation and tuition. Three kids could make anybody daydream about one more crack at youth. Maybe Shirley too, ground down by twenty-four-hours-a-day motherhood, stared out at the driveway every morning, waiting for a *National Geographic* photographer with great cheekbones to pull up in his old truck.

"What you're saying doesn't make any sense," insisted Etheridge. The dry, affable manner I'd appreciated at my first meeting was gone. He was intense, almost laserlike now. Insurance executives probably didn't get the chance to be intense too often.

"How can you say you're in love with another woman, causing your wife and children all this pain, and yet say you don't have any problems with Shirley?" Etheridge's voice was rising. I liked what he was saying, but it wouldn't be helpful if he started shouting. Montgomery was looking almost annoyed, as if some twelve-steppers had appeared out of nowhere and hijacked his civilized men's group. I didn't think he wanted to be part of this conversation. Dougherty hadn't said a word, but his habitual twinkle had vanished.

"What Hal is saying makes sense to me, Rick," I put in. "If you didn't have some sort of marital problem, you wouldn't be drawn to this woman so strongly. If you don't mind my asking, have you had any counseling? Taken any steps to talk this through with Shirley? Will she be stunned to hear this? Because, if she would, you're on slippery moral ground."

Melman looked confused. "Talk *what* through? What is there to say? I'm in love with somebody else. I didn't jump into bed with Amy. I didn't go running off like some horny teenager. I don't need to discuss that for a couple of years, at great expense and personal disruption, before the inevitable occurs. Knowing what I know about what I feel, how could I go back to the way it was? And Amy's no bimbo. She feels horrible about my family, but she doesn't want to be some mistress. She isn't sticking around without some sort of commitment on my part. She says she wouldn't blame me a bit if I stayed with my wife and kids, no hard feelings at all, but I have to decide. She's like that. Look, I feel wonderful when I'm with her. We sit up all night talking. Sex is great . . ."

He put his head in his hands. "Jesus, I'm happy. I'm *happy*. Why is that so bad? Why is that *evil*? Don't you guys want that for me?"

Pretty basic questions. I'm not sure I had the answers. I was happy. Maybe not in the hot-blooded, romantic way Ricky was talking about. Jane and I practically had to make an appointment to have sex these days. But in my life happiness struck through different routes: in a trusting and loving marriage, in a kid's laughter or in a quiet late night walk with the dog, in the eternal fight to hold on through all the complex and often terrifying zigs and zags of daily life. Jane and I were like batters in front of those machines that pitched baseballs, swinging away as one decision, dilemma or requirement after another rushed remorselessly toward us.

They were incalculable, these threads that made up the tapestry of our life together, countless wins and losses, mistakes and solid judgments, victories and defeats. You had no idea how it was going to turn out, really, all you could do was keep acting, reacting, deciding. And loving.

But things looked different to Ricky, evidently. Happiness, for him, meant Amy. She was passion, youth, beauty. How could Shirley compete with that?

Dougherty pounded the table. "Jesus fucking Christ, Ricky, you sound like a graduate student in some bad writing program! You're a social worker, for Chrissake, not some shithead who thinks with his dick! If you're talking like this, what the fuck hope is there for the poor bastards who come to you to help patch up their lives?" That one struck home. Melman's head snapped back, almost as if he'd been whacked.

"NG, no good, not acceptable here," Dougherty went on. "We're a Fathers' Club, not a branch of fucking Club Med. Coming here is a statement that you want to learn how to do things better than men have done them before. And you want us to say, 'Go for it, Ricky. Leave your family. Be with Amy. Be happy.' " He was perilously close to sneering. "No way, at least not for me. If you're going to cause all this damage to yourself and them, you of all people, it should be a considered decision. . . ."

Like Etheridge, Dougherty, too, seemed to feel Melman had violated some strong ethical understanding. It was clear this group wanted the Fathers' Club to be a meaningful place where people brought serious problems. Why hadn't Montgomery expressed that creed to me? For that matter, why was Montgomery looking so uncomfortable with it himself?

Montgomery cleared his throat again. He addressed his words to the group, not Melman, whose eyes still blazed with resentment. "Look, I'm on my second marriage. Things don't always work out the way we want. You can't order somebody to stay in love. It sounds silly, but life *is* short. There are times when you have a right to look after your own happiness. Ricky has a shot at it. Are we so sure he shouldn't take it? Sounds like playing God to me."

No, I thought. We really aren't sure, but I was pretty certain about one thing—he shouldn't take his shot in this way.

"What happened in your first marriage?" Melman asked him, sensing Montgomery was the only person in the room on his side. Was that true? But then I remembered Benchley's caution about men's groups. They don't reflect men in general; they are self-selecting groups. The sort of man who thought it was just fine to run out on your wife and kids with virtually no warning wouldn't be here.

"Well, I guess I just fell out of love. The spark wasn't there

anymore. I just wasn't happy with my first wife . . . That's all."
Montgomery flushed. No doubt he'd begun seeing the woman who
became the second wife even while married to the first.

"You told me you had two daughters, Charlie," I asked. "Are
they from the first or second marriage?"

"One from each," he said tersely. He wasn't volunteering one
word more than he had to.

"How do you get along with the child from the first?" I pressed.

Montgomery looked down at his flowered ceramic coffee mug.
"It's pretty strained," he answered softly. "Lately she won't come
to my home for visits. I want to work it through, but I don't know.
I might just have to wait. That's painful. But otherwise," he insisted, "I *am* happy. That might not be what you want to hear, Kit,
but it was the right choice. Janine, my first wife, she's dating somebody now. She might remarry. Sometimes, everybody turns out
better off when marriages end. It isn't always a dreadful thing. It
isn't always silly or self-centered or piggish. I know how Ricky
feels. I think there's too much self-righteous thundering here."

The room was silent. Montgomery had weight here, everyone
knew he was careful and thoughtful. "It sounds worse than silly the
way Ricky wants to do it, Charlie," I argued. "It sounds callous."

"The point isn't whether Ricky and Shirley can stay married, or
even if they should. We can't decide that here in this room. We
don't even know her—at least I don't. But if you have problems,
don't you try to work them through before you make your decision? Isn't that necessary? Ricky, how long have you been married?"

"Fourteen years. We got married right out of grad school. My
son is eleven and the twins are almost eight. Look, I know this
sounds ingenuous, but I have no quarrel or complaint with Shirley.
She's always been supportive of my work, which pays shit but
which is what I want to do. She's smart and funny; she tries hard to
make me happy; I know she loves me. She'd do anything for me. I
know that. I just, I just . . . love someone else. That's the reality
of it. I didn't look for it, but it happened. . . ."

He groaned. "I think of Amy all day. I want her all the time. Do
you guys remember that feeling? Has it died in all of you? I'm
grateful to be able to feel it, even with all the pain it will mean.
Until this woman dropped out of the sky, like a gift from God, I
had fully intended to be married to Shirley for the rest of my life.

And I mean to be totally candid with Shirley. I'm not going to lie to her."

He searched the room for support. "And look, I hate to bring it up, in light of what's happened. But you're being awfully hard on me. Remember when Dale said he was leaving Linda, that he had to work some things out, that he couldn't be a father and spouse just then, that he had too many problems? Nobody jumped all over *him*. You all said you understood. Where is all the support you gave him?"

I didn't want to speak more than my share—after all, I was still the new kid on the block, and nobody to give moral lessons to these guys—but I don't often get the opportunity to talk about this stuff in advance of disaster. Besides, I wasn't exactly a good candidate for long-term membership in this club. Why not speak my piece while I had the chance?

"Let me paint a picture for you, Ricky," I said, pouring water into a glass that Etheridge slid in my direction. "Shirley will be enraged, totally humiliated, unable to face your mutual friends. She'll drive twenty miles outside of town to shop. She'll be mortified, knowing that for months every person who looks at her will say or think, 'Poor Shirley Melman. Her husband left her with three kids and ran off with some Harvard student.' They'll all dump on you, tell her it wasn't her fault, but she'll think that it was. She'll wonder what she should have done differently, why she couldn't fix whatever problems there were. Then she'll be furious, hating your guts and wondering why you lied to her, snuck around, fathered kids and then ran off rather than raise them with her. She'll have a tough row to hoe, for sure—three kids, no career, no husband.

"As for you, you'll be locked for fifteen years or so into child support and alimony payments, many of which you won't be able to make because as you said yourself, you don't earn shit, yet you'll have two households to maintain. Your kids will be laughed at in school, gossiped about. They'll blame themselves too, as kids do when their parents split up. You and Shirley will try to get them help, of course, but you won't be able to afford much. Troubled kids without money are pretty much on their own. Their lives will never be the same."

I was just warming up. I had seen this scenario unfold too many times and it always made me mad. "Can all this be overcome? Sure.

There are good therapists, and lots of kids from divorced families
do fine. Some couples talk it through, they stay civil, maybe they've
got the resources to find the help they need. But don't dwell too
deeply in your Harvard Square intellectual fantasy. It will be
rough. And lots of times the new relationship doesn't work out."

Montgomery looked at me curiously. "You seem to know a lot
about this, Kit."

"I do," I told him grimly.

Etheridge shoved back his chair and began to pace around the
room. "And that's a bad comparison about Dale, Rick. It's cheap
and you know it. Dale was tormented over business failures. He
had emotional problems. He felt he had to step back from his
marriage in order to get some personal problems straightened out.
It still seems to me that he did the right thing, at the time. He
never said he wanted his marriage to end. He said he wanted to
save it."

Was that true? I wondered. Battelle knew about Dale's affair
with Bev Cadawaller, but obviously this group didn't. Dale hadn't
done what Ricky did, come in and lay it all on the table. It sounded
like he'd cast his dilemma in such a way that the group would
naturally support his leaving Linda—just a temporary thing so that
he could get his shit together. That did seem quite different—
though it certainly wasn't how things had turned out. Maybe it was
never what he really intended. Melman, to his credit, was being
more candid.

Etheridge shook his head. "Dale wasn't mooning about a
younger woman and long nights sitting up and bullshitting about
literature and cinema." Anger was out of character for him, I suspected; he was struggling to contain it.

"I wasn't here for the Dale discussions, obviously," I jumped
back in. "Some marriages don't work. But there's a minimum
threshold of decency, and you're not even close to it." Etheridge,
Dougherty and Rheems were nodding, understanding what I was
saying. I guess they call this male bonding: the four of us were a
cohesive group, as of that moment. We had the same value system.
What a shame our little community couldn't last for very long.

"You owe it to Shirley to talk to her about this," I went on.
"Instead of skulking around, which I bet is what you've been doing,
right? She has to know something is wrong." God, did I have
experience at this. "She's probably noticed money disappearing or

the MasterCard has gone through the roof with unexplained dinner bills, books and flowers. Would that be accurate?"

Melman flushed purple.

"She already suspects something is up, and probably even what,"
I continued. "I don't know what's right and wrong for people; they
do have to make their own decisions. But I'm a believer in process,
friend. What you're planning is a rough thing to do to your partner. You're not only endangering your wife's and kids' emotional
health, but Amy's too. You're casting her in the no-win role of a
home wrecker. And if your new relationship doesn't last, you'll
have nothing left. If you get help with your marriage and things
still don't work out, okay, everybody did the best they could. But
this isn't anybody's best. This is cheap and easy."

Montgomery leaned forward. "We're getting damned judgmental here. We can't say what's going on between Ricky and Shirley.
If he feels he needs to take this step, then we should offer him our
sympathy and any other support. That's my vision of this club.
We're not here to beat up on people for the personal decisions they
make."

For some reason, Montgomery made me angrier than Melman.
Ricky seemed screwed up in the way so many men are as they veer
toward mid-life. Worn out by years of work, stress and conflict,
sensing the limits of their bodies, confronting for the first time the
knowledge that death is no longer incomprehensibly distant, they
often flip out, seeking affirmation of their youth and energy. The
dads I badger for child support are not evil, uncaring men. They
seem instead almost desperate, lunging hungrily for one last round
of youth. That it almost never works or lasts seems as incomprehensible to them as aging does to a high school athlete.

"This is the Woody Allen argument," offered Dougherty, trying
to lighten things up. "The heart wants what it fucking wants."

"The pecker wants what it wants is more like it," Rheems
snapped. The words—the first that he had spoken—stung. "I'm
sorry," he added just as quickly, "that was way out of line. I, well, I
have a lot of mixed feelings about this."

"I'm new here and probably overstepping my bounds," I said,
wading in. "But I can't agree with Charlie. When families fall
apart, terrible things can happen. I know. My father did this to my
family. In his forties, he left us to live with another woman, a
woman he eventually married. I'm trying so hard not to be my

father. To be different from him. I'll do anything for that." I felt my own eyes sting. Only Jane knew how I felt about my father's desertion.

"Are you close to your father now?" Ricky Melman asked.

"I haven't spoken to him for years," I said. "I'll never forgive him for what he did. I considered it an extraordinarily selfish act. I understand that everything doesn't work out, that some marriages aren't meant to be. But when you have a person who marries you in good faith, kids who love and need you, you have to respond in good faith. You have to try to hold things together. You have to be sure of what you're doing. Then, if you don't succeed, you do what you have to do. And I'll be the first one to support you. You can live in my guest room, cry on my shoulder, borrow what little money I can spare. But this? A secret affair with a college student, sneaking around, jettisoning your family with no effort to sort out your problems or find some solution? Your kids will never forgive you. I promise you: you'll face their anger and resentment the rest of your days."

The room was quiet. I'd surprised Melman and myself. Even Jane had never met my father. Ben and Emily knew that he and I exchanged cards once or twice a year, but in response to their questions I'd just say we weren't close. I'd never mentioned him to Luis or Benchley. So I was amazed I'd brought the whole sordid episode up here. For the first time, I realized why chasing after Deadbeat Dads had become such a passionate part of my work.

Etheridge coughed. "Kit, I appreciate that. That took a lot of guts. That couldn't have been easy to say, and I'm sure you haven't said it to a lot of people. Thanks." He looked at Melman and fell silent.

Melman slipped off his spectacles and rubbed his puffy eyes, still looking wretched, but calmer. "So what are you guys telling me to do, exactly?"

"Get thee to a therapist," Etheridge advised. "Like Kit says, don't leave your wife for this kid. Leave her if you have to, because the relationship doesn't work and because you've determined that it can't be fixed. Maybe you won't have to leave her at all." He got up and poured some juice for Melman, who looked as if he might just topple over. "I'm sorry if I've been yelling at you. I apologize. It's just that I want this group to mean something, okay? I want it to matter. You see? I know it's hard, but let us help you do the right thing. Sit down with Shirley. Get help. Be patient. Then do what you have to do. That's the price for my support."

Dougherty hesitated, then nodded. So did Rheems. Montgomery just shrugged.

Melman bowed his head. I wondered how much of what we'd said had filtered through. "Well, thanks, guys. It wasn't what I expected to hear, but maybe it's what I need. I'll have to think about all this. I promise I will." Etheridge leaned over and patted him on the arm.

No more clues at this meeting either. And I'd certainly revealed far more about myself than I'd learned about anyone else. I was feeling scummier than ever about my deception. But if Ricky had to search his soul to figure out the right thing, didn't I have an obligation to do the same?

"Guys, there's something else I have to tell you," I said bluntly. "These two meetings, well, they're not what I thought . . . I never realized what really goes on here.

"I thought you meditated or did readings from Robert Bly, I don't know. But since we're pushing Ricky to do the right thing, I have to do the same."

Deep breath. Inhale. Exhale. "Here's the story. I'm a private investigator. Kit Deleeuw is really my name, and I am really married to a psychologist. And everything I said about my son and my father is true. But I didn't come here for male companionship and advice. I came because Linda Lewis hired me to find out what was wrong with her husband. Dale had stopped paying child support and wasn't even in contact with his kids. Linda was worried about him. Then the day she hired me, he was killed. I found his body, in fact. The next morning Linda told me about this group and how important it was to Dale. She also told me that a couple of you had had business dealings with him. So I came here to find out more. She didn't want me to. And I feel crummy about it. I haven't said a single word about anything that I don't believe—Ricky, I hope you accept that. I'm completely sincere in what I said about your situation. I hope you know that."

The looks from around the table were like daggers to the gut. Rheems and Etheridge were stunned. Melman appeared even more miserable than before. Montgomery looked flabbergasted, then furious. Dougherty alone showed no visible emotion.

"So you lied to us?" Etheridge demanded. "You let us all open ourselves up while you were just a PI hoping to scarf up some useful information?"

I would have put it a little more benignly, but that was about right. "Yes," I said. "And I'm sorry about it. But I'm investigating two murders, and in my book, murder takes precedence over almost anything. I made that decision before I came here, before I knew you all. But there's no question that I came in under false pretenses. I take full responsibility for that. This group seemed the best shot I had at figuring out who might have murdered Dale. And then, Linda, too. But the group didn't turn out the way I thought. I was shocked that I was suddenly talking about my kid. And surprised as hell to be spilling my guts about my father. But I was in an impossible position, confiding details of my life and offering you advice on yours. It seemed like such a charade."

"It is." Dougherty said it coldly.

"Right," I agreed. "But I can't keep it up, for what it's worth. So I don't want to continue it. Though it couldn't have gone on very long, anyway. David Battelle has figured out who I am. I'm moderately well known around New York City and Essex County. Before long, the police will catch on to you and your connection to Dale and they'll be poking around here too. All I can tell you is that I think what you're doing is the Lord's work. I really liked being here. You helped me a lot with my kid. . . ."

Montgomery looked at the others. "Under the circumstances," he said, "I think it best that you leave, Kit."

Rheems was looking wobbly, shaking his head. "This is a real wound. Dale dies, Linda too, and then we take in somebody who turns out to be a *spy?* Jesus . . ."

Etheridge nodded. "I think what Charlie means to say is, get the hell out of here, Deleeuw. Just go."

I stood up. "I understand how you feel, I really do. I'd probably feel the same way myself. I hope you'll be more understanding once you think about the position I'm in."

"GO!" Etheridge thundered. Things were sliding downhill rapidly. I headed for the door.

"Wait," said Melman. "Before you leave, Deleeuw. Thanks for talking to me tonight. I'm not going home tonight and telling my wife I'm leaving. I might do it tomorrow, or in a few days, I just don't know. But I want to think about it. I can't promise anything . . ."

"You shouldn't," I told him. "It *is* your life."

He nodded, lifting one hand in a sad farewell. It seemed pretty clear I wouldn't be attending any more Fathers' Club meetings. I couldn't say I blamed them for throwing me out, but it didn't make me feel any better.

I walked out to the Volvo. Willie, napping in the front seat, snapped instantly awake.

"How was the group?" he asked.

"Swell, Willie. Really satisfying. I just got tossed out for being a self-confessed liar and snoop. Now let's go keep our appointment with the mob."

Sixteen

THE VOLVO steamed down Route 3, heading for the great, dirty, concrete and definitely nongarden like labyrinth that makes up much of the easternmost chunk of the Garden State: refineries, aging highways and bridges, warehouses, soot-tinged slums, crumbling ports and bulging prisons. This is almost everybody's image of New Jersey—the turnpike squeezing between belching towers of flame and mountains of cargo containers.

Of course, fifteen miles in almost any direction brings wide stretches of tree-lined streets and tidy split-levels with carefully tended lawns, but the stereotype endures.

The state has always been kind to its bedroom communities and brutal to its once great urban areas. Wedged between New York and Philadelphia, New Jersey no longer has healthy cities of its own. All of them—Camden, Newark, Trenton, Paterson, Atlantic City—have been raped, pillaged and abandoned. At least Jersey City, where I was headed, was showing some feeble signs of renewed life—a few yuppies seeking cheaper brownstones than Manhattan or Brooklyn offered, thousands of Latin and Asian immigrants joining the more settled Poles and Italians. In Jersey City you could drive by a Cuban restaurant, a mosque, and a hip clothing emporium, all on the same block.

"You okay, Chief?" Willie asked, sounding tentative. I nodded without taking my eyes from the road. I had barely said a word since I got in the car. Willie wisely hadn't pushed for conversation.

"Yeah, I'll tell you about it later, okay? I'm not really in the mood now."

Car dealerships, appliance warehouses, gas stations and burger joints rushed by. It occurred to me that we were driving into the town where Luis lived. But I had no idea where and wouldn't have dreamed of trying to look him up.

There was nothing pretty to look at. Every now and then some poignant old house, synagogue or park stuck out amid the clutter. I wondered what it was like to live twenty feet from a roaring highway.

The cell phone beeped. It was Jane.

"Hey, sweetie," she said. "I miss you and the sound of your voice. I just got home. Ben seems almost chipper. What did you do, drug him?"

I laughed. It was good to hear her voice, too. More than anything, I think I missed seeing her at dinner every night, each of us filling the other in on the day's events, talking about the kids, laughing, staying current with one another's lives. Now, it was mostly catch as catch can.

"I got home almost early tonight," she said. "My evening class was canceled. But I've got two big papers to do. My friend Valerie has invited me to sleep over next week for a couple of nights so that we can both stay late in the library. I know this is a rough time for you, Kit, but I hope I can take her up on it. I don't think I can handle it otherwise."

I sighed, told her it was fine. I reported on my conversation with Ben (as Willie tried tactfully not to eavesdrop), and a few details about the case.

"Kit, I'm worried about you. You've got so much on your plate. I'm sure Linda Lewis's death was horrible for you. And this time with Ben, oh, I just wish I could be around more.

"But listen, Kit, you just say the word and I'll be there. On the phone or in person. Whatever you need. It wouldn't be such a disaster to take an incomplete in a course."

"Jane, I'm okay. Honestly. I feel better about Ben and I'm just absorbed in these two cases. It's a little complex. Today I'm juggling more things than I think I've ever juggled in my life. I'll fill you in when I get home, okay?" Though we both knew she'd be asleep by then.

I pulled off the highway onto Jersey City's mostly grungy, tenement-lined streets, home of the Holland Tunnel and a bunch of singles bars. It was time to focus on Jacob Logovitz and his connection to Dale or Linda Lewis, not Jane or Ben or broken promises to the men's movement.

We passed a few blocks of gentrified townhouses, the bricks pointed and cleaned, fresh flowers planted in window boxes, unshuttered windows revealing living rooms with track lights and oil paintings.

Jacob Logovitz's home didn't turn out to be one of those. Logovitz lived in a dingy, narrow, three-story brick house with a firehouse on one side and a trash-littered empty lot on the other. Willie tapped me on the arm as we pulled up. He gestured toward a gleaming black minivan parked a few houses up the street, the puffs from its exhaust indicating that the engine was running and somebody was probably inside. You would think federal agents would know not to keep their vans that clean. Unless, of course, they *wanted* to be seen.

"Well," I sighed. "They've already got my license plate. So they'll have my name and address in a minute or two. We'll get a visit from the FBI in a couple of days, wondering about our business here." I'm disinclined to be helpful to the FBI, law-abiding citizen though I am. Its investigation of my Wall Street firm had been utterly ruthless. A swarm of agents had burst into our offices at midday and carted out everything in our offices, from computers to family pictures. The FBI threatened me continuously with prosecution unless I talked about my friends and their transactions. But even if I'd known about the insider trading my friends were involved in, I doubt I would have ratted. The feds never believed I was innocent. My only luck came when the U.S. Attorney decided to run for the Senate and, anxious to wrap up the case, agreed not to prosecute me in exchange for my never working on Wall Street again. I promised. But the FBI made it clear that, should I ever stumble, its minions would be eager to run me over. These guys would probably be delighted to see my name pop up in their computers during an organized-crime surveillance. Another excuse to hassle me, and I was feeling pretty hassled already.

Willie seemed edgy too. His knee jiggled nervously. This wasn't really his scene. He'd pulled a worn leather jacket over his dark blue T-shirt and torn jeans. Alas, he still looked and was affable and gentle, chewing gum like a teenager. At least he was exceptionally tall. Most people would hesitate before tangling with him, though I'd never once seen him angry and couldn't picture him hurting anybody.

I hoped I hadn't made a mistake in letting him come along. If he wanted to be a private investigator, he had to come out from behind the monitor sometime. But was it wise to start with a Russian mobster? Well, what could be safer than a discussion with the FBI sitting right outside? Besides, I reminded myself, it wasn't as if we were unexpected. In fact, we'd been invited.

"Do you know anything about this guy you didn't tell me earlier, Willie?" I asked, turning off the car engine.

"Not much," he answered. "He's sixty-seven. Supposedly, his wife and two kids are dead, killed in the Soviet Union under circumstances nobody seems to know much about. There was a profile of him in *Newsday*. Plus *PI Reports* had a big on-line file on him."

Such information used to be available only through police sources or days spent in the bowels of public libraries. Most PI work is confidential and you can't really ask other PIs for much help. But Willie had inputted Logovitz's name and instantly come up with a fairly substantive bio. Civil libertarians could spend years sorting out the privacy questions, but meanwhile I faced a lot less door-knocking and phone-trawling.

"He was a colonel in the KGB, investigators believe." Willie was reading from his printout by the light of the streetlamp. "He tried to clean up some mob which was infiltrating restaurants in Moscow and was nearly beaten to death. Then he went over to the other side. Nobody knows how or why, but three years ago he turned up in Brooklyn. The FBI describes him as a major player, according to the story," Willie summarized. "They say he's absolutely merciless, much feared, supposed to run all the Russian loansharking and car theft operations out of New Jersey. He's also been investigated—get this—for defrauding the government out of millions in housing subsidies. One of his organization's scams was getting people to apply for housing aid two or three times under different names. Another—anyway, this was the charge—was some bribery scheme where HUD officials in regional offices would certify the existence of subsidized housing projects that didn't exist. There were all these paper trails but, according to federal officials, witnesses moved, disappeared and clammed up at an amazing rate. Logovitz got indicted, but the indictment was thrown out. The investigation, as they say, continues."

"Can we get any more specifics on how these scams worked?"

Willie shook his head. "Not yet. But I can get more. The *Newsday* story says that Logovitz runs a $40 million business." We both looked up at the dingy house and shook our heads. Some headquarters for a multimillionaire.

"He's quite a character," Willie said. "He lives simply." To say the least. "He dotes on his younger sisters and brothers and their kids—I don't know yet how many—and operates like an old-fashioned godfather. On the surface, a real warm, courteous, family-type guy. But cross him, and you're sorry." You disappear or change your mind about testifying, I thought. Or you die.

All this was about four miles over my head. No wonder the FBI was on the scene. It occurred to me that a Logovitz connection would also explain the feds' intense interest in Dale Lewis's murder. "Maybe you ought to stay in the car," I suggested.

"Forget it," said Willie.

Why on earth would somebody like Logovitz agree to see me? "Let's just be careful," I muttered. I was nervous. I'd been in a number of hairy scrapes already in my time as a PI, dealt with cold-blooded killers and true psychotics, gotten slugged and shot at. But I'd never tried to question a criminal figure at this level. I had this fleeting thought that it would be nice to be able to tell the guys at the men's group next week about how frightened I was. But that wouldn't happen.

"I'll do the talking," I said, emerging from the Volvo and locking the doors. "If you have a question, be polite. And for God's sake don't get cute. He may not be into the American smart-ass mode of communications. This guy has agreed to see us because he wants something. I don't want to give him anything without knowing what he wants."

We crossed the street and walked up to the front door. Shabby and ill kempt, the brick townhouse would draw hostile stares and scolding clucks in Rochambeau. Grime covered the windowsills. Paint was peeling off the door and windowframes. Heavy curtains were drawn over all the windows.

I noticed a mild roar and looked toward the backyard. The house practically adjoined one of the partially submerged approaches to the Holland Tunnel. Headlights from onrushing trucks and cars flickered on the walls of the houses around us.

The smell of exhaust was gaggingly thick. Unless you moved in next to Newark Airport, I could hardly imagine a worse place in the state to live. Or one anybody with any money at all would choose.

At the door, Willie pulled out his penlight. I thought I saw the black van shift a bit, as if somebody were moving inside. There would probably be infrared pictures of us to go with the license ID. They'd have made me by now, but not Willie, unless he had some history I didn't know about. Was I crazy to be dragging him into this?

I couldn't make out the words below any of the three doorbells. "Shine the light over here," I asked Willie. At the sound of my voice, one of the curtains parted slightly. And as I glanced over, I saw the winking red light of a videocamera through the window. So inside they were taping us, too.

Under the thin wash of light from Willie's penlight, I saw the thin strips of begrimed white paper taped under each bell. The top one said simply "Logovitz." The bottom one said "Bella Properties," the middle "Grove" something. The other words were smeared and unreadable. I pushed the top bell.

The door opened instantly. A beefy young man in a garish floral shirt, too cool for this fall chill, stood in the entrance. Another man, dressed in jeans and a V-neck but like his buddy resembling a tractor-trailer, stood in the hall behind him, arms crossed.

"Can I help you?" asked the Hawaiian shirt guy in a thick, guttural rumble. I studied his muscular forearms and impressively broad neck. He didn't look friendly, or unfriendly either—just *there*, an impassable obstacle unless he decided to yield.

"Kit Deleeuw and my associate, Willie Baker." Willie started slightly. I'd decided not to give them Willie's real last name, so I'd made one up. And if the FBI was listening, in their shiny black van, I'd rather they chased after Willie Baker.

"We were expecting just *you*," objected the Neck. "Not him." Behind us, the Tree stared impassively, chewing gum and yawning. He'd probably sized us up quickly as no threat. I wanted to ask him what it felt like being so obvious a cultural cliché. I didn't.

"Well, he comes with me," I said. "He works with me. No him, no me." Jane would have cracked up over that line. It sounded as if I were talking to a lower primate. But maybe I was, because it worked: the Neck waved us inside, then closed the door, after glancing out at the van. Maybe they brought coffee to each other, these guys.

Without fanfare, Neck turned Willie and me to the wall. The Tree came up quietly for a person about eight feet tall and frisked us thoroughly: up the calves and thighs, around the crotch, up the side, around the belly, and up the back. This wasn't a casual pat-down; it was a first-rate probe. Lots of guards are shy about running their hands up another man's genitals or butt, but not these two. Willie flushed. I winced. They weren't any too delicate.

"Uh, gentlemen, could you take it easy?" I found myself saying. "I understand you have a job to do, but if we were here to hurt anybody, we wouldn't come strolling up to the door and ring the bell, right?"

The Neck startled me by turning me around and smiling. "I beg your pardon, Mr. Deleeuw. But you'd be surprised at the things people would do. Let's just say we prefer to take the surprise out of any meetings Mr. Logovitz holds." Well. I wasn't expecting an articulate, well-spoken response from my wide-necked friend.

"I'm sure you understand that we're just professionals doing a professional job," he added. "As private investigators, I'm sure you and Mr. Paine here"—he winked at me—"oh, I'm sorry, Mr. *Baker*. I'm sure you both do the same for your clients, isn't that right?"

I laughed. "Well, well, don't underestimate muscle men."

He smiled back. "That's right. I wouldn't. Mr. Logovitz is waiting for you in the living room. Not too long, now, okay? He's a bit under the weather."

It was, in fact, a scene from *The Godfather*—the Eastern European, low-budget version. The room, lit by two table lamps with brocaded shades, was bathed in shadow and ringed by sofas and chairs with carved claw feet. An ornate cupboard full of crystal and china nearly filled one wall. Though it was only somewhat chilly out, a fire roared in the fireplace. The room smelled of furniture polish.

A tiny, bald man perched in a big red chair near the fire, his lower body swathed in afghans. As we entered, he peered at us through thick spectacles. A bottle of vodka and three cut-glass goblets sat on a mahogany table next to his chair. I had the feeling this old man had transported his surroundings straight from Mother Russia to New Jersey.

"Hello." Jacob Logovitz had a surprisingly strong, thickly accented voice.

"Hi," I said. "I'm Kit Deleeuw. This is my associate Willie."

The old man gestured us to two antique chairs across from him, his eyes flicking from one of us to the other behind his coke-bottle lenses. The Neck and the Tree took turns drifting past the doorway. They would be just steps away if they heard or saw anything they didn't like. I wouldn't be doing or saying anything they didn't like.

"Did you notice our friends across the street?" Logovitz laughed raspily. This touched off a coughing fit. In a flash, the Neck was in the room with a glass of water.

"So many better things to do with government money and they follow me," Logovitz chuckled, after a sip. He shook his bald head at the utter ridiculousness of it all. I had encountered this before in megalomaniacs. No matter what they do, they believe themselves victims. Someone is always persecuting them.

"Mr. Logovitz," I said, "thanks for seeing me. I appreciate it. Though I was a little surprised . . ."

"Why?" he asked, pulling his lap robes closer and sipping nasally from his water. "I have nothing to hide. Some vodka?" Willie and I both said no. Willie looked nearly paralyzed. I got the feeling he'd never been near a man like this in all his life. Logovitz had the same feeling, it seemed. He kept staring at Willie too.

Under the layer of furniture polish, the atmosphere was thick with medicine and rubbing alcohol. Logovitz didn't look healthy. I might not have a lot of time for this chat.

"I'm sure you don't, sir. Well, as my assistant told you on the phone—"

"Miss de la Cretaz," he offered, letting me know that he missed nothing and that he knew who and where Evelyn was.

"Yes. As she told you, I am investigating the death of a client, Linda Lewis. She hired me to look into the affairs of her husband, Dale Lewis. Not his business affairs," I added quickly, "but to determine whether he was all right. She said he'd been a loving and devoted father, but suddenly had stopped sending child support and even visiting or calling. You may know—"

He waved a gnarled hand impatiently. "I know about Dale. We worked together, as you have already learned."

I mumbled something, a stall.

Logovitz's gimlet stare was almost unnerving. "Mr. Deleeuw, I'm an old man and not a well one. I have a van outside my house twenty-four hours a day filled with handsome young men like your associate here who would like nothing more than to see me die in prison." He clapped his frail hands. The Neck glided in with an electronic wand, the kind that detects listening devices. He ran it around the room and, for good measure, over Willie and me.

Logovitz nodded toward the heavy drapes. "They try everything. If a florist comes in with flowers, we find microphones among the roses. If a maid comes in to clean, we find them under the bed. Now they try to point directional microphones through the windows. We have installed special curtains. And distractions." The Neck snapped on a switch, and classical music swirled from a hidden speaker. He flicked the volume to full throttle and the room briefly rattled before he turned it down. "That will have them jumping up and down in that truck," Logovitz roared gleefully. Say what you wanted about Jacob Logovitz, they hadn't broken his spirit.

"So, Mr. Deleeuw, let us proceed. I knew Dale. Nice young man. We were in land development together." I opened my mouth, but he held up his hand as if to say, "I'll ask the questions around here, sonny." I had obviously been summoned to receive a message from a man who did not intend to submit to any interrogation.

"Our venture was most unsuccessful," continued Logovitz. "Dale did not prove to be a responsible or trustworthy partner. You don't need to waste your valuable time investigating him." I blinked, and Willie couldn't resist a glance at me. Was this man admitting to murder?

"Why not?" I asked, as forcefully as I could.

"You can continue with your investigation, of course, if you wish. I'm just saying I wouldn't if I were you. You know, Mr. Deleeuw—what kind of name is Deleeuw, anyway?"

"It's Dutch. But can you tell me why—"

"Please," snapped Logovitz, taking another sip of water. "I am not interested in Dale Lewis. He reneged on his commitments and met an unfortunate end. You won't learn much about it, in my opinion. That's a prediction, that's all, Mr. Deleeuw, from a man who follows the news."

I waited while another coughing fit shook his frail body. "Then why are we here?" I asked.

"Because of the wife," he replied without hesitation. "He talked about her. I read about her in the news. It bothered me very much that somebody would take her out and shoot her in the head, a young woman like that. A mother of two young children. What happened to her husband was tragic too, you understand, Mr. Deleeuw. But it was probably a business matter. The man had a habit of borrowing money from people, too much money, too many people. I hear he didn't pay it back. I know absolutely nothing about this firsthand, you understand. But I'm giving you advice. Dale Lewis is not worth bothering with. You're never going to find his killer. Bother with the wife. I know what it means to lose family. Do you understand what we're talking about?"

The Tree came in and scanned the room again, maybe to make certain I hadn't activated some listening device. But I had the impression the old man didn't really care. His message was unmistakable: Dale had been killed because he'd welshed on a huge debt. But Linda was killed for other reasons, and not by the soldiers of this dying mobster. For some reason, it mattered to him that I know that.

"Mr. Logovitz, forgive me, but in many ways I'm inexperienced. Do people really get killed for debts of several hundred thousand dollars? Isn't that a little extreme? I hear what you're saying, and I appreciate it, but I just want to put my mind at rest about this."

He sighed, gazed from me to Willie, as if the ways of his world were inexplicable to the likes of us. Which was probably true.

"From what I hear—I wouldn't know personally, you understand—but from what I hear there are other ways to ensure that a debt is repaid. It would be unusual, somebody dying for a few hundred thousand dollars. But sometimes, of course, there are unusual circumstances." His water glass was empty. The Neck refilled it.

"Like what?" I asked Logovitz.

"Like . . . oh, I don't know . . . trying to escape a debt by threatening to go to the authorities with false information about somebody, a lie that might cause other people trouble. In such a situation, somebody might get hurt."

I thought I had it now. Dale had borrowed a half million dollars from Logovitz. He'd also borrowed money from his wife, Jim Rheems and David Battelle—close to a million, all told. He couldn't repay it. So he welshed on Rheems and Battelle and Linda, but Logovitz wouldn't take that so civilly. The old man's organization had probably been leaning hard on Dale. That might explain his unpredictable, erratic behavior in the days before his murder, even his vanishing for a while. He'd have been on the run, moving around. Then, Logovitz was suggesting, Dale made the fatal decision that he could get the Russian mob off his back by going to federal prosecutors with information about Logovitz and his housing subsidy schemes. Logovitz couldn't permit that. So Dale died. It made sense. In this case, it was the first thing that did. It would also explain the heavy federal presence. The van outside was not subtle surveillance but a clear and expensive statement: Logovitz had done something serious and the FBI was all over him.

But didn't this theory make Linda's death even more incomprehensible?

"Mr. Logovitz, I appreciate this appointment even more than I did before. Thank you, sir." He nodded. I meant it. He was sort of a throwback, to the times when even criminals had codes of ethics. During his life, Dale Lewis had violated a big one—maybe the biggest. He'd welshed, then ratted—a double whammy in any criminal enterprise. But Logovitz apparently didn't believe in killing innocent mothers. That offended him. He wanted the record clear that he was not responsible for that abhorrent act.

The old man was taking a risk talking to me, though he'd been careful to say nothing explicitly incriminating. Who knew what kinds of technology the FBI was employing? They could have the tea bags wired. Logovitz had probably calculated the odds pretty well. He was probably not planning on living much longer anyway. Given the way our legal system worked, by the time he was convicted and sentenced, he'd be under a marble tombstone in the Jersey City cemetery. Even if he wasn't, was prison all that much worse than this claustrophobic house arrest? He had the demeanor of a man who had lived his life and was settling up.

Still, this conversation with me was above and beyond the call. I felt a surge of relief. Whether or not I admitted it to myself, I'd been assuming Linda was a knowing partner in whatever crooked scheme her husband had concocted. Logovitz, who would have known otherwise, was telling me it wasn't so.

I had only one more question. "Mr. Logovitz, can I ask how Dale found you? He wasn't exactly . . . connected."

Logovitz pondered that a minute. "He came to me through a business associate who knew of my work in building housing projects in New Jersey."

"Would that associate by any chance be David Battelle?" I asked.

Logovitz shrugged. He said nothing. But I knew I was right. Battelle worked in that field and would have known that Logovitz was bankrolling such projects. Battelle would have been Dale's logical introduction to a world far beyond him.

It would have been a perfect note on which to leave, but my young friend Willie decided to get enterprising.

"Mr. Logovitz," he blurted out in his guileless way, "did you murder Dale Lewis?"

Logovitz didn't have time to react. The Neck was in the room in a flash, tossing Willie effortlessly to the floor. I jumped up to help and never even saw the hand that savagely jammed into my gut and slammed me down so hard that my vision blurred.

We'd been having such a civilized conversation. What the hell had set Willie off? The pain coming from the general area of my intestines was blinding. "Jeez, Willie," I hissed, "I'm glad you spoke up."

I glanced over to see him on his feet with his fists balled and shook off the pain long enough to yell, "Willie, no!" The Neck grinned softly. I think he rather liked Willie. He hadn't hit *him*, just knocked him down. I rubbed my lower abdomen. The pain had subsided from agonizing to horrible.

"Sorry." The Neck came over to help me up. "You came at me kind of fast. Sorry, Mr. Logovitz. Overreacted a little, I guess."

Logovitz clucked a bit and Tree backed off. Willie and I were standing, but shaking. The Neck's speed and violence—this all couldn't have taken two seconds—were frightening. Especially when you considered he was trying *not* to hurt anybody.

"It's okay, Charles," Logovitz told him. "We'll excuse the boy's bad manners. He's young. Forget it, please. Mr. Deleeuw, my apologies. Your partner there could use a bit of training. I *don't* murder people. And it's impolite to ask." I thought I saw the hint of a smile on the old man's weathered face. I think he was enjoying this.

"A discourteous question," Logovitz murmured, mostly to himself. "Charles will show you out, Mr. Deleeuw. Thank you for coming. I'm afraid I must retire now."

Charles and his buddy steered us toward the door. I was still reeling from the pain shooting through my gut; Willie looked pale and shaken.

Back in the Volvo, I breathed as deeply as I dared until the pain eased, then turned on the ignition. The van was still parked, engine running, up the block. Willie and I'd have a good talk, on the ride home, about appropriate versus inappropriate questioning of suspects.

Seventeen

I THOUGHT, that's the big question, the one you just pop," Willie said, struggling to explain. "You know, to rattle him. To catch him off guard."

To Willie, of course, Logovitz was a frightened old man. Maybe he was too young to know how scary old men with lap robes could be. Or was this the danger of spending too much time on computers? Maybe a corner of your brain shorts out and you end up losing a bit of feel for the give and take of face-to-face human interaction.

"Generally speaking," I said, "you don't ask somebody like that a question the way you asked it, and in his own living room, no less. You're adding disrespect to insult. Besides, you don't rattle a mob boss. You work very hard *not* to rattle a mob boss. These people either talk to you or they don't."

"Sorry, Chief," Willie said penitently. "It was just an impluse. It won't happen again."

"It's no big deal," I said. It wasn't, in fact, though in other circumstances it might have been. There *were* times when you had to be plenty careful in this business. But Willie had gotten the message.

"I think Logovitz genuinely hated the idea of a woman and a mother being murdered like that." I felt safer as we pulled back onto the highway west. "In his culture, you can be as vicious as you need to be under certain circumstances, but there are things you don't do. You don't kill innocent mothers of little kids. He was also giving me a gift by telling me not to bother about Dale."

Willie looked puzzled. "What kind of a gift is that? Wasn't he just telling you to stay away from the case? Trying to scare you off?"

"Maybe," I said. "But my reading of it was that he was saving me time. He made it pretty clear that Dale bailed on a big debt, then tried to trade evidence to the police as a way of getting out from under, and got hit because of it. Logovitz knows I'll never solve Dale's murder. PIs don't solve mob crimes, except in books. Sometimes the feds can, because they can squeeze people, offer immunity and protection in exchange for information. But I'd have no way of doing that. So, if we believe him, and Linda's death isn't connected to Dale's, it saves us half of an investigation."

"And do you believe him?" Willie asked.

"He has no reason to deal with me at all. He may not be disclosing his true motives, but I do believe what he's saying."

Willie was looking at me oddly.

"What?"

"Well, Chief, there's a moral issue here, right?"

"What moral issue?"

"You're saying what a relief it is that we don't have to look into Dale's killing because the old man told us not to. You're saying I was wrong to ask him about it because that's bad mafia manners. You're saying how convenient it is to skip all the work we'd have to do checking out Dale's death. But I'm thinking to myself, Is that okay? Do we just write off a murder like that? Especially if the guy who arranged it practically confesses, right in front of us? Doesn't that seem just a bit cynical?"

The giant concrete ovals of the Meadowlands sports complex loomed up on our right. This had to be one of the more bizarre architectural accomplishments of our time—a massive racetrack, football stadium and arena surrounded by acres of parking lots, all plunked down in the endless meadows a stone's throw from Manhattan. Only New Jersey would permit so hideous a despoiling of its environment.

Willie had a point. Had I already been doing this too long? Had I become so opportunistic and cynical that I needed a twenty-five-year-old kid to tell me that a person's death, no matter what the circumstances, is serious stuff? That perhaps I ought not be so overjoyed at the corners we could now cut?

"And, Kit . . ." I knew this was serious because Willie rarely called me Kit. He hesitated. "I can be honest, right?"

"You'd better be."

"I got mad when he talked about murdering Dale, that's why I was in his face about it. But you didn't. I wondered why, and I came up with an answer, I think. You don't like Dale Lewis, because of the way he treated his wife. You don't really care that much who offed him because you think he was a creep. But you care a lot about her, don't you?"

That was pretty clear thinking on Willie's part, about murder and about me. I was happy, sort of, to say so. "Okay, Willie. Good points. Well taken. I guess I don't think much of Dale. He seems to have been a leech, sucking money out of everybody, abandoning this lovely woman . . ."

"And maybe you're a little jealous?" Willie was half smiling now.

"Whew. The kid shows his stuff. Maybe, but mostly . . . oh, fuck it. It's none of your business. I'm a happily married man. I don't go swooning over other women. Anyway, what does it matter now?"

Willie nodded, this time sympathetically. "But I saw your face this morning, after you found out about Linda. You were pretty shaken up. The only point I'm making is, I guess you've got to be careful. That's what you've told me a hundred times: when you get personally involved, be careful. It clouds your judgment. I'm just reminding you of your own advice."

"Okay, thanks, I get it," I barked. "Now stop being so astute and start coming up with some answers on the goddamn case, okay? Like who benefits from Linda's death? If she wasn't murdered at random—and I refuse to believe she was—then somebody killed her because they had something to gain by her death. Either there's a motive like love, or financial reward, or some kind of vengeance. One of the names we know about has got to have had a reason to want her dead. I'm going to see Bev Cadawaller tomorrow morning. You might run her through your computer in the meantime and see if anything else pops up. I'll have Evelyn call Lieutenant Tagg in the morning and see if we can't get the state police file on Logovitz. Okay? Salve your conscience?"

Willie nodded. "Okay. But do we go to the feds and tell them what Logovitz said about Dale Lewis?" He wasn't going to give up easily.

"I don't know, Willie," I said wearily. "Let's sleep on that one, okay?"

We sat quietly, whizzing west. By the time we'd reached his Jeep, Willie had his headphones on and was tapping his giant sneaker on the Volvo floor, head rocking back and forth so hard the car almost swayed. He waved and bounded off.

I wasn't surprised by what I saw when I got home. I'd thought they might wait till morning, but they aren't the patient sort. Even though it was past midnight, a black sedan sat at the curb outside my house, squeaky clean, idling quietly, the two men in front sitting up straight. I couldn't make out the faces of the men inside, but there wasn't much mystery about who they were.

I pulled into my driveway. Belatedly, Percentage started to bark. Half the Federal Bureau of Investigation could sit there with their engines running all night, and he would snooze undisturbed, snoring away on his back with his three good legs and one gimpy one sticking straight up in the air. But let his beloved master arrive in the car Percentage rode in nearly every day, and he instantly turned into the world's most ferocious watchdog. Ah, Labradors.

I got out of the car, walked to the end of the driveway and waited. If I could keep them out of the house, so much the better. All Ben needed now was to see the feds questioning me in our living room.

Special Agents Andersen and Hirschorn flashed their IDs, politely holding them out long enough for me to actually read them. "Kit Deleeuw?" the tall one asked. "I'm Agent Hirschorn." I didn't know if it was the time of day or the new informal FBI, but both men wore sneakers, jeans and windbreakers. My guess is that they'd been part of the surveillance unit keeping tabs on Logovitz and, in my honor, had broken off from the others.

It was getting chilly, and my resolve to keep them outside began to soften a bit. It seemed rude. These guys were just doing their jobs. What had happened to me on Wall Street wasn't their fault.

"Welcome. I'd invite you in . . ."

"No, thanks," Andersen, the short one, snapped. "We only have a few minutes." "What were you doing visiting Jacob Logovitz, Deleeuw?" My resolve to keep them outside stiffened again. "You know who he is? Given your background, it takes a lot of cheek to go see him. . . . You should consider yourself lucky you're not in jail, my friend."

"Given my background?" I sputtered. "Excuse me, Agent Andersen, but I'm not aware that I've been convicted of any crime. Or even indicted for that matter. And I'm not aware that I have to stand out here past midnight and even discuss this with you, either."

"We've checked your file. You're only out of jail because we didn't have enough evidence to charge you. That could still change."

Calm down, I told myself. Getting hot won't help anybody. "It will only change when you could find a bleeding elephant in the snow," I said. "And you won't. It could only change if there were something to find. Which there isn't. So we can talk tough with one another until I go inside and you go back to sit on your butts in Jersey City. Or you can ask me what you want to know and I'll try to cooperate. Your choice. I'm not afraid of you. I have no reason to be."

Hirschorn shrugged, although Andersen was itching to throw a few more verbal punches. They didn't really have a lot of options, when all was said and done. "Okay. Let's try it," Hirschorn said. "What were you doing at Logovitz's house? And who was that with you?"

"He had nothing to do with this," I said. "I'm investigating a murder. The victim's name was Dale Lewis. A local land developer, young guy. His wife was killed a day later at a convenience store at the edge of town. Logovitz, as I'm sure you knew before I did, was a silent partner of Dale Lewis. So I called and asked if I could come see him. To my surprise, he said yes."

"Who was inside?" Andersen asked.

I described the Tree and the Neck.

"What did Logovitz tell you?" Hirschorn asked.

"He said Dale owed him money. That's all he said."

"Did he tell you that Lewis was a potential witness in a federal investigation, which makes his killing a possible capital crime and federal offense? That it makes *you* a possible witness in a federal investigation of a capital crime?"

"I'm flattered to be involved in so important a case, but the fact is, he told me nothing. And if you read your files, you ought to know that I am not so easily bullied. If I had information on a criminal act, I would share it with you. I'm not hiding anything, I just don't have anything to hide. I walked in and out through the front door. I have a right to do that. I wasn't secretive or indirect. And you have no right to make me uncomfortable about it."

"When you left," Andersen continued, as if I hadn't spoken at all, "you were bent over as if you'd been hurt. Was there any rough stuff?" I'm sure they would have loved to get Logovitz on an assault charge, if nothing else. And Logovitz had been at least partially responsible for offing a witness in a federal investigation, not something I wanted to endorse or ignore. But if I took on the Russian mob, it wouldn't be over a punch in the stomach. The trickier issue was whether to tell them what Logovitz had said about Dale.

For the moment, I decided, I had no real information to offer and my own work to tend to. "No," I lied. "Just middle age. I pulled a groin muscle." That wouldn't help my credibility any, but these people didn't think I had much credibility to begin with. They believed I'd weaseled out of the jail time I deserved for insider trading. They wanted to charge and sentence me. Barring that, they'd managed to drive me from my work. I fantasized sometimes that they had second thoughts; that in secret they turned to one another and said, "God, I'll never forgive myself for what we did to that Deleeuw guy. He was completely innocent. We drove him from his career, almost bankrupted him, nearly wrecked his life, and all for no reason."

But I knew they didn't think like that. Instead, they waited for the next round, when they intended to finish what they'd started five years ago. But if they think I've stashed my ill-gotten gains, they ought to look at my kitchen. Nobody with money would eat under a ceiling like that.

In any case things, as they often do, had worked out for the better. My belief is that men almost never change their lives voluntarily. They have to be hit on the head, laid off, run over. Men aren't much inclined to introspection. But when your career goes up in smoke and a lifetime of expectations is swept away, well, it gets a guy thinking about his choices. These days, a lot of men have been shocked this way. They make up a sort of secret brotherhood—like the Fathers' Club in some ways. I felt a stab of pain almost as sharp as the one still in my gut. No time to fuss about that, though.

"Deleeuw, the file on you is still open," Hirschorn said. "It would be in your interest to help us out, make things even. Are you planning to go back to see Logovitz? Would you be—"

"No," I interrupted emphatically. "Don't even think about it. I won't wear a wire. I don't trust you and I won't work with you. I don't need to make things even with you; you need to make things even with me. And if I had any relevant evidence, I'm obliged by the state of New Jersey to give it to you. But I don't. Is there anything else?"

There wasn't. I didn't feel great about my harrumphing. They had a rough job, and they needed the help of people like me to do it. Willie was right in broad moral terms, but he hadn't seen what smart lawyers could do with the wishy-washy, circumstantial ramblings of a sick old man. I'd have a vicious crime syndicate on my tail, and in the end nobody would even go to jail.

I said goodbye, walked up my walk, unlocked the back door. Inside, I bent down to scratch the dog, and groaned in pain. That was a mistake. Jane, awake and going over files in the kitchen, heard me.

"Kit, you look pale as a ghost. What on earth . . . ?" Percentage wiggled around me in circles, bringing me one gift after another—two chewbones, a ball, a ragged piece of rawhide.

First, we went through a family rundown—how she was, what Emily's teachers had said, how Ben seemed, how Percentage was walking. We had a shorthand term for this—"Do the rundown," one or another of us would say on a busy day. It was a way of staying abreast.

Only after that did I tell Jane about my late evening adventures in mafia-land. The Neck knew how to inflict damage. The pain where I'd been punched was a small but vivid reminder of how powerful and frightening this bunch could be. Imagine what they could do if they really meant to cause harm. Dale Lewis had been crazy to get mixed up with these people; he'd paid dearly for his hubris.

Jane ordered me into bed and administered ice packs and herbal tea, clucking and fussing. She muttered about my going to the emergency room and fired off several grade B platitudes like, "Internal injuries are nothing to fool around with, Kit." Mothers are mothers, no matter what else they choose or need to do with their lives.

Snuggling in bed, we talked about Ben—she thought he seemed less angry, "easier"—and I asked her advice about my case. Why, I asked, would Jacob Logovitz be helpful to a meddling PI?

"He's doing life review," she replied. Psychotalk. Therapists, like bureaucrats, have special words for everything, as though people won't appreciate their wisdom if they use normal language. That's how problems become "issues." Life review, she explained, noticing my skeptical expression, meant Logovitz was increasingly conscious of his mortality, toting up his achievements and debts and unfinished business, considering how he would be remembered after he died. Clearly, the old man had different standards than most of us: he was willing to be remembered as a gangster. But he had his limits: he wanted his slate clean of Linda Lewis's murder.

My head swam with unexplored theories, undigested information, confusion, guilt. Should I take Logovitz's advice and forget about Dale, thus permitting a vicious mobster to direct my investigation? Did I have a single clue or reasonable theory about how or why Linda was killed? Had I begun the process of patching things up with my son, or was I kidding myself? Was my infiltration of the Fathers' Club appropriate under the circumstances or a smarmy betrayal of a group of gutsy men sincerely trying to help one another?

I'd felt stunned by the depth of feeling that surfaced during the Ricky Melman discussion. I had never seen anything quite like it. It seemed a small, commonplace thing—one more man deciding whether to torpedo his family or preserve it—but I knew it was an enormous one for the people concerned. And we had gotten involved, altered the proceedings, perhaps even saved his family great suffering. Even if Melman ultimately left his wife, it might be less shattering, a considered, supervised decision everyone could prepare for. I saw so many families busted up, not just in my work, but simply as a neighbor, a resident of this town. Jane and I often shook our heads when we thought of the families who had moved to Rochambeau about when we did—Sue and Billy, who split up because she cared about nothing but redecorating her house; Jan and Peter, who divorced over some ugly affair; Donna and Stan, whose relationship disintegrated when his career fell apart and hers took off. Such couples seemed to pass out of our lives. They sold their houses and moved; their kids went to different schools; they made new friends. We lost the thread of their lives, kids and adults alike. Maybe the Melmans' story would have a different ending.

Jane had drifted off to sleep, her dark head on my shoulder, but I was still wound up from my day. I was supposed to meet with Bev Cadawaller in just a few hours and the marathon would begin again.

I had to start making some headway in this case. Aside from the fact that I wasn't getting paid—and I wasn't some hotshot corporate lawyer who could work pro bono for weeks—I had a growing list of other cases that needed tending.

Yet I seemed to have few avenues to explore in terms of Linda's death. I hadn't learned one new thing about it, didn't have a single promising lead. I decided I should explore Battelle's relationship with Linda and Dale more thoroughly, learn something about Cadawaller and her involvement with Dale (and maybe somehow with Linda, too?) and untangle the monumental mess that represented Dale's business. I wanted to talk to Jim Rheems, too. I had to at least consider the possibility that he was angrier at Dale than he let on. But if that made him a suspect in the first murder, it hardly explained the second. Why would Rheems kill Linda? What motive could he possibly have? I also had this nagging feeling that I'd overlooked something at my audience with Jacob Logovitz.

Eventually, even my racing mind slowed down and I fell asleep.

I often wake up muttering, with sheets and blankets knotted around me, but I can never remember what I've been dreaming. I remember this dream, though.

Ben was sitting on a bench, in what looked like Rochambeau Municipal Park. Blood trickled down his face from a wound on his forehead. It ran in a dark stream down into his lap where it spread in a widening stain. He was partially slumped over, unnoticed, completely alone. He sat quietly, not crying or calling until he looked up. "Dad?" he asked softly. "I got hurt. I'm sorry."

I couldn't reach him. I had the sensation of running but not going anywhere, of shouting but not being heard. I watched the life drain out of him as he kept apologizing. He didn't seem to hear me or, if he did, he couldn't or wouldn't respond. Yet he showed no trace of anger or resentment; there was a soft, almost baby-like sweetness about his face, the look I remembered so well from when he was small. He closed his eyes.

Then I noticed Linda Lewis sitting on a bench across the park;

Dale stood behind her. She was smiling as a long parade of baby strollers rolled slowly by. The park was filled with happy sounds—dogs barking, kids laughing, mothers calling out soft admonitions to "Be careful," "Watch the swing," and "Don't get too close to the pond." Other than Dale, there were no men anywhere.

I screamed at Ben to wake up, but he didn't. Shouting for help, I ran frantically out of the park, and was suddenly on my own street, tired and panting. Sweat poured down my face.

My street was deserted and absolutely still—no minivans or station wagons, no wagons or toys on the lawns, no sounds of leaf blowers or mowers, no men with briefcases rushing for the train to the city or ambling back home. Rochambeau looked as if a neutron bomb had wiped out all the people but left the buildings intact. Or as if, without warning, it had been evacuated. Why, I remember thinking, wouldn't there be signs of panic, stuff left behind, barking dogs? The houses had been emptied of life.

When I entered my own house, Percentage didn't greet me. He sat in the playroom staring out the window, angrily, as if somehow I had offended him. I called out for Jane, but she wasn't home; she must have been at school. Emily didn't answer either. Upstairs, I saw a light on in Ben's room. I tried to open the door, but it was locked.

I woke suddenly, pulse pounding, teeth clenched, haunted by the image of that locked door.

"A suburban nightmare," said Jane when I told her about it in the morning. I guess it was.

Eighteen

I NEVER GOT BACK to sleep. At dawn I slipped out of bed, showered and decided to take Percentage for an early morning walk. He struggled to his feet, wiggled his off-balance retriever wiggle, and brought me a present from the laundry hamper, a pair of Jane's underpants. Percentage's little perversion: he adored Jane's undergarments, snatching them off the bed, sleeping with them if he could, presenting them as gifts to dinner guests, in the days when we used to have dinner guests. I pried this pair out of his mouth, which necessitated a friendly little tussle. Jane, fortunately, was dead to the world.

As I did every morning, I tiptoed past the kids' rooms. Ben's door was usually closed, but it was open this morning, I was relieved to see. A pile of CDs and music magazines was climbing at the side of his bed, as always. He'd forgotten to turn off his computer monitor; I bet he'd been up half the night yakking with invisible girlfriends on-line. As in my nightmare, he looked deceptively sweet-faced and angelic in his sleep.

I thought of how true all the clichés are: life is short, kids grow up in a blink. I wanted to be able to talk with Ben easily when he was an adult, to have lunch in the city now and then when he could take time off from the important drama he was directing or the case he was trying. To trade books and squawk about how the country was going to hell in a handbasket. I wanted to go for long walks at the shore, exchanging insights about the meaning of life. I'd give him sage advice; he'd fuss about my getting more exercise. I pictured lots of laughing and pats on the shoulder, not blood streaming from his head.

What did a dream like that mean? Jane would say it was easy: the helplessness of the parent, the child moving beyond reach, the fear opened like a vein by the week's events, my anguish at losing a client.

I wanted what I think most men want, at the core—to die knowing I had done well by my children and family, worked hard for them, given them safety and support and guided their way into the world as gently and wisely as I could. If I died today, I wouldn't have that conviction. So many things were unfinished. My relationship with Ben was being tested. So, in a way, was my partnership with Jane. My tests with Emily were yet to come. I didn't want to blow it. I didn't want to be one of those men who spend years lamenting the distance between them and their kids, forcing themselves to have tortured, uncomfortable talks with their offspring to try to mend the damage, most of which couldn't be repaired.

Emily was tossing and turning a bit. Unlike her brother, she liked her room organized—books here, stuffed animals there, five garish colors of nail polish on the shelf, everything in its proper place. Like her mother. Ben seemed only to care that his possessions were in his general vicinity and lived amid growing piles of clutter. Like his father.

The coffee smelled tantalizing as I headed downstairs. Despite our woeful financial state (it was beginning to dawn on me this would not be a temporary thing) Jane and I had indulged in a $125 automatic coffee maker that could be preset the night before so that we woke to freshly brewed coffee. Mornings were always hectic—feeding and walking the dog, getting breakfasts going, rousing the kids, bringing in and clucking over the paper. Besides, there was no such thing as a crisis-free morning. Sometimes Percentage had barfed on the floor. Emily's favorite time to remember overdue science projects was 7:30 A.M. Jane had to testify in a sex abuse case in two hours and couldn't find her file. God, how I envied June Cleaver.

So all labor-saving devices were cherished. I poured coffee into my favorite mug, a huge white ceramic affair with Percentage's photo reproduced on the side, a birthday present from both kids.

They liked to rib me about how I loved Percentage more than I loved them. My stock reply was, "No, I love you more than the dog. But not by all that much."

I wanted this to be a longish walk, if the dog's leg held up. I had a lot of thinking to do before I finally met Bev Cadawaller at the Roadway Diner. Outside, the lights were beginning to pop on in the houses of legal titans and Wall Street go-getters, who liked to be on the six-fifteen to Penn Station. And somewhere down the road someone had managed to set off his burglar alarm while bringing in the paper.

At six-thirty the Hedenbergs would start screaming at one another, four doors down. It had taken me a while to figure out that this was just their method of communicating: they were from Brooklyn. Accordingly, no one in the family thought it out of the ordinary to hear Harold Hedenberg bellow, "This is the *third* time I've told you kids to get *up*. I'm *not* going to tell you *again!*" Sometimes I heard them shrieking back, "Okay, *Okay*. We're *not* deaf!" The Hedenbergs' bellowing had become a part of my morning routine. I was stunned when I met them a few months ago at Emily's school: they were sweet, loving, soft-spoken.

Soon the first wave of dog walkers would appear, people holding scoopers in one hand and coffee mugs or papers in the other, in a rush to get the dogs to do their stuff so they could head off to work. On weekends the dog walkers loved to chat and let the dogs sniff each other, but workday etiquette required that you save your visits for another time. It also permitted people to dash out of their houses for the morning paper in bathrobes or pajamas while passersby looked the other way.

At six-forty-five there'd be a major flurry, especially in homes where both Mom and Dad worked, or where there was only Mom or, as was the case with our neighbors, two working moms. The exodus would be in full tilt, men and women rushing the kids off to day care, greeting incoming nannies, walking briskly toward trains and buses.

At seven-thirty the town came alive with the roar of school buses. With the commuters going or gone, this was the moment when control passed to the stay-at-home moms, once the most powerful element in towns like Rochambeau, now a dwindling, increasingly uneasy minority. Moms were only visible for a few years, since sometime in middle school it became uncool to be escorted to the bus by your parents. Before that, though, kids and mothers gathered in clusters by the bus stops, the moms reminding them to turn in their homework, eat all their lunch and not throw things on the bus, pretending to wave cheerfully but no doubt feeling little stabs of pain each time the bus pulled away.

At eight, the workers came out: yard crews with blowers and trimmers, plumbers and roofers, town workers cleaning sewers and collecting the recycled newspapers.

By nine things had quieted. The town was left to the housewives and the nannies and their little charges.

My work was at odds with the rhythm of life of my own community. I'd moved here a new suburbanite, an applicant to the great dream of comfort, safety, education and pleasure, of languorous backyard barbecues and pretty parks to walk your big slobbery dog in.

But my career change had dramatically altered all that. I had deliberately inverted my life; I lived on the darker edges of the dream. I had become an outsider, different, now, from the people I strolled past every day. And they could sense it. They were perfectly cordial, but there was always distance between us. I could never be like them again, never have the same sense of safety and opportunity, never feel the well-being many of them felt when they got all their furniture unpacked, first saw the kids off on the bus, visited the gifted and talented department of the crafts shop downtown to buy their gifted and talented chunks of clay.

The irony was, the work that took me into the innermost corners of their lives doomed me to a lifetime outside. There was no going back to the old sensibility. However many times Percentage or I walked by, nodded and smiled, bantered about the weather, I was now a stranger in paradise.

Nineteen

ASIDE FROM a few precious acres of horse country and five blocks of Hoboken, the beautiful people shun New Jersey like the plague. Models and performance artists do not gather at nouvelle hot spots in Jersey. Painters don't come here for the light.

We do, however, have diners. Quick, sensibly priced, rotating desserts in glass cases, surrounded by plentiful parking. Great, gleaming diners that dot the state's many ugly highways like wondrous beacons amid the miles of malls, banner-festooned car dealerships and discount warehouses.

The Roadway, where I was meeting Bev Cadawaller, was a proud representative of its species. Above its shiny aluminum roof a neon sign advised, EAT HEAVY AND OFTEN. The Roadway's menu was vast, a trove of cholesterol, hundreds of offerings on laminated sheets.

I had never managed to finish any order at the Roadway. Toast came in eight slices, slathered in butter unless you gave explicit instructions to serve it dry. Sandwiches came in three tiers, surrounded by masses of french fries. The shortest pancake stack was four.

The waitresses wore spotless pink uniforms and looked like linebackers. You got coffee refills whether you asked for them or not. If you had a problem with the food, it was immediately returned to the kitchen without elaboration or discussion. The check came instantly. The staff did not tell you their names, make recommendations, advise you what was good today or chitchat about the weather. The only thing that made them smile and kibbitz was children, who were slipped free cookies.

I spotted Bev Cadawaller before she spotted me. She'd been reading the business cards thumbtacked to a corkboard in the vestibule, though I doubted architects advertised there. "Kit Deleeuw?" she asked as I approached her. Tall and slender in slacks, a white silk blouse and a dark blazer, she was quite beautiful, with thin, angular features and intense eyes. She stood out as distinctly from the half-asleep regulars as if she'd been holding a flaming torch.

"Yes. How did you know?"

"Just a guess. You're not wearing gold, your shirt is not unbuttoned down to your waist, and you're not in jeans." She smiled.

We shook hands and were led by a hostess in pink to a booth with aqua seats. Cadawaller set her oversized briefcase—stuffed with sketches, I presumed—on the seat next to her and studied me.

"Come here often?" I asked.

"All the time. Every architect loves diners," she replied. "They're a uniquely American expression, a chance to blend fun with utility." Her teeth were gleaming white and straight. She wore a thin silver chain, holding some sort of green gemstone, around her neck. If she felt any discomfort or unease about meeting a private investigator to discuss a murdered lover, it didn't show.

Rita—the waitresses all wore name tags—hovered in her pink uniform. "Help you?"

"I'll just have coffee. Black," said Cadawaller.

"Coffee and wheat toast, dry," I said. I had eaten at home after my walk with Percentage, but I was afraid of what Rita might do if we occupied a whole booth for just two cups of coffee. Rita shrugged as if to say, "I don't give a shit what you eat or don't eat, pal."

Cadawaller glanced at her watch. "I've only got a few minutes. How can I help you, Mr. Deleeuw? I know you're going to broach some delicate subjects relating to Dale and his family; I'm prepared for that. I'll answer your questions the best I can. I've already talked to the police and told them all this as well. It would probably be best if we got it over with as quickly as possible. Okay?"

"When did you talk to the police? And to whom, if you don't mind my asking?"

"I don't remember her name. A black woman, very direct, very sharp. Began with a P."

"Danielle Peterson?"

"Right. I guess some of my stationery and papers were still in Dale's office. I told Officer Peterson all about our business relationship."

Rita slapped two steaming cups of coffee and an aluminum pitcher of milk down on the table. "Toast's coming," she said, sailing off to the next table, which was occupied by four elderly women out for breakfast, their pantsuits the colors of tropical birds.

"About your working relationship with Dale—I'm not exactly clear on the details."

She ran her finger over the gleaming Formica tabletop, making no move to drink her coffee. "The last five years have been rough on architects, Mr. Deleeuw. A lot of firms went under, money was scarce. My father—he passed away last year—was a real estate lawyer; he urged me to get involved in housing development. There aren't many grand design opportunities in New Jersey, although occasionally an interesting residential opportunity presents itself, but there is a lot of work. The government has earmarked millions of dollars in grants and subsidies for building housing in suburbia for moderate- and low-income families and the elderly. So I work as a free-lance architect. I go from firm to firm, as these housing projects come in, and help them with blueprints, mock-ups and sketches. I take jobs where I can find them, and so far," she said, "I've held my own. I don't want to do this forever, but I've had a far easier time of it than my classmates, many of whom are building strip malls in places like Galveston."

My toast arrived. Rita deposited it without comment.

"Dale first called me two years ago to work on a project called Cedar Ridge. He was a land developer, he told me, who was working more and more in this area, getting grant money from HUD to design garden apartment complexes for people who couldn't traditionally afford them. He had come up with what he called a 'utopian vision.' "

My eyebrows went up at that. She noticed.

"It *was* a pretty exciting idea," she said. "Dale wanted designs for new kinds of small communities, with a few dozen free-standing homes adjoined by T-shaped apartment complexes. His notion was for all the single-family homes to be upper-income. A fourth of the apartment units would be for the elderly, a fourth low-income, and half middle class. Those who could afford it would buy their houses and apartments; the poor families would gain equity by occupying and maintaining their units for ten years. Each development would have a magnet school, a community center and a sports and recreational complex with a swimming pool. Dale had this elaborate rebate system worked out—the longer you stayed, the lower your mortgage payments were. To encourage people to hang in there and not leave at the first sign of problems. I loved the idea. I was happy to design it."

I took a few notes. "Sounds like a pretty ambitious concept for somebody who didn't have much of a background in housing."

"Not completely," she answered coolly, sipping her coffee. "Dale studied architecture before he switched to finance. He visited a bunch of public and private housing developments, talking to people, taking an idea here or there. It's a shame about him. . . ." She sighed. "He had a lot of talent, a lot of drive. He just had this habit of overreaching. He wanted to give his family everything: money for college, for grad school, vacations, his retirement. He had this fantasy that he could take all the big worries off his kids' shoulders; all they'd have to do was pick work they loved. It was sweet. But I warned him that you couldn't buy happiness for other people, not even your kids. You had to leave them their own successes and failures."

She'd urged me to get down to business, so I did. "Did you discuss these things while you were having an affair?" I asked.

"God, I hate that word," she muttered. "Affair? What does it mean, anyway? We had a relationship, yes. We loved each other for a while. I'm not ashamed of it; it was lovely for both of us. I'm sorry his wife found out, I'm sure it caused her great pain. But I really cared for Dale. He had a powerful vision and we shared it. It could have transformed the suburbs. This was one thing the suburbs hadn't figured out how to do: get different kinds of people to live together in the same community. But he was having horrid problems getting anybody to give him financing for Cedar Ridge. He was borrowing money from his friends, from his wife . . . It was getting scary." She shook her head. "He seemed obsessed with it. I guess his wife was getting suspicious. One night when he was leaving my apartment she was sitting out there in her car, watching. She was classy about it, told him they'd talk when they got home. They tried to work it out, but I guess the marriage never recovered." She flipped her dark hair back over her shoulders.

This was a very poised Other Woman. No, I volunteered, the marriage didn't ever recover. "Linda never gave you a hard time? Threatened you in any way?"

"No. In fact, I never spoke to her, before or after that night. She looked at me from her car that night, then just drove off. Dale told me she was upset, of course, and soon afterward he and I both agreed to stop seeing each other socially. But we continued to work together. I used his office in Rochambeau. I gave him a series of designs for different kinds of mixed-dwelling communities, different percentages of private homes versus apartments, different combinations of incomes and ages. Kimball Associates still owes me $10,000 for these designs. I doubt I'll collect now. And before you ask: I never really knew many of the details of his business. He never was very specific about the financing he was getting."

I took a few more notes. "Bev, do these names mean anything to you? Ricky Melman?"

"No. Never heard that name."

"Jim Rheems?"

"I met with Rheems and Dale once. He wanted to look at the designs for one of our communities, the best one, I think—Sharing Grove. I believe he lent Dale some money."

"What was Sharing Grove?"

Her eyes took on a faraway look. "Oh, it was a dream place. Dale really thought he was going to make his mark with it. Frankly, so did I. I see now that we were playing God, in a way, trying to create a whole new world. Sharing Grove was going to revolutionize housing, be a new kind of multi-use, mixed-income community. Dale even bought a chunk of land out near Newton. We would drive out there once or twice a week—the school would go here, the lake would be there, the cultural center, the day care center up the hill." I saw she had teared up. I had never heard about the land before. I wondered if Dale had told anybody else about it.

"That was the beautiful part of Dale, the part I fell in love with. It's always the dreamers like that who do the beautiful things, who create things that last." She sighed again. "Unfortunately, these people rarely have mastery of details, like money or zoning. Or politics. They can dream, but they never have any economic clout or other kinds of know-how. So they make messes."

"What kind of messes?"

"Oh, financial and legal messes. Dale was always ducking phone calls, evading some bill collector or creditor. He preyed on his friends for money. He was desperate to get funding. He got more and more agitated, tired and strung out. He even said he wanted to stay away from his family for a while . . . which really shocked me. He and Linda had separated by then, but he was utterly devoted to Liz and Noah. He and his wife had worked really hard to stay in touch, work out problems together, be civil. They were quite good friends, actually. I admired her for that."

"Was Dale seeing anybody else that you know?"

"I can't say for sure. But I doubt it. When we had our fling, he was nearly taken over with this dream, what Sharing Grove would do for him, his family and the suburbs. He was building a new kind of suburb, he said. Suburbs would never be the same."

It did sound revolutionary. Racially and culturally, the suburbs were more diverse than ever these days, with the African-American and Latino middle class moving into communities like Rochambeau in a steady flow and gay parents showing up at PTA meetings. But the burbs sure weren't economically more diverse. You could move to Rochambeau if you had three heads and green hands, but if you wanted a modest four-bedroom, those hands had better be clutching a check for $250,000.

Obviously, Linda's version of events had at least some truth to it. She and Dale *had* been close, and it did sound like he was a devoted father. It also sounded like he was fearful, toward the end, that he might endanger his family by being around them too much. Seemed like he was right, too.

"And what about David Battelle?"

At that name, she winced visibly, showing more emotion than she'd shown about anything so far. "Where are you getting these names? Were they all in Dale's address book?" Cadawaller obviously had never heard about the men's group. She reached into her canvas bag and pulled out a pack of menthol cigarettes. Smokers were still welcome in the Roadway.

"David Battelle is . . . well . . . was another one of Dale's friends, another person who loaned him money, I think. One of the people we met with and showed designs to. He . . . I didn't like him. He was nasty and patronizing to Dale, as if Dale was some ignorant kid who didn't have a clue." And he might have been right, I thought, but didn't say so.

"Somehow, Battelle found out about Dale and me. He called me up, I guess this was six months ago, well after Dale and I had stopped . . . seeing each other outside of work. . . ." She took a long drag.

"I remember him saying that even though some people figured it was dangerous to play around with people you worked with, he thought it was a great idea. Then he asked if I wanted to play around with him. There was something creepy about him. I mean, I'm a single woman who's interested in men, but this guy . . . And Dale told me Battelle was really furious about the money Dale owed him. He also told me—I guess I ought to tell you this—that Battelle had repeatedly come on to Linda. Dale was none too happy about that."

"So you never went out with Battelle?"

"No, I'd rather go out with an eel." I was a little taken aback by the level of her hostility. Battelle seemed acerbic and edgy—and he clearly had a temper—but he didn't seem as vile as she described. I pressed her, but all she would say was that he "creeped her out."

Cadawaller told me she had at least a dozen projects going, and one of them looked as if it might lead to a job in a hot young Washington firm. So she would be leaving New Jersey soon. It was sad, she said, that Dale's dream wasn't going to materialize.

"But why not?" I asked. "If it was such a good idea and the federal government is so hot to see mixed-income housing in the burbs, why couldn't someone make it fly?"

She waved to Rita for a refill, then smiled thinly. "Well, that's what I mean about Dale being a dreamer. First off, the mob is all over land development in New Jersey. Everyone seems to have known this except Dale and me. It runs all these scams to get subsidies and construction grants, using dummy companies. The dummy companies collect money, then they default on loans or find toxic waste . . . a million things can derail a project. The mob controls all the construction unions, too. One project I worked on, this front company applied to HUD for a subsidy for mixed housing in Bergen County. It got a million dollars up front, followed by a raft of environmental, zoning and other delays. The 'company' went bankrupt, the 'plan' got put on hold, its real owners stay hidden behind twenty layers of corporations, banks and holding companies. For a million dollars in taxpayers' money, all you had to show was one huge hole in the ground and some crummy plans from a lousy architect they probably own. But you probably know about these things, being a private investigator. There are all kinds of land-use and construction scams going on. I don't even know if the government knows much about it."

Oh, I thought, it does, it does. But there was no point in passing that on. The less anybody knew about it, the better. I didn't even like knowing about it myself.

She turned her coffee cup in a slow, lazy circle on its saucer. "Dale had so much—a wife he loved, two kids he was crazy about. Why would he throw all that away?"

I frowned. It was an odd statement. "What makes you say he threw it away, Bev? For all we know, some crackhead followed him off the street and killed him for the ten bucks in his wallet. Why do you assume Dale helped bring about his own death?"

I thought I saw a flicker of fear behind those self-assured green eyes, though not for very long. "At first, I thought he'd killed himself," she said. "He was so deep over his head, I figured he just despaired about paying back what he owed. When I heard that the police thought he'd been murdered, I assumed he'd somehow gotten in over his head. Fallen in with the proverbial bad crowd. I don't have any inside information for you, Mr. Deleeuw. The whole time we were together, Dale was digging that hole that got him killed. Day and night—big ideas, more and more loans, more desperation. It was hard to be stunned when the hole swallowed him up."

"Were you sad?"

"Sure. But I'm not the falling-apart-and-sobbing type. I'm over Dale. What we had together was really finished. I came to see him as wonderful but profoundly self-destructive."

"And how angry was Linda?" I asked.

"Not angry enough to kill him."

"And she never did anything to you? Never tried to get you fired? Made threats?"

She shook her head. "If you're looking for some reason in this universe for me to kill Linda Lewis, Mr. Deleeuw, you won't find it. My relationship with her husband was over. I'm an architect with prospects, and no reason to jeopardize that." I couldn't think of one either.

She looked up at the clock. She was getting antsy.

"Look, Mr. Deleeuw, I have to be in Philadelphia in two hours. You've probably already talked to this man, but if you haven't, you ought to check with Dale's adviser, his lawyer. . . ."

I waited. Surely she didn't know about Logovitz. "Battelle?"

"No," she said, "Dale never took Battelle's advice. This was an attorney who went over all Dale's paperwork. What was his name? I was at his office once, waiting in the car while Dale dropped some documents off. A big old restored Victorian in Livingston."

"You mean Charlie Montgomery?"

"Yes, I think that's it," she said. "He knew all about Dale's business affairs."

We said our goodbyes by the cash register and I watched her hop into her gleaming new Saab and roar off down Route 46. Then, in the vestibule, I fished the cell phone from my jacket pocket, called Information, then dialed Charlie Montgomery's office.

It was a bit early, but he came right on. He was obviously not happy to hear from me, though. His voice was like dry ice. "I didn't expect to hear from you again, Kit. Not after last night. I felt extremely responsible. . . . I should have checked you out more thoroughly. . . . I—"

"Charlie, I appreciate this, but we'll have to do the postmortem some other time. How come you never mentioned that you were Dale's lawyer in his development deals? Did the others in the group know?"

There was a long pause. Then Montgomery said, "No. They didn't."

"Why not?"

"Dale wanted it that way. Attorney-client privilege. I can't tell you anything about it, other than I was his lawyer, and I was very concerned about him and the direction he was taking. But he was adamant that our working relationship be kept absolutely separate from the men's group and that I never discuss his business with anyone. And I won't."

"Not even with the police?"

"Not unless I am compelled to do so by a court or grand jury. Look—I'm not a believer in arguments, especially when they're pointless. But what you did to our group was awful, Kit. A total betrayal. We talked openly, we tried to help you, and Ricky was very appreciative of your advice, I know. We were staggered to learn your real agenda. Staggered," he repeated.

I listened to the trucks whining by on the highway. Cadawaller was probably already twenty miles down the road. She would go far, I suspected—literally and metaphorically.

"I told you I'm truly sorry about that, Charlie. I was impressed by the group, and I learned a lot from it, too. I would be happy to meet with everybody, together or individually, if you thought it would do the slightest good. But I felt I had no choice but to do what I did. And I'd probably do the same thing again, if I had to."

He remained polite but chilly. "I can mention it, maybe after they've cooled off. Feelings were running pretty deep last night. I can understand your position. Murder is pretty serious stuff. At least we weren't betrayed for something trivial, for insurance fraud, as Hal put it."

He didn't go further and I didn't press him. I would have liked to talk to the people in the group again. I felt I owed them that. But I still had a dead client on my hands and on my conscience.

"So there's nothing you can tell me about Dale's business dealings?"

"Only that he didn't take my advice. Frankly, I don't even know why he paid me for it. He was headed on a self-destructive course, and I told him that many times. I also told Jim Rheems to stay the hell out of it. I torment myself constantly with the thought that I should have done more. But you can't force a client to do what you suggest or a friend, either." He sounded pretty low about that.

"I wish you the best," he said in a let's-wind-it-up tone. "What you said to Ricky the other night, well, it bugged me. It struck close to home, as you probably sensed. But it was on-the-money advice, just the kind men sometimes need to hear. If I'd heard it a few years ago, my daughter might not hate my guts now."

Twenty

I HUNG UP the phone, walked out to the diner's parking lot.

The lawyer-client stuff made sense, sort of. I could see Dale wanting it that way, wanting a wall between his men's group and his business. But if that was his preference, why blur the lines so much? Why turn your group members into your creditors? And there were other lawyers. Maybe Dale knew that members of his own men's group were far more inclined to take him seriously and might lend him money for his great scheme more readily than banks or strangers.

Everyone in the group seemed to have a connection to Dale— except for the onetime teacher Frank Dougherty, and I expected any second to learn that he'd given Dale title to an old family property outside Dublin.

I noticed that my ancient Volvo was blocked by a car angled in front of it, which was strange. I didn't notice until I got closer that the other car was the black Chrysler sedan I'd last seen as I'd ridden in it on the way to Totowa General to look at Linda Lewis's body. Detective Sergeant Danielle Peterson sat behind the wheel munching a glazed doughnut. A foam cup I'd bet held coffee was on the dashboard.

"Aren't you out of your jurisdiction, Sergeant?" Actually, I was glad to see her.

"Not as far out of my jurisdiction as you are over your head, Mr.

Deleeuw. Hell, I sashayed in there as plain as day, the only African-American in the joint, to order my doughnut and coffee, and Rochambeau's most famous private eye was sitting ten feet away with the knockout other woman."

"Following me? Hey, you had no business—"

"Oh, chill, Kit. I'm just bored. Evelyn told me where you were. I got nervous 'cause you hadn't checked in lately. The chief *always* gets a little cranky when you and the Rochambeau PD are working the same homicide. Maybe that's 'cause you wiped his ass on the last two. He doesn't want any more surprises. Are there any? Besides your having tea with Russian mobsters in Jersey City?"

"So that's what brought you out? The Feebies yanking your chain?"

"You bet that's what brought me out, Deleeuw. Two mightily pissed-off organized-crime task force agents were in the chief's office this morning before he could even unscrew the Cremora jar. You walked right into their surveillance, and now they're freaking out about what the hell you were doing there. Seeing as how they regard you as Ivan Boesky's confidant, anyway, you sure rang their bells, pal. Seems you were not exactly a cooperative little private eye. They want the chief to squeeze you by threatening to go to the state licensing board. For refusing to cooperate in an ongoing felony investigation. So the chief sends me out, knowing, I'm sure, that we're pals."

She shook her head. Danielle Peterson was awestruck at the amount of trouble I could manage to get myself into in one middle-class New Jersey suburb. "The Feds want to drag you along the parkway behind one of their cars, leaving pieces of you all the way to Asbury Park. They do not foresee a warm relationship with you. And of course, taking your license is always a tempting proposition for the chief. Not that he dislikes you, but you have proven to be a giant pain in his butt. So here I am."

Danielle knew how to squeeze. She was my friend, genuinely concerned about me, but foremost, she was a good homicide cop. She wanted to know what I knew. One thing she already knew damn well was that I could not afford to lose my shield. She wanted some cooperation, meant to get it, and knew just how to get it.

I scraped one foot back and forth in feigned aw-shucks shyness.

"Well, maybe I know a couple of little things that you and the chief don't," I said, smiling.

"Get in the damned car. Then we'll both know." I climbed in and she pulled into a quieter corner of the lot, turned off the engine, picked up her coffee and turned to me. Her expression was serious.

"Look, friend, I'm worried about you. You have just gone from sandlot ball to Yankee Stadium. You've nobody behind you but that retired witch from the library, your cute computer freak and a Cuban fast-food guy. What the fuck is going on? You know who Logovitz is? You know who these agents are? They're crack anticrime ball busters from Washington, the crème de la crème. They'll get a warrant and take the insulation right off your walls just for kicks if you get smart with them, understand? They'll have your license for a snack, then go suck your money right out of your bank account and hold it for ten years while your ass gets bounced from one grand jury to another. You know what these people can do? And if *they* don't do it, the Russian mob will. These guys have iced twenty people in the last few years. Man, I never thought you were this dumb."

Put that way, she had a point. The Russian mob and the FBI were a lot to take on for no fee. Not to mention the Rochambeau PD, which had already thrown me in jail once for obstructing justice and would be only too happy to do so again. "All right, I hear you, Danielle. I even appreciate what you're saying. But somebody killed my client. That makes it something I can't run away from, okay? I'm not flexible about my clients being killed. I get a little stubborn about that."

She knew it was true. I'm no hero. I've never once taken my gun out of my safe. Almost anybody who wanted to punch out my lights could, and a diverse array of vermin, Deadbeat Dads, insurance cheats and outraged citizens already had. But nobody killed my clients. Nobody harmed my family. Those were just two things I couldn't let go of.

"Look, Danielle, I do have some stuff I don't think you have," I offered. "I'll trade it. But I need a huge favor. And I need it now."

Her eyebrows went up. "Your response to what I just told you is to ask ME for a favor? Is this what they mean by balls the size of a dinosaur? What the fuck—"

"Look, Danielle, give me a break, okay? Get me this one bit of information. Then be at my office at three and I'll tell you every-thing I know, I swear it. You can tell the chief. You know I wouldn't set you up like this and not produce."

She emptied her cup before replying. "What's the favor?"

I pulled out a Post-it and scribbled several names on it.

"Maybe your FBI buddies will help you. Maybe Tagg can. I just need to know if these names ring any bells on the FBI's surveil-lance records from Logovitz's house in Jersey City. The old man can't go out much and he can't trust the phones: almost anybody doing business with him would have to go there to him. I need to see if any of these people show up as visitors. Please. And if you can't help, I'll still spill everything at three at the mall. My office. Okay?"

She glared, looking both worried and pissed. "You're a smart investigator, Kit, you know I think so, but you have this reckless streak. Understand that I can't push these people. They say no, it's no. I won't stick my neck out another inch. You can be the rebel investigator on your own. I've got a pension to protect, and I'm a single parent."

My own son's face flashed through my mind. "Agreed."

"And don't go getting yourself killed before this afternoon. Hear me?" she shouted as I dashed for the Volvo.

I eased onto the highway, checking my rearview mirror to see if anybody was following. I pulled over suddenly into a gas station to see if anybody behind me hesitated or pulled over as well. Back on the highway, I darted suddenly for an onrushing exit to see if any-body else did the same. Satisfied that I wasn't being followed, and feeling intensely wily, I called Evelyn on the cell phone.

She sounded upset. "Kit, Danielle Peterson said it was life and death that I tell her where you were. I thought you might be in trouble. Normally, I—"

"It's okay, Evelyn, you did the right thing. You can trust Dan-ielle. And you have to use your best judgment. I'm heading out to Lincoln Township. Can you look in the phone book and find an address for a Frank or Francis Dougherty? And can you put Willie on?"

He came on in a heartbeat. "Hey, Chief. How are you feeling?"

"Better. Are you?" I told him about the FBI's late night visit and my talk with Bev Cadawaller. "Willie, have you made any headway on looking into Linda's will?"

"No, Chief, it's too soon for it to show up. The probate court clerk won't even tell me over the phone if it's been filed yet. Want me to go to the courthouse?"

"Sure, and I also want you to check out a few things in federal bankruptcy court, okay? I'm just fishing, but maybe we'll catch something. I'd like to know more about who's broke and who isn't. If the will isn't on file yet, call Linda's mother. Maybe she knows something." He said he was already on the way.

Evelyn came back on the line with Dougherty's address—56 Hope Street—and with directions she'd gotten from a county street map while I'd been talking to Willie. Evelyn can be chillingly efficient.

Lincoln Township was half an hour away, a recently rural community rapidly being suburbanized, judging by all the new construction. Hope Street was a holdover from its less developed past: its streets were paved but the sidewalks weren't. A couple of dogs ran loose. Amid the newer condos, you could still make out an old farmhouse here and there. The effect was ugly, a hodgepodge of competing strip malls and housing styles. Maybe it would look better in a decade or so.

I drove past number 56 twice. The name "Dougherty" was stenciled on the mailbox that stood at an angle next to the street. There were a couple of softballs and a bat tossed on the lawn, and a beat-up Corolla in the driveway. Pulling in behind it, I glanced around for the ubiquitous busybody, the person in the neighborhood who starts looking for the mail carrier at 11 A.M. and checks out every strange car as if it were carrying Jeffrey Dahmer. Every block had its own resident PI, just waiting to receive some justification for his inveterate snooping. I saw the curtains move in a small split-level across the street and down the block—number 40.

The door of the Dougherty house opened before I could ring the bell. The face staring at me looked very familiar, not because I knew her, but because I knew her type. The woman was in her late thirties, skinny to the point of looking haggard. Her brown hair hung limply around her face. There was a purplish semicircle under one eye, an angry welt on her cheek. She wore an Ohio State sweatshirt under a navy windbreaker, worn jeans, a pair of old sneakers. Before becoming a PI, I had never seen a face like hers. I'd seen it dozens of times since. It was the face of a beaten wife. I was stunned to find it here. But you didn't need to be a PI to see that you don't get bruises like that doing housework.

"You want to pay admission or you gonna tell me what you want?" she hissed.

"Are you okay?" I asked impulsively. Probably a mistake, but I couldn't help it. Over her shoulder, I saw some magazines on the floor and a lampshade tilted at a crazy angle.

"Fine," she snapped. "Now, who are you?"

"My name's Deleeuw. And you are . . . ?"

She hesitated. She didn't have to answer but, after all, the name was on the mailbox. Maybe she was curious about what I was doing there.

"Tessa Dougherty."

"Well, I'm happy to talk to you," I said. I took out my shield and my card. "Look, Ms. Dougherty, I'm a private investigator, checking into a case back in Rochambeau. I had this question that was bugging me. You probably can answer it for me in a flash. Or your husband can. Is he home?"

"Maybe." She was much too suspicious to tell a stranger she was alone in the house.

"I know your husband. I've met him a couple of times." I wondered if she had a clue he belonged to a men's group. I also wondered why he'd joined one, if I was seeing what I thought I was.

I went on cheerfully. As long as they were talking, you had a shot. "Frank told me he was a schoolteacher, here in the township. But I need to reach him, and when I called the school system they said he didn't teach there anymore. Could you tell me where I can find him?"

She looked at my shield again, then back at my face. Anger was replaced with resignation and, I thought, a dose of fear.

"You'll have to talk to Frank about what he is or isn't doing," she said coldly. "I don't speak for him. He'll be home tonight. I have to leave for work now. I was on my way out when you came up on the stoop."

I decided to push a bit. "Look, just tell me where he works; I'll go talk to him there."

She shook her head. Her rush to get out was probably the only reason she had opened the door in the first place. I didn't want to coerce her; she might pay dearly for any wrong judgments. Wherever she worked, she'd probably dealt with lots of questions, enough stares and curt denials and dumb stories about falling down the stairs.

"Look, Ms. Dougherty," I said, "if you need help, you can call me. I know what's going on. I can refer you—"

"You don't know *shit*." She cut me off savagely. "You have no business coming up here and talking to me at all. My husband won't like it. Now please move your car. I'm late and I don't need your help. I don't need *anybody's* help."

I nodded, but slipped my card into the pocket of her windbreaker. "It's not your fault," I said softly. "No matter what, you don't deserve to be hit. Understand? It's not your fault."

She just stared, then closed the door behind her, walked swiftly toward her Corolla without looking back. She sat in the car long after I'd driven down the block and into the back parking lot of an auto upholstering company, where I waited for her to drive past. It wouldn't amaze me if she called at some point. I hoped it wasn't from a hospital emergency room. Jane had taught me that abuse was amazingly complex, that some abused women loved their batterers and protected them to the end. They often saw themselves as responsible, so worthless they had it coming.

I whistled out loud. Frank Dougherty had appeared to be one of the sweetest members of the men's group, genuine and almost elfin in his charm and warmth. Could he really be punching this waif around? I knew that almost any kind of person could be a wife beater, especially when alcohol was involved; I'd already met too many of them in Brooks Brothers shirts and wingtip shoes. But Dougherty was in AA, wasn't he? And he surely appeared to be on the evolved end of the scale. But somebody was beating up this woman. Either Dougherty was doing it, or he wasn't helping put a stop to it.

I decided to go back to the house, to peer in windows or maybe even force a lock, if I had the chance and the snoopy person across the road didn't spot me and call the cops before I learned anything.

I was not pleased, as I sat watching the traffic, to find myself considering Dougherty a possible suspect. There were far too many already.

Bev Cadawaller had no obvious motive to kill either Linda or Dale, with the affair over and her career moving forward. But I suppose it was possible that she had lied to me, that Linda had provoked her or threatened her in some way or forced Dale to end the relationship against Bev's wishes. Bev had seemed notably nonremorseful about an affair with a married man with two small kids. Most people in that situation at least *pretend* to be abashed.

David Battelle might have wanted Dale out of the way to have a shot at Linda—at least he might think he had one. Or he might have been furious at Linda for rejecting him; that was not unprecedented as a motive for murder. And Dale owed him a large chunk of money.

But Logovitz had all but admitted he'd had Dale killed, or had he? I had to be careful not to read more or less into the old man's statement than he'd intended. All he'd really told me for certain was that I shouldn't waste my time poking around into Dale's death. One thing appeared to be true: the world of government-subsidized housing development was a morass of corrupt bureaucracies, graft and organized crime. Maybe the FBI could penetrate it, but Willie and I? It was out of our league.

Battelle had obviously gone after Cadawaller too, and something about the way he did made her think he was a creep. Linda hadn't reacted that way. Why? Just because she was way over on the trusting and forgiving side? Had Battelle done something to Cadawaller that she didn't want to talk about? Her venom toward him didn't quite match the fact that he had expressed interest in her. Maybe there was something there, something in his background, some psychosis or history of assaults on women. It was a long shot, but worth checking out. I made a note on a Post-it.

Of the other group members, Jim Rheems had a powerful motive for being furious at Dale for losing a chunk of his money. He'd admitted he both loved and hated Dale. If Rheems had it in him to kill somebody, I sure hadn't picked up on it.

But I apparently hadn't picked up on Frank Dougherty's real personality either. What else might he be capable of?

Montgomery had withheld knowledge of his relationship with Dale from the men's group, but lawyer-client privilege was a perfectly valid excuse for doing so. I'd have done the same if a client asked me to. It was hard to picture this cautious, successful pillar of the legal community committing a cold-blooded murder. Most murderers I'd met didn't start men's groups. And yet, I was bothered by his role in our discussion the other night; he'd seemed wishy-washy, uncomfortable with blunt talk. Why had he formed a men's group if he didn't want to talk about these things? Maybe it was even more to his credit that he had.

Maybe it was, after all, some drugged carjacker who'd panicked during a botched robbery and shot Linda? It had happened before. Sometimes the truth is obvious, easy, right there on the surface. Tagg could have a point: if it quacks like a duck and waddles like a duck . . .

Finally, I saw the old Corolla and its sad driver leave the block. If Tessa Dougherty had been telling the truth, she was going to work and I had plenty of time alone in the house. But she might have said that just to get rid of me. For all I knew, she'd sped off to warn her husband that I was looking for him.

I got out of the Volvo, inconspicuous in the corner of the empty lot, and locked it. The upholstering company was open, but there didn't seem to be any customers. Three different streets led in and out of the lot. Thick woods bordered both sides of the road back onto Hope Street. It took me less than five minutes to walk there, not bothering to duck when a car passed. In my usual uniform—khaki trousers, blue oxford-cloth shirt, navy blazer—I wasn't suspicious-looking, particularly. Nobody would figure me for a burglar. But everybody would spot me as a stranger, and nobody was favorably inclined toward strangers these days.

There were about twenty houses on the block, two of them old clapboard structures probably dating to the time when the area was mostly farms. The rest were boxy little bungalows like the Doughertys', probably not very old, but not holding up well. People here didn't have the home-maintenance money that went into Rochambeau's Victorians and colonials, though a few of these had been spruced up with flowers in window boxes. I saw two small children playing at the end of the block, fully absorbed in their toys. Trucks and cars whined on the highway nearby and a cat yowled somewhere down the block. In answer, a dog started yapping.

Hope Street was a long cul-de-sac. There'd be little traffic, and only one way out, which was not good. Normally, I would spend a half hour or so checking the street out carefully for housewives, people who were out of work or who worked at night. Maybe I'd even concoct some door-to-door salesman persona. But I couldn't spare half an hour.

I cut over to the south side of the block. Across the street from the Doughertys', the curtain hadn't moved. I walked slowly through the woods until I came to the rear of the Doughertys'. That put me in full view of the rear windows of neighboring houses, but out of sight of the house across the street which, I suspected, housed the block's resident snoop.

I behaved as if I had business there, whistling and looking around. The rear yard was tiny, enclosed by a wire mesh fence with a gate. I walked up to the back entrance, which had a bare light bulb mounted over it, and tried the door. From the adjacent kitchen window, a picture of Jesus stared sadly out at me. Forgive me, I prayed silently, pulling a small lock pick from my jacket pocket. The door's old-fashioned lock popped open in two seconds.

The kitchen smelled of stale food. The porcelain sink was filled with dirty dishes.

I moved through the kitchen into a living room with a big color Sony in one corner, a CD player and VCR piled on top of it. There were a frayed sofa and a couple of love seats. No paintings on the walls, just blown-up family photos of Frank, Tessa and two heavy-set, sullen-looking girls.

I went upstairs to the master bedroom. It, too, was nondescript: queen-size four-poster, a pair of nightstands on either side of the bed, two dressers, a walk-in closet. It looked as though the girls shared the smaller room to the right, festooned with posters of Brad Pitt and Keanu Reeves.

I didn't see a study, books, tapes, papers to grade, or anything else that would indicate a schoolteacher lived here.

Quickly and surgically, as I'd been taught to do, I "tossed" the bedroom, groping under the mattress, opening the drawers of the nightstands. Nothing. I looked through the first dresser: it held women's undergarments and sweaters. It was in the second dresser that I came upon a metallic-smelling, .9mm pistol wrapped in gauze beneath a neatly folded row of boxer shorts.

I'd heard the schools were rough these days, but not that rough. This was an expensive, professional's weapon, not the kind a nervous homeowner keeps around for security. I wondered why Dougherty had left it in a place where any determined searcher (not to mention his own kids) could find it. I wondered if he had a license for it. It was loaded and another clip, oiled and in a cardboard box, was right next to it. I also found a pair of expensive infrared binoculars, ugly spiked brass knuckles, and a knife with a six-inch blade that flicked open at the push of a button. Also nestled among the underwear was a small blackjack, only six inches long but startlingly heavy; applied to the back of the head or the groin, it could put you down in seconds.

Dougherty was a goon, not a teacher. And maybe a killer. Nobody carried brass knuckles for protection. They were for frightening and torturing people. And binoculars like these weren't meant for bird watching. No wonder Tessa Dougherty was terrified.

A siren wailed in the distance. It could be an ambulance or a police car headed for some car crash, but the sound seemed to becoming closer. An instinct told me to get the hell out of there and, when all is said and done, instinct counts. I closed the drawers, sorry to leave the closets unexamined, and trotted back downstairs. Being found in some stranger's house would cost me my license for sure, and for good.

I left by the front entrance, figuring that anyone who'd gotten a look at me entering from the back would be looking for me to leave the same way. I closed the front door as slowly and deliberately as if I were a realtor checking out a prospective client's home, then walked briskly across the street and between two houses, surprising the hell out of the ugly little mutt who had obviously been barking earlier. He was chained, but he raised a din worthy of a Newfoundland, lunging desperately against the chain that tethered him to a pole, eager to take a bite out of me. I bolted into the woods.

Aside from dog walking, I'm not much for exercise. But I'd been a runner in college and, every now and then, had gone through running phases in Rochambeau. I wasn't in as bad shape as I'd thought, maintaining a steady clip through the woods as the dog's barking faded but the sound of sirens drew closer. I could hear the police cruisers screeching onto Hope Street behind me, followed by door slamming and confused shouting.

The cops would go into the Dougherty house—someone on the block probably had a key—and would find nothing missing or disturbed. If some dotty old lady had called in the supposed burglary, the cops would be dubious. Seeing the house intact and the VCR and CD player still in place would quickly make this a low priority and a nonevent. But as soon as somebody called Tessa, and the cops asked about suspicious persons in the vicinity, she'd supply my name. How could I have been that dumb? But I hadn't planned on breaking into her house. I'd thought she'd just tell me where Frank was and I would go talk to him. Breaking and entering was an impulse, and it had paid off. Though if he was really a wiseguy, she wouldn't tell the police. And if she was the classic battered wife, she might not tell anybody.

Wheezing, I broke through the woods into the parking lot, slowing to a dignified walk. Two more squad cars, sirens on and gumdrops blazing, rushed past the southern road heading onto Hope Street. I got into the Volvo and drove out the lot's eastern entrance. One of the police cars was already blocking the cul-de-sac. In a few minutes, it would occur to somebody to check the parking lot, but by then I would be long gone. The entrance to 280 was two miles down the road, and soon I was steaming toward the mall. I called the office.

"Evelyn, put Willie on and stay on the line."

"Willie's over at the courthouse, Kit. He called to tell you he'd found some interesting stuff and was on his way back."

"Okay, Evelyn, listen. If anybody asks, I was in the office until two minutes ago, then went out for coffee, okay? I was there all morning. Have you got that?"

There was no response. Evelyn is not a good liar. She's had no experience at lying, and, being a deeply religious person, is concerned about the afterlife implications. But she'd done it several times now, and seemed to be coming to terms with it.

"Okay," she said, having briefly considered the spiritual costs and deciding she could live with them. "You were here until 11:30 A.M. You just went out for coffee."

"Thanks," I said. "Put some insurance files on my desk, stuff we could've been going through. The Calderone case and the Edwards file. I'll explain when I get there in five minutes. If anybody calls and asks for me, remember: I've been working on files all morning and just stepped out for coffee. I'll call them back."

I called home and was surprised to hear Mrs. Steinitz answer. Jane must have been feeling awfully persuasive this morning to engineer her return. "Ben's up on the computer," Mrs. S. reported disapprovingly. About the only activity she approved of, to my knowledge, was reading Shakespeare. "But we're getting along fine today. He's behaving pleasantly." That was good to hear, though probably short-lived. I asked if I could talk to him.

"Yup," he said.

"How's it going?"

"Fine. Dad, can I go out with some of the guys tonight? We just want to go to the park and see what's up."

"Well, what could possibly be up?" I asked.

"I dunno."

I considered reminding him he was grounded, then decided to honor our truce. "Okay, but be home by nine-thirty. I don't want any reason to regret it. Fair?"

"Cool," he said, and hung up.

I called Jane at the clinic but she was unavailable, which could mean anything from "in the ladies' room" to "at the ER with a client who's getting her stomach pumped."

I parked in my space at the mall and came in through the main atrium. A ghost had been added to the Cicchelli family in the window. I sometimes fantasized about Mr. and Mrs. Cicchelli having wild sex on the plaid Herculon sleeper-sofa while the seniors taking their daily strolls around the mall fled in horror.

Plain James perched on his stool, puffing on a Camel, looking disheveled and listening to Etta James.

"Hey, Kit," he said. He looked a wreck, his mascara smudged around his right eye, his wig tilted. His spike-heeled pumps were off and one bare foot was tapping in rhythm with the music.

"Bad night?" I asked.

"Hell night," he said, tossing his Camel into the ashtray. "Here's your gorgeous amanuensis," he said, nodding toward the main entrance.

Willie was strolling in. I waved him over to the Lightning Burger where Luis was patiently explaining to a glassy-eyed teen-age employee that you had to turn the fryer on in order for the french fries to cook. He went through this several times, carefully and courteously, tossing me a nod and a wink.

"Hey, pal," I said, leaning over the counter. "I know we're heading for lunchtime, but I could use a few minutes, if you could spare them. I've got a lot of information to process quickly and so, prob-ably, does Willie. We might have a trip to take before Danielle is scheduled to show up here this afternoon. And by the way, if any-body asks, I was here all morning. Okay?"

Luis raised his eyebrow. No reason to tell him more.

"I've been to the Federal Building and county courthouse," said Willie. "I think you might want to take a drive to Livingston, too."

"Gentlemen," Luis said, emerging from behind the counter, straightening his tie. "Allow me to show you to a table."

Twenty-one

I WAS STILL JUMPY from my excursion to Lincoln Township. Not only hadn't I expected to find a battered wife and a small arsenal in Frank Dougherty's house, but now I was expecting a county SWAT team to come storming in at any second and haul me away for breaking and entering. Pounding through the woods ahead of pursuing cops isn't really up my alley. I actually stiffened when two men who looked like plainclothes cops came into the mall. But they headed for the Food Court, not my office.

I wondered what Tessa had done. If she hadn't fed my name to the cops, she'd surely told the well-armed Frank. I kept my eye on the door.

Luis ordered burgers for the three of us, and I quickly filled him in on all that had happened to me that morning—my days were sure getting full. He took it in, then looked at me thoughtfully.

"There are certainly a lot of people in that men's group one wants to know more about, isn't that right, Kit?"

"You trying to tell me something, Luis?"

"Nothing that isn't already crystal clear to you, I'm certain." This was always Luis's way of pointing out some obvious point that only a blockhead (like me) could have missed. He asked, "This group, which has so many connections to these murders—who started it?"

Willie had been busily wolfing down his burger, but he jumped in. "Funny you should ask, Luis. Guess who filed for bankruptcy two weeks ago in federal court in Newark?"

"Not Montgomery? He's got a booming law firm."

"Not Montgomery," Willie said triumphantly. "Grove Properties, of which Charles Montgomery is the president." Grove Properties. Why did that name set off a minor buzz in the depths of my brain? Where had I seen or heard it?

I sat very still, letting the memory surface. Grove. It took a while. "I saw a folder on Montgomery's desk that was labeled Grove Properties," I said. "And wasn't that one of the names on the doorbells at Logovitz's house? Remember, Willie? Three names, and one of them said Grove something." And there was something more, if I could just put it together. "The big project Dale wanted to build, the one he was borrowing all the money for. Bev Cadawaller said it was called Sharing Grove."

"If that was the name on Logovitz's door," said Luis, "and it was the company Montgomery was president of . . ."

"Montgomery has to be fronting for Logovitz," I finished. "Let's go, Willie. I have to wrap this up before Danielle shows up with the Third Army. I can't put her off past three."

It took us half an hour to thread through the highway traffic to Livingston. On the way there, Willie filled me in.

"Kit, I got the probate file on Linda's will. The family property and stocks that showed up on that loan application? There was a clause inserted into her will that, in the event of her death, those holdings go to Grove Properties. *Not* to her kids."

I whistled. "So Montgomery gets the money and property that Linda put up so that Dale could build his Emerald City. That's just bizarre."

Willie leafed through the copies of legal documents he'd made at the courthouse. "Kit, the mob doesn't go bankrupt, does it? I mean, guys like Logovitz don't file for bankruptcy in federal court, do they?"

It was a good point. "Willie, I just don't think we know what was happening here, whether Montgomery was only fronting for the mob, or whether he had something else going on on the side. Or whether this is some scheme to make it impossible for the federal government to collect the money it's owed. There are probably a dozen companies to wade through before you ever get near Jacob Logovitz."

Willie groaned. "God, it took me two hours just to get this stuff. Unless I know the mob's passwords, we'll never be able to put all that together."

"That's why God made an FBI. Willie, did the ME release what kind of bullet killed Linda?"

He shook his head. I called Tagg's private line as we drove, got a recording, then dialed the state police switchboard and said it was urgent. The operator patched me through. Tagg didn't seem delighted to hear from me.

"Jeez, Deleeuw, you're off the reservation again, aren't you? You've already pissed off the feds, I hear. All I need is for you to be calling me and ruining my day, too. What the fuck are you up to?"

"Look, Lieutenant, I don't have solid evidence. But remember how I helped you on that drug case?" He growled in my ear, but I had his interest now. "I might be able to do it again. Mind you, it's just a lead. I don't have anything hard—"

"Except your fucking head," he snorted.

"What kind of bullet killed Linda Lewis?"

".38 police special. Why?"

Well, I thought, no pro would make life *that* easy.

"Check out Frank Dougherty, 56 Hope Street, Lincoln Township. Fell from grace as a schoolteacher couple of years ago. You might want to talk to him. But be careful. Dougherty has a .9mm pistol in his bedroom, along with a mean-looking knife and some vicious brass knuckles. Check and see if the gun is licensed. If it isn't, you can get him on that alone."

"And how would you know there's a gun in this gentleman's house, Deleeuw?"

"Just that brilliant intuition that all the great ones have. I'll be at the mall this afternoon if you need me. This guy might be the shooter, Tagg. Could've been a professional hit. It's a hunch, but I know he has stuff that most schoolteachers don't have much use for. That's all I can say. Run his name around and see what you come up with. And if I'm right, you owe me again." I clicked off the cell phone.

We found the gracious restored house where Montgomery, Raskin & Jones did business and sat in the Volvo for a moment, taking in its imposing size and meticulous landscaping.

"Willie, do we know anything about this firm?"

He leafed through his folder again. "Well, to be honest, I can't swear to it, but I don't think there's any Raskin or Jones. I can't find them in any database and, when I called asking for them, I was told they're not taking cases. They're not members of the New Jersey or New York bars. So they seem to be phantom lawyers. I didn't mention it because it isn't that uncommon—the Bar Association secretary told me lawyers love to have high-sounding names on their doors and often make them up. But it seems more significant now, I think."

It would never have occurred to me in a million years that there was no Raskin or Jones in Montgomery, Raskin & Jones. But I guess a plaque that read "Charles Montgomery, Esq." just didn't have the same cachet. I remembered walking into this building just a couple of days ago, thinking that in this tasteful, respectable setting, an oasis in a sea of split-level yuk, I would be more than happy to turn over my most intimate legal affairs. Now, I wondered if anything about it was real.

"Does Montgomery's name show up in court records?"

"Yeah. He does a lot of work in the land development and real estate acquisition field."

The place seemed deserted, with no lights on the second floor. Inside there was only one secretary where there had been several, and an apparent dearth of clients, too. There was certainly less bustle than before. Our steps actually echoed in the paneled entrance hall.

A matronly woman who could have been an attorney herself stood to greet us. She wore a well-tailored navy dress and jacket. "May I help you?"

"We're looking for Mr. Montgomery."

"Mr. Montgomery's not here, I'm afraid. He's gone for the day."

"Everybody seems to be gone for the day."

She didn't respond to that. I didn't remember seeing her the last time I was here.

"It's urgent that we speak with Mr. Montgomery."

"I'm sorry, but that's not possible. Please leave your names and numbers and I'll let him know you were here."

"Excuse me, ma'am . . ." She offered no name. "But has something changed here? It's so different from when I was here a few days ago."

"I'm sure I don't know what you mean," she said. "If you'll

excuse me, I have a great deal of work to do." She nodded toward the door, then sat down at her desk. She wasn't going to volunteer anything.

I looked at Willie; he nodded imperceptibly. I hoped that meant he had Montgomery's home address. It did.

"It's just a mile or so from here," he said, poring through his folder stuffed with printouts when we were back in the Volvo. He pulled out a county map. "Go right here, then left, then right again."

Montgomery's house was another Victorian, this one a white frame that seemed to ramble up, down and around. A squat turret occupied the northeast corner, overlooking a lovely flower garden. The Mercedes was parked by the front door. Two or three acres swept away in the back. A white-muzzled golden retriever strolled out to greet us, tail wagging.

"This is a lot of house for a small family," I said.

"It *is* pretty roomy, isn't it?" Especially to Willie, who lived and worked in dark, cave-lit rooms, by the eerie glow of his PowerMac.

As we stood gawking Montgomery came out onto the porch, wearing a green pullover and gray slacks, arms crossed over his chest. Still the embodiment of the trusted lawyer, but his eyes were much sadder than I remembered.

"Kit. Nice to see you. I don't believe I know your friend."

I introduced Willie. "Charlie, you act like you're expecting us."

"Well, I am, Kit, I am. Janice called from the office and said she was sure you were headed here. Although ever since you called me and asked about my work relationship with Dale Lewis, I thought you'd be by."

He led us into a gracious sitting room, with windows of beaded glass. There he pointed us to sofas and took an upholstered rocking chair. Arrayed around the shelves and end tables were family pictures in silver frames.

"Beautiful photographs," I said. "The women . . ."

"This was my first wife Janine. My second Billie, died of cancer a couple of years ago. My girls, Caroline and Lynne. Both at boarding school. Just me now. I date a woman from Short Hills from time to time, but I don't see marriage in my future. Especially now."

Willie and I glanced at each other. He'd never mentioned being a widower. Did the other men in the group know? Had he been lying? This was beginning to feel strange.

"Charlie, your law firm seemed empty today, almost deserted."

He poured each of us a snifter of brandy from a decanter on a sideboard. He nodded sadly. "It is, it is. I told everybody to clear out this morning. I'm sure most of them are gone by now. Some will probably want to stay and face the music."

I leaned forward. "Charlie, I have this feeling we're moving on parallel tracks here. I wonder if we could get on the same one. What music? What's going on?"

He stood up to pour himself another shot of brandy.

"Kit, you know the basics. That Logovitz and his organization murdered Dale. But you'll never be able to prove that, and Logovitz won't be alive much longer anyway. And I'm sure you've figured out that I fronted for the organization. Bought land. Wangled millions in federal housing grants for developments that were never built, or were never built properly, or were started but never completed. No point going into all that. It's very complicated. The FBI will unravel it, eventually, but even they will be surprised at how clever these people are, how ruthless. I don't think they've grasped how much money was at stake."

He looked out at his beautiful gardens with pleasure and pride. You could see from his expression that no hired gardener had created them.

"I had a very prosperous career until a few years back, Kit. Then I developed an unfortunate gambling habit. Was generously comped in Atlantic City, lost quite a bit, built up substantial debt, enormous amounts. I had to borrow from some rather unsavory sorts to keep playing.

"Enter the Russians. This is familiar territory to them—they are all ex-KGB, they turned agents all the time by getting them involved in something, then recruiting them for the agency. It's in all the LeCarré books. I used to love those books. . . . Anyway, same principle here: once you're in, you're never out. Logovitz offered to pay off my debts if I fronted for him. Just once or twice, he said. He stole my whole life, of course, as I knew he would. I never had any illusions. But the alternative was disbarment and ruin. You see, I had embezzled some of my clients' funds to stall my creditors. I couldn't just go into Gamblers Anonymous; I would have gone to prison.

"My firm was in Short Hills at the time, but with the new . . . backer help, I bought the current building—it's quite beautiful, isn't it?—made up some fake partners' names and started doing business. Logovitz and his crew were my only clients. My secretaries never quite knew what was going on. Janice knew. But she hired only temps, and if anybody asked too many questions, they were gone. There were surprisingly few questions, really. People generally don't really want to know what they suspect."

He shook his head, sighed. "I made a lot of money, but I lost everything. My first wife won't speak to me. My second is gone. My daughters are out of state, thank God. I lied to them all the time. They sensed it, I think. Who can blame my older girl for staying away?"

I tried to process what was happening, but it was a struggle. I had barely opened my mouth when he began pouring his heart out. Some need for confession, apparently.

"All that will come out soon enough and it's not really your concern, is it?" He continued his monologue. "Your concern is the Lewises. But I feel I ought to explain some of this. We members of the Fathers' Club stick together, right? And I admired your speech to Ricky Melman. I did. I thought, That man has a lot of character. He wouldn't have bartered his life away in this corrupt fashion, would he? You wouldn't, would you, Kit? You believe in family too much, don't you?"

I nodded, feeling strangely close to tears as the reality of what he was saying began to sink in. "I hope I do, Charles." I felt he was being sincere about the Fathers' Club. We were both in it. There was a community in the group, perhaps a twisted one, but a community.

"Dale died because he owed a lot of money to Logovitz and because he hoped to get out of his mountain of debt by going to the FBI and offering to testify against him. Well, that could really only end one way. I did my best to warn him; I actually begged him to let me negotiate another way out. I yelled, pleaded, finally even tried to slap some sense into him." He grimaced, probably at the memory of his own slide into violence. "But he left my office, saying he was on his way to the FBI office in Newark. He never made it, of course. I wasn't there, but I can imagine what happened. . . . I ask myself every single day what in hell he thought he was doing, and I can never come up with a single decent answer."

"And Linda?" I asked, not wanting to risk his clamming up now. I wondered if he had gone mad or, perhaps, sane.

"Linda. An unforgivable tragedy," he said softly. "The moment I crossed the line from having any vestiges of humanity left to . . . well, they turned me into a monster." His eyes welled up.

"You see, Kit, I was desperate to get out from under this deal with the devil. I'm in my fifties, I didn't have a lifetime ahead of me. I loathed myself, my cowardice. This project of Dale's, well, I really believed it could work. Dale had a hell of a dream there, and I thought it could help me be independent, get away from Logovitz and his kind. Help me flee, if I had to. I figured I could make some money from this project too. All the companies connected with the development were called Grove. The holding company was Grove Properties. The name of the new community was Sharing Grove. My own little company was called New Jersey Grove, Inc. I was siphoning cash from the block grants and loans we were receiving. I'd set up this fake corporation and was overcharging for surveying and environmental impact. I stood to skim nearly $500,000 if the project went ahead. I already had $300,000. Dale, you see, was in on this with me. He was helping me. One or two projects, and I would just vanish. I could, you know. I really have nothing much left in my life but this house. I'm just a crook and a gardener." He said this venomously.

"I won't go into the details. 'Lawyer-client privilege,' and all that. The FBI will explain it soon enough. But when Sharing Grove faltered, Logovitz's 'company' sent in auditors. I had to put the money I'd pocketed back into the special accounts. The local township went crazy at the prospect of housing that might attract minorities. It got stalled in court, became a mess. Meanwhile, trying to keep it afloat, we borrowed more money, from everybody— Rheems, Battelle. And from Linda. She'd put up $500,000 after Dale told her he was in terrible trouble, that he really had to have the money. It was amazing, actually. Here this couple had been through everything—he'd had that affair, they'd split up—but she didn't blink. She signed over everything she had, even changed her will. Imagine."

I thought of Jacob Logovitz's dirty little townhouse by the Lincoln Tunnel. Montgomery's splendid suburban period piece could have been a movie set, but he wasn't in control of any part of his life.

He gulped down another brandy, a man trying to firm up his resolve. This had to be a nightmare for him. "Bit by bit, you get more desperate, they drag you in deeper. I had so much ambition, so much pride . . . But I can't blame them. I let them. I'm responsible. I know that."

He turned suddenly to us. Willie looked at me in near panic. He just didn't know how to react. Take notes, maybe? Run and call the police? I held up my palm, in a gesture that said, " 'Just stay put.' " When somebody was talking like this, there was no need to do anything.

"Mob killings—well, there's hardly ever an arrest," Montgomery was saying. "Nobody will find Dale's murderer."

"Dale's murderer was Frank Dougherty," I said. "You hired him. You paid him to kill Dale." I stated it as absolute fact.

Montgomery's eyes strayed to his flower gardens again. "No, that's wrong. I would only know the matters I controlled. We were very compartmentalized. But Logovitz wouldn't trust a drunken ex-schoolteacher for a job like that. He used a pro, somebody who flew in from Houston, killed him, then flew out the same night. Flew to Pittsburgh, maybe, rented a car. Almost impossible to trace. Probably in Mexico City now."

He smiled crookedly at the sight of the retriever bounding outside after a rubber ball, tossing it in the air, stalking it as if it were alive.

"You're quite good, Kit. We checked you out. I knew all about you ten minutes after you called me, of course. But I dismissed the warnings. You were a green private investigator, only in the business five years. Your training was Wall Street . . ." He shook his head. "I was not afraid of you. I underestimated you. But when I look back at all this, maybe the only thing I can say for myself is that I really wasn't cut out for it. I'm immensely relieved for it to be over." He looked back out the window.

I was working hard to piece it together. "But you recruited Dougherty," I said. "Whether some guy flew in from Houston for that particular assignment or not."

"Yes, I hired him. Dougherty was desperate, another life thrown away. Fired from his school job for drinking. He applied to work on one of the construction sites we controlled. The foreman tipped me off, said he had a man desperate enough to do almost anything and smart enough to pull it off. So he did various jobs for us. We both went on the same journey, due to our separate addictions and our refusal to get help, all the way down the road to murder. Good work, Kit. You're worth every penny you make."

Ha, I thought. "Did you bring Dougherty into the Fathers' Club?"

"Yes, the Fathers' Club. In a way, one of the worst things I ever did. I live in a world of false fronts and dummy corporations, so it came naturally to me to create a false Fathers' Club. Though Lord knows I could use a real one. We asked around the church—nice move, don't you think? being falsely religious, too—and recruited Jim Rheems and Ricky Melman. Rheems brought in Hal Etheridge. They were the genuine members of the group. You and I and Dale and Dougherty were just using the others." I winced at being placed in that company, and walked over to pour myself another shot of brandy.

"I created the group under fake circumstances but, like you, I came to value it. I actually looked forward to those meetings. I think Dale did too. We could actually talk to other men about things going on in our lives. Not the *really* difficult things, of course, I couldn't do that. But about being a man, healing from a broken marriage, struggling to talk to your kids. We had some great talks. Especially at night in the winter, with the fire going and mugs of hot cider. I'd never had a group of men like that around me. I'll really miss it."

You will, I thought. They probably don't have men's groups in the prison at Rahway.

"So," I said, gulping down my second brandy and offering the bottle to Willie, who seemed both fascinated and paralyzed at the same time, staring at Montgomery as if he were a viper. "If Dougherty didn't kill Dale, then he killed Linda. And you ordered him to." Montgomery turned to me. His eyes had gone vacant, disturbing.

"You wanted her $500,000 to put back into the accounts you'd been embezzling from, before Logovitz's auditors got wind of what you were up to and brought the guy back from Mexico City to put a bullet between *your* eyes. Dale was killed for threatening to go to the feds. Linda died because she was goodhearted enough to put up all she owned for a brainless dreamer ex-husband, and because she was trusting enough to alter her will to turn over all she owned to you. Will you lose any sleep over two small children with no parents and no money, Charlie? And you'll miss the men's group? You are a totally amoral disgrace."

His eyes narrowed. "Don't get all high and mighty on me, Deleeuw. You're no saint. You were run out of Wall Street, weren't you? Forbidden to return? Why—because you're such a sharp bond trader? And you betrayed the men in the Fathers' Club. You got them to open up their hearts to you, to tell their secrets and fears. You pretended to tell them yours. Does that make you an honorable man? You're on the same road as me. . . ."

"No, no," I said. "Too easy, Charlie. I feel terrible about the men's group. But that doesn't make me a thief or an assassin. I could never have Linda Lewis killed. No decent human being could have offed that woman and left her kids orphans."

Montgomery sighed quietly. He'd gone through four or five moods in minutes. "I'm sorry. I can't tell you how I came to do it. I don't think I'll ever really know what was missing in me, what was broken so badly. I'm sorry you cared so much about her."

His dreaminess infuriated me. "I did care about her," I said coldly. "And you killed her. For money. To save your wretched hide. You're not some inner-city kid with no father, bad schools, drugs and guns to blame for what you've become. You had every advantage. You have no excuse. You are the most contemptible person I've ever encountered." I couldn't bear to look at that distinguished, handsome, pathetic face. I turned away.

I shouldn't have. I didn't see at first why Willie had jumped to his feet and was rushing toward Montgomery. When I whirled back around, Charles had a pistol pointed at me.

"No, Willie—," I shouted, too late. Montgomery raised his arm and brought the gun butt crashing down on Willie's head. Willie crumpled. Blood trickled from his scalp into the elaborate pattern of the rug.

"Don't hurt him," I said quietly. "Please. If you have a beef, it's with me."

"I didn't hurt him badly," Montgomery stammered wildly. "Just stunned him." He looked around frantically, as if he'd heard something. "I won't hurt him," he said. "I don't even know him. I'm not a killer, don't you understand?" He kept the pistol pointed at me.

My heart almost jumped out of my chest. But Montgomery was

right: he wasn't really a killer. Instead, he turned and ran down the hall. I heard a door slam somewhere on the first floor. I heard the gunshot seconds later, echoing through the empty wooden house.

Then, even as I leaned over Willie, tires screeched nearby, a helicopter thrummed overhead. Four or five vans pulled up onto the beautifully maintained lawn, one plowing right into the glass wall of the greenhouse a few feet away. Men in black jumpsuits with "FBI" stenciled on their backs, wearing black helmets and carrying shotguns and machine pistols, scrambled out. A string of Livingston and Rochambeau PD police cars careened onto the lawn behind them.

Three of these commandos crashed into the sitting room where I knelt, still dumbstruck. One leaned over us. "He shot?" he demanded.

"No," I said, "just thumped hard on the head." I pointed down the hallway where Montgomery had run, but the corridor was already aswarm with agents. I heard a door splinter. Then a voice crackled over the radio of the agent bending over Willie.

"Suspect has self-inflicted gunshot wound to the head. Looks bad. Send the paramedics."

Fifteen minutes later, covered by a blood-flecked sheet, Montgomery was carried off on a stretcher. They took Willie away in an ambulance. I stood on Montgomery's beloved lawn watching the ambulance and the hearse head down the gravel drive.

Chief Leeming and Danielle Peterson came up, shouldering their pistols.

"You okay?" Danielle asked me.

"Naturally," Leeming said. "Deleeuw's always okay. It's everybody else that drops dead. It's a good thing the FBI had you under surveillance, Deleeuw. Otherwise, you'd be dead too."

I think Montgomery knew, from the moment I called from the Roadway Diner, that his house of cards was starting to totter. And I think he had been immensely relieved to watch it fall.

I sat down on the lawn and wept, startling Leeming, who skittered away. Danielle leaned over and patted me on the back.

Linda had died to keep the Russian mob off a pathetic man's back. Who was going to explain that to her kids?

Twenty-two

SHARING GROVE turned out to be a big rubbish-strewn lot north of Newton, near the New York border. It was hard to picture Dale Lewis's utopia ever rising on this barren site, but Bev Cadawaller had given me very explicit directions. A highway ran along the eastern edge. Strips of rubber tire, beer cans, condoms and slats of wood littered the dusty ground. Newspapers and plastic trash bags whipped around in a cool wind.

It was Halloween morning—in child-centered suburbia, the closest thing going to a national holiday. That night I'd go out with Emily, keeping a discreet but watchful distance as she went from house to house. I always refused to dress up in a costume myself, but I provided directions, security, a flashlight to illuminate darkened sidewalks, and occasional exclamations about how much people liked Emily's costume and how much great candy she was getting. And for that, I think, my daughter was grateful.

But this was probably the last year I'd go trick-or-treating with either of my children. For the past several years, Ben would rather be caught reading Milton than walking around with me on Halloween. And Emily was approaching middle school, not a time when you wanted dads in tow.

Jane was looking forward to coming home early that night to coo over the trick-or-treaters and to quietly roll her eyes at the grown-ups who had lost their parental marbles and whose costumes were more elaborate than their kids'. We knew this wasn't generous but, in our defense, neither of us had ever yielded to our shared impulse to scream, "Get a life, please!" After all, these fanatics were our valued neighbors, the people who signed for our UPS packages.

So I didn't plan to stay long at this phantom housing development. It was a disappointing place, anyway.

Percentage ran in circles, tracking a fantasy rabbit he would never catch, though I doubted any rabbit would live here voluntarily. I'd decided I owed it to Linda to mark the disintegration of her family and the death of the man who'd wanted to be a good husband and father, but somehow lost it along the way. So I'd brought a bunch of daisies. "For you, Linda. And your family," I said, tossing them into the breeze. They landed in a heap in front of me.

Dale Lewis was sincere, I'd come to believe, about transforming this lot into an Eden, a new community where rich and poor, young and old, black and white, lived with all the advantages our suburbs offer: safe and clean streets, good schools, well-tended parks, a strong sense of community. Eventually, he'd become obsessed with his vision, and it had killed him. Maybe, one day, it would happen. But not here.

I couldn't bring myself to mark Charles Montgomery's passing in any way. I didn't really even care much why he did what he did. Good people did bad things and bad people did good things. I could learn every intimate detail of Charles Montgomery's life and have no real grasp of how one human being could do that to another. But Montgomery would be judged by an entity better equipped for the task than I was. One of my most closely guarded secrets—even from Jane—was that I believed in God.

I'd had a frantic couple of days following the horrible scene at Montgomery's house. Willie had sustained a minor skull fracture, and he'd spent the next week under the loving scrutiny of some young and quite attractive nurses in Livingston Hospital. The sponge baths were the best part of the day, he informed me. Willie would be fine.

Danielle was enraged, as I had predicted, that I'd withheld information about the men's group. I tried to explain that this was a matter of honor—Linda was my client, not just a citizen—and I'd felt obligated to track down her killer myself. To date, Danielle was not mollified, but I think it was a notion she understood quite well and would come to accept. I don't think she'd mentioned any of this to Leeming; if she had, I probably would be bagging groceries by now at the A&P.

I did pay off the other I.O.U. I'd incurred in this case. After Montgomery's body was taken away, I called Debbie Silverman, the television producer, and told her that a prominent Livingston attorney had just shot himself dead and that the police would soon be arresting an ex-schoolteacher named Frank Dougherty for the murder of Linda Lewis. I even told her that the murderer of Dale Lewis was believed to be a professional hit man for the Russian mob. The producer had her exclusive. The condition was that she not mention my name.

"Why not?" she asked. "It would be great for business."

I told her I didn't need any more of this kind of business.

Sure enough, within hours the Lincoln Township police had called Chief Leeming and asked him to pick me up for breaking and entering. I had also underestimated the FBI, which had been tailing me ever since my visit to Jacob Logovitz and which, humiliatingly enough, had actual videotaped footage of my break-in at the Dougherty home. They threatened to turn it over to the local police if I didn't cooperate and, for good measure, they took another whack at getting me to turn in my Wall Street colleagues. I agreed to disclose what I knew about Sharing Grove and told them yet again to go to hell on the Wall Street stuff. They filed their tapes away, but I probably haven't heard the last of them. They didn't give a damn about my little break-in, but they might care about some future case.

The local burglary charges were quickly and quietly dropped, all mention of my name expunged from the records. Maybe it was because the FBI was eager to debrief me. Or maybe because Danielle drove out to the township and "reached out," as she put it, to a friend of hers who worked there. Nothing was missing from the house, she pointed out. And though Tessa Dougherty had in fact turned my business card directly over to the police, she didn't seem to want to go to court and testify against me. All I really suffered were some harrumphing lectures from Chief Leeming on what a pain in the ass I was and wouldn't I ever learn to behave halfway professionally and how could I be so unspeakably stupid as to break into somebody's house in broad daylight.

Lieutenant Tagg followed up on my tip and, with the FBI's help, nailed Dougherty when he came home that night. On the advice of his lawyers, he cut a deal and pled guilty to the second-degree murder of Linda Lewis. The state cops found his .38 at the bottom of the Passaic River. Montgomery had paid him $10,000 to kill Linda and destroy the Lewis family.

I didn't envy Dougherty his Judgment Day either. But in this world, he avoided life imprisonment, not to mention a possible death penalty, by providing some damaging testimony on a couple of Logovitz's lieutenants he'd done jobs with. He also led the FBI to Montgomery's computer disks, stashed in the very sitting room where we'd had our last conversation. On them were enough leads, dummy corporation records and zoning board bribes to keep a federal grand jury in business for decades.

Tagg, knowing my need to learn what had happened the night Linda was killed, sent me the transcript of Dougherty's confession. He explained it all: how he called Linda at home, said he needed to talk with her about Dale and asked her to meet him at the convenience store. How he was able, courtesy of his attendance at the Fathers' Club, to sprinkle in convincing personal details. How he waited in the parking lot for her to arrive, walked up to her car and pointed a gun at her. He told her that nobody would get hurt if she would just take a few minutes with him. She went behind the building with him, calmly, bravely.

He told her he was sorry. She begged to see her children one last time, to say goodbye. He shot her only once, hoping to fool the police into thinking it was a botched carjacking. He was sorry he hadn't thought to bring an accomplice along to steal her car and make the crime more convincing. But he never touched her body, he insisted. He was not a rapist. I heard that he repeatedly tried to kill himself while in prison, and had to be kept under twenty-four-hour surveillance.

His wife sold their Lincoln Township house and moved away; nobody knew where.

Predictably, whoever executed Dale Lewis was never identified, let alone apprehended. But Jacob Logovitz was indicted on fifty-two counts of conspiracy to defraud the federal government, one count of conspiracy to commit murder, and various counts of conspiracy to commit interstate theft. No one really expected to make the murder charge against him stick, Danielle acknowledged, nor was the old man ever expected to set foot inside a jail. His doctor testified that a trial would kill him and a judge ruled that all hearings be postponed pending improvement in his health. I did not picture this happening. But a number of people would be convicted, and his organization disabled, perhaps permanently. The investigations would go on for months and result in many trials over many years. I didn't have much heart for following them.

When the dust settled a bit, I drove up to Connecticut where the two Lewis kids were living with Linda's mother, brought them a sackful of toys and explained to them how terrific their parents were and how the people who had hurt them had been caught and punished. We agreed to exchange letters and presents each year. The sadness in their faces was heartbreaking; I had this awful feeling that it would never go away.

My relief over my repaired relationship with Ben was short-lived, of course. I was living in fairy-tale land, psychologically speaking; Ben was a good kid but had some problems to work out. More "space" and a few heart-to-hearts wasn't going to do the trick. One day he told his bullying, jockstrap-for-a-mind gym teacher where to get off when the guy called a friend of Ben's a "retard," and was suspended again. This time I silently cheered for him but agreed with Jane that he probably needed some help, even if his heart was in the right place. We started seeing a therapist together. It wasn't so bad, actually. It gave us both a place where we had to talk for an hour a week, with a truly impartial referee who listened and taught both of us how to listen, too. Unlike the movies, there would be no cathartic moment, when I explained to my son the pain and travails of my own early life and he shouted "Dad!" and flung his arms around me while we both shed copious tears of joy. This was work, sometimes painful work. But I believed it would come out all right. We all wanted it to.

Jane considered dropping out of her doctoral program, but the whole family raised so much hell about it that she promptly abandoned the idea. We'd all seen how hard she'd worked for years to get this far, and much as we missed her, none of us wanted her to stop now. She only had one year to go, and even Ben conceded that my cooking was improving. Still, I was uncomfortably aware that the way I'd reacted to Linda Lewis had raised some questions about my marriage. I was never close to leaving or wanting to— quite the opposite. I wanted more of Jane, not less. But the simple truth was, I felt lonely. And, like other housepersons, a bit put upon, squeezing murder investigations between calls from the school and pediatrician's appointments.

I took Ben and Emily out to Lightning Burger one night a couple of weeks ago, and went over the case with them. Luis, to my amazement, joined us; I had invited him but assumed he wouldn't. I went through it all with them, skipping over some of the details but hitting the high points.

I also told them we all had one more year to pull through before Jane would be back in our lives on a more predictable basis. "Look at it this way. We miss her for a year, but we get years of a happy Mom. A great trade." When the dust settled, I wanted Jane to see me as somebody who had helped her get there, not somebody whom she'd succeeded in spite of. I'd seen enough unhappy marriages to want a happy one. And I didn't want a life in which I'd be drawn to other people. Jane and I are going to Key West for a long weekend next month, farming the kids out to friends' families and the dog to a kennel. Meanwhile, we've drawn up elaborate plans to stay in communication daily, via fax, e-mail and telephone. We'll be fine.

Still, Linda Lewis's death rattled me. She was the first client I had lost, and it was hard to shake the feeling that I should have protected her somehow. Sometimes, Plain James and I sit by his cart, eating Luis's burgers, listening to Ruth Brown or Muddy Waters, watching the polyester parade and feeling blue together.

Say what you will about the suburbs, though, life goes on with a vengeance. Back-to-School Night was followed by the Autumn Harvest Concert (more Thunder Drums), soccer games, and, soon, the Science Fair. Emily wanted to invite eight friends to sleep over and in a distracted moment I agreed. It will not happen again. They were still giggling and shrieking at 3 A.M. Among the guests was "She's Not Ready" McGann's kid, Alison. Turned out Alison was more than ready—she was shrieking loudest of all.

There was just one loose end left to attend to. I called Jim Rheems last night and left a message on his machine that I'd like to attend a meeting of the much-diminished Fathers' Club, not as a member, just as somebody who had some things to say. I said he could call and tell me not to come but, if he didn't, I'd show up at the next get-together. So far, he hadn't called back.

I thought about the group as I stood amid the rubble of what could have been Sharing Grove and tossed stones at a tin can. There was something quietly, mundanely heroic about these men. Nobody had made them attend club meetings or forced them to talk. Their friends and often their families joked about their being "new, sensitive men" who beat drums, just as I had. But they'd struggled to overcome their own history. Talking is a pretty rare thing for men outside of World War II movies to do.

I missed it. I missed telling them how Ben and I were struggling to work through our differences. I wanted to tell them about the determination Jane and I had to stay happy and in love. I wanted to chuckle over Em's slumber party. And to explain about those other kids, Liz and Noah Lewis. Maybe then the Fathers' Club would understand why I'd done what I'd done.

Epilogue

TREES BENDING in the stiff wind cast wavering shadows across the stone facade of the church in Springdale. Sheets of cold rain swept nearly horizontal, drenching me, turning my umbrella inside out the instant I opened it. You could almost smell winter, just weeks away.

I walked slowly down the hallway lined with photographs of past rectors and church officials. The library door was closed. When I knocked, Jim Rheems's hearty voice boomed, "Come in."

Someone had lit the logs in the fireplace and the blaze added to the sense of being sheltered from the tempest outside in a cozy corner of some ancient castle. Rheems, wrapped in a heavy wool sweater, had taken Montgomery's old seat at the head of the table. Battelle, a cashmere scarf draped rakishly around his neck, sat to his right. Hal Etheridge was tossing a small sponge-rubber ball up in the air, and catching it; when I entered, he nodded at me. Ricky Melman sat across from him. "Hey, Kit," he said quietly. "I've missed you." Etheridge nodded, as if he agreed. Battelle just stared. A pottery pitcher of warmed cider and a heaping bowl of pretzels sat at the center of the table.

The wind buffeted the building in great gusts, driving rain against the windows and drafts down the halls of the old church.

Rheems pointed to my old seat. I took off my sodden trench coat, hung it on the back of a chair near the fireplace, rubbed my hands together and sat down.

"Welcome to our depleted ranks," said Rheems. "Finding out the truth about Dale, Frank and Charlie the way we did, I wonder if any of us are real. Or if any of this was."

"It was real for me," Melman jumped in. "It made a difference for me. I don't care what those guys were in it for. I'm sad for them: we sat here for a couple of years and poured our hearts out to them and now two of them are dead and one is going to jail. Maybe it was all fake for them. But it was real for me. I want to tell you, Kit"—he turned to me—"that my family is still together. I'm grateful that you guys didn't just let me walk out of my life that night."

I smiled. It would be great if we'd saved one.

Battelle poured himself some cider. "How sweet," he said. "Forgive me if I'm feeling a little bitter. A bit used. Montgomery needed a front and a fund-raising source, so he started the Fathers' Club. A man who said he was a teacher turned out to be a thug and a hit man. A guy who claimed to be a developer turned out to be disturbed and dishonest and got killed. His wife"—Battelle faltered—"was murdered too. And our warm, sensitive new member"—he pointed to me—"was a spy. Some men's group. Makes you sort of nostalgic for the old days, when we just went to war and killed each other without apology."

"David, that's a bit harsh, don't you think?" Rheems asked gently.

"No, I don't," said Battelle. "I came here with an open heart and talked to other men honestly for the first time in my life. And what did that reap? An unbelievable trail of murder, deception and betrayal. I should've joined the damn drumbeaters."

No one bothered to argue. A great sadness hung over the room. The empty seats haunted all of us. It wasn't just that those absent were gone, but that they had metamorphasized into completely unknown, even frightening, creatures.

"I'll just never understand how Frank could sit there and joke about his kids like that," said Melman softly. "He was so smart, so funny . . ." He shook his head.

I cleared my throat. "Look," I said, "I appreciate being given the opportunity to come here tonight. I think I know how you feel. I'm basically here to say I'm sorry I was one of the deceivers."

I waited for a particularly ferocious gust of wind to finish rattling the windowpanes. I wanted a chance to explain.

"We all live by our own codes. Part of mine is that my clients aren't just people who bring me business. They're usually in trouble. I believe them, work for them, take them under my wing. Linda Lewis was my client. She didn't understand why her husband had turned away from his family. She came to me because she was frantic with worry about him. She didn't tell me how heavily in debt he was, if she even knew, or to whom, though she suggested some of you had given him money. Then her husband got murdered and, as you know, bringing a murderer to justice justifies quite a bit, in my book.

"Even then, Linda was against my joining this group. Maybe she knew what I didn't know—that this was a sensitive mechanism that operated on trust. I thought it was just a bunch of guys shooting the shit once in a while, so I overruled her. I didn't know. I'd never experienced it. I thought finding Dale's killer took priority over other social considerations, manners, or even truth."

The fire hissed as a gust of wind pushed down the chimney. Battelle was staring at the flames, but the others were watching me.

"I had a lot of feeling for Linda. Nothing happened, of course, but meeting her . . . well, it gave me a taste of that feeling Ricky was talking about, something I hadn't felt in a while. I realized I was lonely. My wife has been away a lot."

I looked around the table, trying to read people's expressions, wondering if I was making any sense to them, if I had even a small shot at redemption.

"Linda had entrusted her safety to me and when she was killed I felt a strong obligation to continue on her behalf. So I decided those considerations added up to a greater moral imperative to solve two murders than to be truthful with you."

Silence. I went on. "I don't know if I'd do it again. When we talked about my son Ben, that was a revelation. Men had never helped me that way before. Like a lot of guys, I don't have a lot of real friends. I've always been too busy working. It takes time to make friends, and the right environment—like here. And let's face it, most of us don't know how. I don't.

"So I was stunned to find myself talking about my kid with all of you and getting helpful information. It changed the way I looked at all this. That's why I'm not sure I would have infiltrated the group if I'd really grasped what goes on here."

I stopped. I wanted them to absorb what I was saying, to think about it, to really understand why I'd done what I had.

"I felt that closeness the other night, too," Ricky said. "I understand what you're saying. But we've been through so much."

I nodded. "I know, believe me. Dale. Montgomery. Dougherty. Jesus—that's how I knew something was wrong here. Too many trails crisscrossing. I sensed all along that the answers were here, and I was right, sad to say. The answers *were* here."

I stood and walked over to get my coat. "I'm not going to belabor the point. I just wanted to try to explain myself and make my case for rejoining the group. You're a remarkable group of men. I admire what you're doing, and, more importantly, I need it. If you can agree to readmit me, I'll be grateful. If not, I understand. I'll wait outside while you decide."

I walked down the hallway, out of earshot, and settled into a big red vinyl-upholstered sofa. Through the far doors I glimpsed the church sanctuary itself, with its arched stained-glass windows.

When I closed my eyes, the ghosts of this case danced in front of me. Linda—earnestly explaining to me that her ex was a good and decent man. Dale's blank eyes. Charles Montgomery's tortured face. Tessa Dougherty's bruises. The haggard, sickly Jacob Logovitz trying somehow to make peace with a murderous life.

Complex stuff, investigating other people's lives.

Twenty minutes or so later, I heard Melman calling my name. I opened my eyes. I walked back into the library like a prisoner awaiting a verdict.

Their faces told me before Rheems spoke. "Kit," he said. "I'm afraid we can't take you back in."

"It isn't just you, Kit," Melman said, before I could respond. "We're disbanding. You're right about one thing: a group like this is based totally on trust. When that trust is betrayed, you can't just pick up the pieces and pretend it didn't happen."

"We do understand why you acted as you did." Etheridge looked miserable. "But you betrayed us, too. You might have had better reasons than the others did, but it comes out the same. The Fathers' Club is over. We just don't think we could trust one another again, not with this group in this setting. Maybe some of us can start new groups, with different people, in new places. But for this group, it's our last meeting."

There was no more to be said. We all shook hands and everybody wished everybody else the best. I got into the Volvo and drove back to Rochambeau on rain-slick highways. Maybe I ought to start a men's group myself. Maybe Luis would join. Maybe Plain James, too.

At home, Percentage came bounding out the back door as soon as I turned the lock, wriggling for joy, taking my hand gently in his mouth the way Labs do to tell you they love you.

We went for a walk, despite the storm. Percentage was a good friend. Maybe we could find a room somewhere in Rochambeau, schedule meetings on Thursday nights after dinner. He could lie on the floor next to me, dreaming of woodchucks, while the other guys talked about their problems and fears. I leaned over and patted his damp head. My face was wet, too. It was the rain.